a Duke
TOO FAR

JANE
ASHFORD

sourcebooks
casablanca

Published by Sourcebooks Casablanca, an imprint of Sourcebooks
P.O. Box 4410, Naperville, Illinois 60567-4410
(630) 961-3900
sourcebooks.com

Printed and bound in the United States of America.
OPM 10 9 8 7 6 5 4 3 2 1

Prologue

HE SHOULD NEVER HAVE EATEN THAT EEL PIE, THOUGHT Peter Rathbone, Duke of Compton, as he strode along the London street toward St. James's Square. It had tasted all right, but three hours later, his innards were uneasy. He put a hand to his midriff as he walked. Unfortunate that this should happen just now, when he was on his way to an important appointment.

Well, he would endure. He sprang from a long line of stalwart folk. They'd come over with the Conqueror, gone on Crusades, swung broadswords in various battles, borne generations of children, and held their lands through civil war and plague. He might be the last Rathbone, but he wasn't going to cast up his accounts over a damned fish pie. He hoped.

He'd been walking for hours on this filthy March day, despite the tendrils of icy fog that pervaded London, ever since his uncomfortable meeting with his banker. His family had been banking with Coutts since they began keeping their money in banks rather than a simple strongbox in the muniments room. The representative there had been respectful, but he'd made it clear that there was no more to be wrung from the overdraft. Regretfully, he could not help Peter with the improvements he wished to make on his acres.

The long trip to plead his case in person had come to nothing. So Peter had walked, grappling with various knotty problems, and only noticed he was famished when he passed a pie shop. Cheap and filling fuel, he'd thought. Both of which had proved true. And possibly lethal as well, he concluded with a humorless laugh that ended in a resounding belch.

Perhaps he should have sent his regrets to the Earl of Macklin about this mysterious dinner. Food was the last thing he wanted just now. But Peter didn't receive invitations from a leader of society every day. Or any day, really, since he lived in Shropshire. A man on the edge of ruin was not sought after by the *haut ton*, even if he was a peer of the realm. He had *seen* the earl, who had happened to be present when Peter called on relatives of his mother—a visit that had not gone well. But he couldn't imagine why the older man had asked him to dine. Of course it wasn't a case of help for his situation. Peter knew that very well. But he couldn't afford to ignore such a connection. So he was going, even if he felt sick as a dog.

Stepping into the brightness of White's made him stop and blink, dazzled by the ranks of candles. Rich wooden paneling, a hum of conversation, clinking glasses, and warmth replaced the icy fog. He'd never been here before. His grandfather had been a member. Both of them, actually, if he remembered correctly.

His father, who'd disliked London, had never bothered to join any club.

Savory smells rode the air. Usually welcome, tonight they made him feel even more queasy. He would rise above his stomach, Peter told himself. Metaphorically, if not literally.

A servitor took his much-worn greatcoat, hat, and gloves, leaving Peter in his one decently fashionable coat, black, purchased for his father's funeral. Worn with gray pantaloons, this was the only ensemble he had that was worthy of White's. And his shirt only just made the grade. The place teemed with dandies and Corinthians and others who paid vast sums to their tailors. And then there was Peter, whose attire barely sustained the character of a gentleman. Following a waiter into the dining room, he swallowed a hint of bile. "Where is Lord Macklin?" he asked the man.

"There," said the waiter, indicating a small party in a private corner.

Peter easily identified Arthur Shelton, Earl of Macklin, from his one previous sight of him. Not only was he the oldest of the trio ahead, but he exuded an easy authority. Old enough to be Peter's father, his hair showed no gray. He looked strong and assured and...trustworthy somehow. He was talking to two younger men, closer to Peter's age. The shorter one had a snub-nosed face, dun-brown hair, and dark eyes. The other was ruddy, with reddish hair and a choleric manner. Macklin looked over the latter's shoulder, spotted Peter, and nodded.

Peter joined them. Lord Macklin acknowledged him with a smile. His face showed few lines, and those seemed scored by good humor. He gestured toward the snub-nosed man. "Daniel Frith, Viscount Whitfield." He named the other as Roger Berwick, Marquess of Chatton. "And Peter Rathbone, Duke of Compton," he told them.

Peter greeted the others. He didn't know any of these gentlemen, and he still had no idea why he'd been asked to dine. Whitfield and Chatton looked a bit older than his twenty-four years. Their curious gazes told him nothing.

His innards heaved. He tapped his fingers uneasily on his flanks and looked away. The room was filled with diners. The rich smells of food swirled around him. His gaze passed over a mirror hanging on the wall, and returned. He looked as uneasy as his midsection felt, Peter thought. No Adonis at the best of times, his long, somewhat bony face showed strain. He should have had a haircut; his black hair was too long. And his hazel eyes, which often sparkled with humor when he examined his own reflection, were full of anxiety. So would his companions' be, Peter thought, if they were worried about shooting the cat in White's, at the Earl of Macklin's table. Should he mention the eel pie? No. Not while they were anticipating their dinner.

Peter turned back. The redheaded fellow, Chatton, who looked almost as dyspeptic as Peter felt, gave him a positively vulpine smile. Peter suppressed a start.

"And here is the last of us," said Macklin. "Gentlemen, this is my nephew Benjamin Romilly, Earl of Furness."

The new arrival resembled his uncle, similar

coloring and frame and features in a younger genera-
tion. He looked startled and not at all pleased to see
the party, however. As far as Peter could tell, none of
them were well acquainted and none had expected to
see the others. This was distinctly odd. It would have
been quite interesting if he'd felt better.

"And now that the proprieties are satisfied, I hope
we can be much less formal," their host added after
providing the others' names to his nephew.

They stood gazing at one another. It was the sort of
august company a fellow would like to impress, Peter
thought. As he was unlikely to do even at the top of
his form, not to mention in his current condition. His
stomach twisted. He *would not* moan!

"Sit down," said their host, gesturing at the waiting
table. As they did, he signaled for wine to be poured.
"They have a fine roast beef this evening. As when do
they not at White's? We'll begin with soup, though,
on a raw night like this." The waiter returned his nod
and went off to fetch it.

He didn't dare swallow a morsel of beef, Peter
thought. The mere idea revolted. He might just
manage soup. Perhaps wine would help. Could he
drown that wretched pie? He drank.

"Vile weather," Whitfield said. The others agreed.

He should say something, Peter thought. Not just sit
writhing in his chair. "A fine claret," he contributed.

The rest merely nodded as bowls were set before
them.

Peter toyed with his broth as the others spooned it
up. Chatton leaned forward as if to speak, and then
seemed to forget what he'd meant to say. He downed

his wine instead. He was immediately given more. Like him, the other young men were taking full advantage of the claret. Peter tried a bit more as his full bowl was removed.

A waiter set a steaming plate before him. The beef was thick and juicy, perfectly cooked. The roast potatoes looked crisp and savory, the carrots seared sweet. Peter didn't dare taste any of it. Horseradish sauce! He clamped his teeth and held quite still.

The others tucked in. Frith in particular seemed to enjoy his dinner. Peter cut bites and pushed them about, trying to give the impression of eating.

"No doubt you're wondering why I've invited you—the four of you—this evening," Macklin said. "When we aren't well acquainted."

Chatton leaned forward again. He looked like a fellow who wanted an explanation.

"You have something in common," Macklin went on. "*We* do." He looked around the table. "Death."

What? Peter wasn't sure he'd heard that correctly. He wasn't familiar with the conversational habits of the leaders of the *ton*, but he was pretty certain they didn't usually drop the word *death* at the dinner table. Peter was aware that he had the social graces of... someone with no social graces. But the other young men looked equally surprised.

Macklin nodded across the table, indicating Furness. "My nephew's wife died in childbirth several years ago. He mourns her still."

The man glared at his uncle, clearly not pleased with having this information shared with strangers.

The earl turned to the viscount. "Whitfield's

parents were killed in a shipwreck eight months ago on their way back from India," he continued.

Whitfield looked around the table. Bewildered but determined not to let on, Peter judged. "Quite so," said Whitfield. "A dreadful accident. Storm drove them onto a reef. All hands lost." He shrugged. "What can one do? These things happen." His expression suggested that he didn't wish to say any more about this subject.

"Chatton lost his wife to a virulent fever a year ago," Lord Macklin said.

The marquess positively bared his teeth. "I didn't *lose* her," he replied, his face reddening alarmingly. "She was dashed well *killed* by an incompetent physician and my neighbor who insisted they ride out into a downpour."

This Chatton had difficulty with his temper, Peter decided. He'd take care not to cross him. But now he'd best brace himself for the inevitable.

"Compton's sister died while she was visiting a friend, just six months ago," their host finished.

His preparation did no good. Peter flinched. "She was barely seventeen. My ward as well as my sister." His innards spasmed, sharper for a rush of sadness and guilt. He rested his head in his hands. He couldn't help it. Just for a moment. This was turning into one of the most trying evenings of his life. But none of that. He straightened. "I ought to have stayed with her," he said. "I wouldn't have allowed her to take that cliff path. I would have…done something." Which was a wish rather than a reality. Delia had never heeded his advice. Much less his orders. And she'd ignored her host's clear warnings about the dangers of the path. Still, Peter had been responsible for her, and he'd fallen short.

"I've been widowed for ten years," said Macklin gently. "I know what it's like to lose a beloved person quite suddenly. And I know there must be a period of adjustment afterward. People don't talk about the time it takes, different for everyone I imagine, and how one deals with it." He looked around the table. "I was aware of Benjamin's bereavement, naturally, since he is my nephew."

Furness visibly gritted his teeth. Peter thought he was going to shove back his chair and stalk out. Whitfield looked ready to do the same. But the earl spoke again before they moved.

"Then, seemingly at random, I heard of your cases, and it occurred to me that I might be able to help."

"What help is there for death?" said Chatton. "And which of us asked for your aid?" he muttered. "*I* certainly didn't."

Whitfield pushed a little back from the table. "Waste of time to dwell on such stuff. No point, eh?"

A belch rose in Peter's throat, sour, unstoppable. There was no choice about releasing it. He tried to make it sound like a mournful sigh. Deuce take it, he *was* mournful.

"Grief is insidious, almost palpable, and as variable as humankind," said Macklin. "No one can understand who hasn't experienced a sudden loss. A black coat and a few platitudes are nothing."

"Are you accusing us of insincerity, sir?" Chatton had clenched his fists on either side of his plate. His face was as red as his hair, and he looked as if he'd be delighted to punch someone. Peter edged away from him.

"Not at all," answered the earl. "I'm offering you the fruits of experience and years of contemplation."

"Thrusting them on us, whether we will or no. Tantamount to an ambush, this so-called dinner." Chatton glared at each of his companions in turn.

"Nothing wrong with the food," said Whitfield, soothing. "Best claret I've had this year."

"Well, well," said Macklin. He didn't seem bothered by their responses. "Who knows? If I've made a mistake, I'll gladly apologize. Indeed, I beg your pardon for springing my idea on you with no preparation. Will you, nonetheless, allow me to tell the story of my grieving, as I had hoped to do?"

Peter was fascinated by the offer. If only he felt better, he'd have been happy to listen.

"And afterward, should you wish to do the same, I'll gladly hear it," added the earl. He smiled.

Macklin had a wisely benevolent smile. He looked like the father any man might wish to have, Peter thought.

The earl said his piece. And then the others spoke, briefly, with varying degrees of enthusiasm and candor. When his moment arrived, Peter surprised himself by coming very near tears. He hadn't talked to anyone about Delia's sudden death. He'd had no one to confide in. Macklin's sympathetic manner and the other men's openness gave him a place to speak his regret. The outpouring nearly overset him. Why must he feel ill on *this* night, his every move curtailed by physical discomfort? Even so, he appreciated the chance to express his sorrow about his sister.

When they were done, Peter returned to his inexpensive hotel and gave in to his condition. Through a miserable night, he vowed over and over never to touch another eel pie as long as he lived. But despite these trials, he felt better than he had in months when he started for home a few days later.

One

KNEELING ON THE FLOOR IN THE DOORWAY OF A BED-chamber in his decaying pile of a house, Peter whittled at a sliver of wood. The panels of the door had shrunk, and the latch no longer caught properly, which allowed the door to drift open at the slightest breeze. As if a ghostly presence was slipping inside, Peter thought, though they had no known ghosts at Alberdene. Perhaps the place was too dilapidated even for the departed.

Still, the errant door would be disconcerting for a guest, should he ever have any. He slipped the small slat into a narrow cavity to the left of the latch, wiggling it to fit. This third time, it did, pushing the latch out a bit. He tried it. The door closed properly now, and held. He shook it to make certain, opened it, shut it, opened again. The slat showed no sign of movement. Yes. He'd done it.

Peter savored this tiny triumph. He liked working with his hands, and in recent months he'd been overcome by an impulse to repair, going so far as to assemble a personal tool kit from various sources about the estate. His crumbling home provided endless opportunities to indulge himself. Besides latches that wouldn't close, there were doors that stuck, cracked windowpanes, loose floorboards that creaked and tripped up the unwary, stair treads that could not be trusted, and chairs that threatened to collapse when sat upon. And these were just in the modern, habitable wing of Alberdene. The older parts of the place had much bigger problems, too large for him to tackle, though he was learning to lay brick, to the amusement of the local stonemason. Still, it was satisfying to do what he could—to mend a small hurt in the midst of so many defects he could do nothing about.

Conway, one of Alberdene's two aged footmen, appeared around a corner and walked slowly up the corridor toward him. Most of the household staff had been in service here since his father's time, or even his grandfather's. All of them except the cook and her helper were decades older than Peter and had known him since he was born. They didn't hesitate to express their disapproval when he offended their sense of what was proper, though they did it silently, for the most part. It was more like having a houseful of aged relatives than servants, Peter thought as he rose from his knees. "Yes, I know you don't like to see me doing carpentry work, Conway. There's no need to hover and scowl."

The old footman didn't deign to reply, though he eyed his master's toolbox with disdain.

"I learned my skills at school, you know," said Peter. "The one Papa chose." Rather than send him to Eton or Harrow or Winchester, with other scions of noble families, his father had put him in the hands of an old Welshman with eccentric educational theories. "I think he expected me to come back as some sort of wizard," he muttered. His father had specialized in forlorn hopes.

Conway's lips turned down further. "A visitor has arrived, Your Grace," he said.

Peter was startled. He wasn't expecting anyone. He couldn't recall when Alberdene had last had guests. And passing travelers were exceedingly rare here at the western edge of Shropshire. "Somebody who's lost his way on the road?"

"No, Your Grace." Conway held out a visiting card. "He has a post chaise and all."

Peter took it and read. "The Earl of Macklin!" He scanned the words again with a mixture of astonishment and delight. In the six months since that unusual dinner in London, he and the earl had corresponded a bit. Peter had greatly enjoyed the letters, but Macklin had given no hint that he meant to visit Shropshire. Yet here was his card. Peter brushed the dust from the knees of his buckskin breeches and reached for his old blue coat, conscious that his ensemble did not even approach fashionable. Due to its origins, his shirt had a fall of lace at the neck. Well, he had nothing much better to change into. This would have to do. He picked up his tool case.

"You won't receive an earl carrying *that*," said Conway, aghast.

"Well, I won't if you will take it for me."

"Of course, Your Grace."

"And put it where it belongs. Not in some forgotten

cupboard." Peter's tools had gone astray more than once, as if Conway thought he could end the duke's plebeian endeavors by hiding the implements.

"Yes, Your Grace," replied the footman stoically.

Peter found Macklin in the main reception room of the modern wing—the one chamber at Alberdene that nearly met the standard of a ducal residence. Behind the earl stood a man who was clearly his valet and a lad of perhaps fifteen. "How good to see you," said Peter, striding forward to offer his hand.

"And surprising, I know," said Macklin, shaking it. "I would have written, but I wasn't certain of my plans until just lately. And since I was on my way south, I thought I would visit."

"You're most welcome." Peter was pleased to see him, though Alberdene was hardly on the way to anywhere.

"Your letters made me curious about the place."

"I must warn you that I can't entertain in the style to which you are undoubtedly accustomed. We're rather ramshackle here. Though I do have a good cook."

"Much can be endured for a fine dinner," replied the older man with a smile.

Peter remembered how ill he'd been at the last meal they'd shared, in London. "Please sit down. And excuse me for a moment while I just see about…" He left the sentence hanging. No need to list the items that must be checked on. And the earl would soon learn that the bellpulls didn't work. Peter hadn't been able to trace what had gone wrong with the wires.

He found the entire staff of Alberdene in the

cavernous kitchen, clustered around a long wooden table and clearly agitated by the appearance of a noble visitor. Conway and his fellow footman, Evan, were lined up on one side as if to support each other. Rose and Tess, the middle-aged housemaids, stood nearer Mrs. Anselm, the cook. The latter's young helper, Gwen, lurked behind them.

The butler of Peter's youth had died when he was away at school, and his father had never replaced him. Peter had tried to hire a housekeeper, but several very competent women who'd applied had walked once through the house and declined the position. Mrs. Anselm now wielded a kind of loose general authority, because no one else wanted it. "Lord Macklin will be with us for…a while," Peter said. He hadn't thought to ask how long Macklin meant to stay. Surely a few days, at least? "Have we a room that will do? He has his valet with him and a lad who will also need quarters."

Conway muttered something disparaging about a grand lord's valet. Peter ignored it.

"The blue bedchamber, I expect," said Mrs. Anselm.

"Curtains are threadbare," said Tess.

"Yes, but that fireplace doesn't smoke," replied the cook. "The boy can have the room across. We'll see to the linens."

"They've all been patched," said Rose. "What's an earl going to think?"

Suspecting that Macklin wouldn't be surprised, having seen the state of Alberdene, Peter left them to prepare and returned to his guest.

Macklin made no complaints about his accommodation. Of course he would be too polite to do so, Peter thought as they sat down to dinner that evening. Fortunately, Mrs. Anselm had conjured a tempting spread out of next to nowhere. She might never ask him what he would like to eat, or pay any heed if he tried to express a preference, but every dish she provided was delicious.

Conway ladled soup into Peter's waiting bowl, releasing a wonderful aroma on a wisp of steam. Peter picked up his spoon.

"That is good!" said the lad Tom as they all tasted.

Peter didn't know quite what to make of him. Tom apparently had no last name, which made it vanishingly unlikely that he was related to the earl. He'd argued that he should eat in the kitchen, then given in with a shrug when Macklin said, "Not this time." He had a pleasant, homely face and an engaging manner. Macklin treated him as one might a young nephew. Peter let the matter go. No doubt he would learn more with time.

"Alberdene is quite venerable, I believe," said the earl.

"First established in the eleven hundreds," replied Peter. "Normans subduing the Welsh Marches, you know. And then added onto in a slipshod way. I think of the place as rather like a dragon lying along the ridge. The head is the ruined Norman tower on the high point, and the tail is the modern wing where we are now. With a mass of muddled masonry in between." Once he'd said the whole thing out loud, he wondered if it sounded odd.

"Dragon, I like that," said Tom. He'd finished his soup in record time.

Peter picked up a knife to carve the roast chicken. "I say 'modern,'" he added. "But this bit was built a hundred years ago." He stopped himself from warning them again about the amenities. Or lack thereof. They'd seen by now. He served the chicken, offered sauce. They ate, and Peter enjoyed the company at table even more than the food. He'd had more than enough of dining alone.

A bat swooped under the stone archway and into the dining room, veering this way and that in the breed's characteristic erratic flight. It looked like a bit of black cloth jerked this way and that by an invisible puppeteer.

Peter set down his fork and lifted a moldering implement that was routinely set beside his plate at meals, an open wooden paddle strung with a grid of sheep's gut. With a practiced eye, he gauged the creature's trajectory, and when it passed close to him, he reached up and gave it a sharp rap. The bat fell to the floor.

Peter turned back to find his guests staring at him. They glanced at the recumbent bat, then back at him. Peter felt a flush spread over his cheeks. This was what came of the sort of upbringing he'd been given. And of living alone for too long. He'd become a dashed eccentric. What must Macklin, one of society's leading lights, think of him? "Ah," he said. "Er, sorry. It's a… technique I developed…for dealing with the bats."

Tom laughed in such an easy way that Peter silently blessed him. He set the paddle on the floor and gave Macklin a rueful smile.

For his part, Arthur had been wondering why there was an ancient bit of wood sitting beside his host's plate on the dinner table. Here was the answer.

"They fly in now and then," said Compton, looking embarrassed. "No one can find any holes in the roof, and yet there are always bats. I was trying to track them down when I found this paddle in an attic, years ago. Used for tennis in the Tudor courts, you know. No good for any sort of game now, but it works on the bats."

Arthur watched one of the aged footmen bend laboriously and pick up the bat with a napkin from the sideboard. He wrapped it as if he'd often performed this service.

"Is it dead?" asked Tom.

"No, just stunned," said Compton. "I can't bring myself to kill them. We put them out on the battlements."

The footman sighed audibly.

"And I know they probably fly right back in," said his master. "But even so."

"Reckon I couldn't kill them either," said Tom.

The footman carried the small bundle out of the room.

The young duke was an interesting fellow, Arthur thought, as they returned to the well-cooked meal. He'd thought him shy and anxious at the dinner in London, but Compton showed no sign of those traits now. A bit odd undoubtedly, but intelligent and amiable. Kind also. He oughtn't to be living alone in this huge, silent house. Arthur would have to see if there was anything that could be done about that.

A heave of the post chaise dipping into a rut jerked Ada Grandison out of sleep and the dream that she'd hoped to outrun on this journey. No such luck. It had set its claws into her again, as it did most nights. Ada ground her eyelids together, but she couldn't banish the image of Delia huddled at the bottom of the cliff from which she'd fallen, even though the accident had happened more than a year ago.

The horrible mixture of grief and revulsion wrenched just as hard. The awful blankness of her friend's dark eyes, the pallor of her skin, the *wrongness* of the way Delia lay on the muddy earth, a glowing, animated girl reduced to a husk—they all seemed even more vivid in the dream. Ada had touched her dead friend's neck, hoping to find a pulse, and it was as if she could still feel the dank chill on her fingertips.

Ada rubbed them together, eyes still closed. Why couldn't she forget? Or not forget. Delia shouldn't be forgotten. But…remember less sharply. This stomach-churning dread felt like a weakness. It should be gone by now, not getting worse. The months of broken sleep were wearing on her distressingly.

She clenched her fist. Somebody must know how to banish such things, but she wasn't acquainted with anyone who had found a friend lying cold and dead on the earth. If this journey didn't help, she didn't know what she was going to do. Actually. But it had to. It would! She'd arranged it for just that reason, or hope. She squeezed her eyelids even tighter. She was not going to cry. She shoved the images away, shut them out.

After a time, the tremor passed. Ada opened her eyes and stared out the chaise window at the countryside passing backward away from her. Shropshire was wilder than her home county of Essex. And it seemed they'd had an early cold snap here this September. The morning light showed swathes of leaves turned from green to yellow or russet. The effect was quite lovely, Ada told herself. She should concentrate on that.

They would reach their destination today. She would see the place where Delia had grown up and learn her secrets. It *was* going to help. She was determined that it would.

Ada shifted in her seat. Her small deceptions would also be exposed. There were several items she hadn't mentioned, even to her best friends, and these were all likely to come out in the next few hours. That would be a sticky bit to get through.

A low growl made her look down. Her small dog, nestled in the pile of rugs that warmed their feet, was worrying a kid glove. Bits of it lay scattered around her. "Ella, no!" said Ada. The dog stopped chewing and raised her pert, triangular face. Shreds of glove hung from her teeth.

"Wretched mongrel!" cried Ada's aunt Julia, looming on the carriage seat opposite. Her trumpetlike voice filled the carriage. She held up the mate of the mangled glove.

Of course Ella had mauled Aunt Julia's glove, Ada thought. To say the two had not taken to each other would be a woeful understatement. Why had her aunt removed her gloves? "She is not a mongrel," Ada couldn't help replying. "She's a Pomeranian, like the old queen's dogs."

"And the worst trained animal I've ever encountered," said her aunt. "Overindulged, unintelligent. I don't know why anyone wants a lapdog."

"She is trained." Ada knew she shouldn't argue, but this wasn't fair. "She never chews my things. She's bored. She doesn't like being shut up in a carriage all day."

"The only thing on which we agree," said her aunt. "I can't think why I consented to come on this quixotic journey of yours."

She'd come because she enjoyed thwarting her younger brother, Ada's father, Ada thought. She'd taken advantage of that.

"I feel we should be returning to school at this time of year," said Sarah Moran, sitting next to Ada, in a clear bid to change the subject. Sarah was always a peacemaker. "It's so odd that we're finished with all that."

"To very little purpose as far as I can see," said Aunt Julia. "Ada cannot even speak Italian." Her gaze raked Ada from head to toe.

She could practically feel the critical scrutiny, Ada thought, like a beam of light flashing over her. She reviewed the image the mirror had shown her when she dressed this morning. Her brown hair was neatly coiled. Her round face had been freshly washed then, her cheeks rosy from the towel. The eyebrows that either gave her face character or wrecked any claim to beauty, depending on the observer's point of view, brooded over her dark eyes. Her determined chin made its customary statement.

She looked down. Her blue pelisse was plain, as was the hat on her head. Indeed, Ada knew she still dressed like a schoolgirl, even though she had recently turned eighteen.

Some girls in her neighborhood had gone to London last season and returned with modish clothes and dashing haircuts and superior attitudes. She had ambitions in that direction herself, but she had to make this journey first, had to clear the slate of the past before she could enjoy herself again. She'd convinced her three best friends to come along. It hadn't taken a great deal of persuasion. They were curious, too.

"If you think to get by on a pretty face, you are a sapskull," said her aunt.

Ada suppressed a sigh. She had *not* been thinking that. She never would. Why would Aunt Julia say so? She reminded herself that this expedition wouldn't have been possible without her aunt's chaperonage. This truth didn't make her an easy companion, however.

They'd had to hire two carriages because her aunt was such a large person. And then Ada's friends had, secretly, drawn lots to see who would ride with the formidable lady. Sarah had lost, and so she was with them here. Charlotte and Harriet rode in the other chaise with Aunt Julia's grand lady's maid.

Well, there were always obstacles to be overcome in planning an expedition, thought Ada. Desperation had carried her through. She'd managed to cajole four sets of parents, recruit Aunt Julia, and set them all on the road. She would continue to manage when they arrived at the home of Delia's brother, the duke.

Ada felt her cheeks flush. She turned to gaze at the scenery once again. No one could accuse her of having made friends with Delia in order to scrape an acquaintance with her brother. She hadn't met Peter Rathbone until much later, when he'd brought Delia to visit Ada's home last year. He'd stepped out of the post chaise, handed Delia down, turned to greet the Grandisons, and somehow shaken Ada to the core. A tall, slender young man. Not conventionally handsome, with his long, oval face, straight brows and prominent cheekbones, his dark hair a bit long. But when he'd looked at Ada, she'd felt as if she was falling into his brown eyes. She'd actually been dizzy for a moment. *That* had never happened to her before.

He'd stayed only long enough to see Delia settled. They'd had no private conversation. But Ada had felt it whenever he was nearby. Her whole body had reacted to his presence. And his departure had left her curious and wistful.

Afterward, she'd found herself bringing the young duke into conversations with her friend. She'd hinted to Delia that she would enjoy being invited to Alberdene. And there she'd met with resistance, making Ada wonder about the Rathbones. Somehow, it was only then that she realized how little Delia talked about her family. Her home, yes; Delia had waxed lyrical about Alberdene at the least opportunity. But very rarely its inhabitants. How had they not noticed? The rest of them chattered about their families all the time at school.

And then came Delia's death, a shocking rupture, a dreadful tragedy. The sadness of it would be with

Ada all her life. And yet it also created a link between Ada and Delia's brother, didn't it? They would share that grief forevermore. Ada imagined gazing into his fathomless eyes, taking his hand. No, he would take hers. That was better. And then—

"Oh, look," said Sarah, pointing out the window.

Ada obliged and saw a stag standing on top of a ridge, gazing down at them. As she watched, it sprang away.

"Majestic," said Sarah, who relished such sights.

Ada's aunt made a sound rather like *pish*.

Ada let her thoughts drift back to their destination. A few hours and she would see him again. Would he also be glad? Surely he remembered her. But what, precisely, did he think?

⤙⤚

Peter was startled when two post chaises pulled up in the drive at Alberdene that afternoon. Another arrival so soon after Macklin's! This was unprecedented. What the deuce was going on?

He saw the carriages from the drawing room, where Tess was showing him the dreadful state of the sofa cushions, most of which had rips and frays. Peter was even more astonished when the vehicles began to disgorge females—a whole flock of them it seemed at first. What could this be?

Abandoning the maid as she was demonstrating the impossibility of mending the cushions without the stitches showing, he went down to the entry. Conway would require some bolstering to deal with this new influx.

Indeed, the old footman stood frozen in the open doorway, staring at the newcomers. The travelers resolved into only four young ladies, standing behind an older woman built like a mountain. She wasn't fat, merely massive, nearly as tall as him and sculpted on heroic lines. "I believe you are expecting us," said this colossus in the voice of a town crier.

"I?" said Peter. They must have the wrong house. He thought of his neighbors. None of them seemed likely candidates for this feminine visitation. He hoped they weren't meant for Preston's place. The old man had grown irrationally crusty. He would shower them with oaths they had undoubtedly never heard before.

"You are *not* expecting us?" asked the woman.

She, and the others, turned to look at one of the girls.

Following their gaze, Peter recognized her. It was Delia's school friend Ada Grandison. He'd met her and her parents when he'd taken Delia to the place where she died. A stab of grief went through him. What was she doing here?

"My letter must have been lost," she said.

The way she evaded her party's frowns suggested deception to Peter. Her young companions' faces hinted that they suspected the same. The older woman merely looked indignant.

"The mail is exceedingly reliable," said the latter. She frowned at Peter as if the missing letter was his fault. Indeed, as if he were some species of repellent insect.

"We've come because of Delia," blurted out Miss Ada Grandison.

He winced. He didn't want to hear that.

"Her last wishes," the girl added.

Peter stared at her. What in the name of all the gods was this?

Macklin came out of the house and flanked him. Peter welcomed the support of his illustrious houseguest, particularly when the earl said, "Julia Grandison? How are you?"

"Macklin?" replied the large woman. "What are you doing here?"

"Visiting."

"Indeed?" The colossus scanned her surroundings, with special emphasis on the ruinous bits of Alberdene up the hill.

"Seeing my friend Compton."

The claim of friendship lent Peter consequence, and as the target of five pairs of feminine eyes—no, six, there was a superior servant behind them—he appreciated it. The elder Miss Grandison looked a bit less forbidding.

A tiny, cinnamon-colored dog jumped from the leading post chaise, first to the step and then to the ground. It trotted over to the pillar flanking the door and raised a leg.

"Ella!" cried the younger Miss Grandison.

The dog looked back at her, frozen in position. The girl hurried over and moved the little creature behind an overgrown yew.

A tremor shook Peter. Not a laugh exactly. More a frisson of concern mixed with amusement. Obviously, his situation was primed for disaster. And yet it was rather pleasant to welcome company. "Do come in," he said. The day was waning. There was nowhere else to send them. Whatever was going on would have to go on here. They must be accommodated. As they filed in, he wondered if Mrs. Anselm would resign her position over the demands of so many guests. One of them clearly a high stickler.

His entryway filling with appealing female figures and high-pitched voices, Peter thought of ways to placate his cook. He'd find something to say. Surely they could manage for a day or so. And just as surely, no gently bred female would want to stay in his crumbling home longer than that.

It was astonishing to see the place bustling with people. He'd spent far too much time in empty rooms and echoing corridors.

Except, what had the girl meant about Delia's last wishes?

Two

"I APOLOGIZE FOR THE STATE OF THIS NECKCLOTH, MY lord," said Clayton as he handed Arthur the square of linen. "The flatirons here leave much to be desired. They all appear to date from the last century."

Macklin could see no flaw in the cloth, but his valet's standards were often higher than his own. He began to tie it. "I've thrown you into some odd households this summer, haven't I, Clayton? What do you think of this one?"

"It hardly qualifies as a household, my lord." The valet tidied away the shaving gear. He'd been with the earl for more than twenty years, and Arthur valued his canny insights as much as his personal services. "Mrs. Anselm is a fine cook, and she tries her best to manage the rest of it, but she wasn't trained as a housekeeper. As she would be the first to admit, my lord."

"I wonder Compton doesn't hire one."

"He has tried, I believe. No one found it a…desirable position."

Arthur gave his valet a sidelong glance. Clayton was an unassuming figure in middle age, with a round face that was pleasant rather than handsome and brown eyes. He had the ability to...exude criticism, however. Clearly, he didn't think much of Compton's large, crumbling house, or their host's obvious lack of money. "Understandable, I suppose."

"Indeed, my lord."

This was the greatest contrast so far to the luxurious house parties where they usually spent their summers, Arthur thought. He would have to find some way to reward Clayton for his outstanding service. If he could just find something the man wanted. He'd offered more than once to help the valet into another profession, one befitting his sharp mind and deep well of common sense. Clayton always refused. "I'm sorry for any difficulties the place is causing you," he told him.

"I like a challenge, my lord."

"You always rise to them admirably."

"Thank you, my lord." Clayton helped him into his evening coat, smoothing it over his shoulders. "If you don't mind me saying so," he added. And stopped.

"You know I want you to say what you think," replied Arthur.

The valet acknowledged this with a nod. "The traveling matchmaking—"

Arthur burst out laughing. "Oh lord, what a phrase. Makes me sound like some sort of marital mountebank."

Allowing himself a brief smile, Clayton said, "Hardly that, my lord."

"I suppose this was prompted by the arrival of a bevy of young ladies? Seemed almost like a sign, eh?" He sometimes teased Clayton, just a little.

"I was…concerned you might see it that way, my lord."

"Because?" Arthur asked. He was fairly certain he knew the answer, but he wanted to discuss it. Clayton was a valuable sounding board when he was working out a course of action. And Arthur reasoned better by talking aloud than through introspection.

"A young lady's parents require certain attributes in her husband."

"And no fortune at all is not among them." The signs of poverty were all over Alberdene, from the state of the furniture to the ill-kept gardens to the nearly empty stables.

"Disappointment seems likely," said the valet.

"Compton *is* a duke. An heiress is the traditional solution."

"Yes, my lord." Clayton's voice was expressionless.

"But it seems rather too much to expect that one has dropped by uninvited, eh?"

Clayton nodded. He appeared to suppress a sigh. "Perhaps a family set on…acquiring a title?"

"A rich merchant or a nabob's daughter? I'm not so taken with matchmaking that I'm willing to hunt one down, Clayton." Arthur shook his head. "No. We'll follow our customary course and watch what happens. And what may be done to…ease Compton's situation."

"Yes, my lord." His concern voiced, the valet visibly put the matter from his mind. That did not mean he looked happy, however.

Julia Grandison's voice boomed from the hallway. The words were indistinct, but the tone was plain.

"Miss Grandison would have made an excellent sergeant major," said Arthur. He'd been loosely acquainted with this lady for nearly thirty years. They were of an age and had entered London society at the same time, Julia Grandison with an impact rather like a cannonball striking the venerable walls of the *haut ton*. Even at seventeen, she'd *loomed*, taller than most of her dance partners and built along such heroic lines that they'd appeared feeble. Her voice carried over the buzz of any evening party, and her opinions were strong even then. She seemed to flout the rules of convention simply by existing. Yet Arthur couldn't recall one instance when she'd actually transgressed.

Clayton said nothing, but his expression spoke volumes.

"You don't like her?" asked Arthur.

"I wouldn't presume," said the valet. "But a person might see that there's no sense barking at the staff over things they can do nothing about. As you saw, my lord."

There had been a misunderstanding about a bath, which had been sensibly resolved in the end.

"The elder Miss Grandison changed her room three times and then scolded one of the maids for the *abominable* state of the house. As if Rose or Tess could replace fifty-year-old draperies with a snap of their fingers."

"Ah."

"And the footmen are not accustomed to carrying so much wood," Clayton continued.

Or up to it, Arthur thought. Conway and Evan were undoubtedly older than he was.

"Tom has taken to helping them." Before Arthur could express any concern, Clayton added, "He says he's happy to be busy, and he does seem to be. He's pitched in with Rose and Tess as well, when they seemed like to break down. He's a good lad."

"That he is." Arthur hadn't meant Tom to work as a servant, but he couldn't quite say that to Clayton. "The influx of young ladies seems to have rendered him tongue-tied for the first time, however. He's flatly refused to dine with us."

Clayton looked amused. "Indeed, my lord. But he's the only one who can manage Miss Tate."

"Who is Miss Tate?"

"Miss Julia Grandison's dresser. Absolutely at the top of her profession, according to *her*." Clayton's tone was dry.

"Oh yes, tall, forbidding woman. Turned-down mouth and a stare designed to depress pretensions."

"All but her own."

Arthur smiled. Clayton seldom allowed himself such comments. Miss Tate must have irritated him personally. "I hope things are not too annoying in the servants' hall."

The valet's amusement grew sly. "She won't trouble *me*, my lord."

Arthur had no doubt. Clayton was more than up to the challenge. "I must go down to dinner."

Clayton opened the door and bowed him out.

His dining room had been transformed, Peter thought as the evening meal was served. His table had gone from a silent, empty stretch of boards to a brightly colored festival. The change seemed more engaging with each passing moment. He just hoped the higher level of noise would discourage the bats. He'd put the paddle on the floor, praying he wouldn't have to use it under Miss Julia Grandison's censorious eyes. Macklin's startled amusement at their first dinner had underlined the oddity of his method, and Peter very much wished *not* to demonstrate it before a bevy of young ladies. Yet he couldn't let the bats run rampant. That would be even worse. And there was no better means of removing them.

Miss Grandison loomed on his right side, a monumental presence in blue satin. Her brown hair was dressed in a way that must be all the crack, Peter thought. One could just tell. A diamond necklace and a cashmere shawl draped over her shoulders added to the impression of fashion and wealth. She ought to have been born a monarch, he thought. She was larger than life.

The lady smiled, and Peter was surprised to notice that her features weren't harsh. Indeed, her oval face, straight nose, and bright-blue eyes were quite attractive. The impact of her personality simply outweighed any details of appearance.

Peter had wished he could place Macklin on the woman's other side to help carry the conversation. But with only two gentlemen in the party, he'd had to put the earl at the opposite end of the table. They were separated by a stretch of young ladies in bright dresses, chattering to each other nonstop. He found it difficult to tear his eyes away from this charming sight.

Peter had never had the chance to stand in a fashionable ballroom surveying the range of potential partners, deciding which to choose. He supposed he never would. But here he had a bounty of beauty at his own board, and he was even confident he remembered all their names.

The one on the other side of Miss Grandison was Miss Sarah Moran. She was the shortest of the four, a smiling, round little person with sandy hair that made her brows and eyelashes indistinct and a sprinkling of freckles. Her light-blue eyes sparkled with intelligence, scanning continually, as if she couldn't get enough of the house. Her interest was gratifying. Peter had worried that his domestic arrangements might inspire disdain.

Beyond her sat Miss Charlotte Deeping, the tallest of the young ladies. Indeed, if Miss Grandison hadn't been present, Miss Deeping might have been thought quite tall. The effect was made more pronounced by her slender frame. She had black hair, pale skin, and a sharp, dark gaze. When it fell on him, Peter was suddenly more conscious of his shabby evening dress. There was an edge of dispassionate analysis in that look. She'd cut her roast beef into precise bits, all the same size.

After her came Macklin. Seeming to sense Peter's regard, the earl looked up and smiled. His solid presence was reassuring. Indeed, Peter didn't quite know what he would have done if this feminine influx had descended upon him alone. They definitely needed more gentlemen in their party, he thought, but young Tom had refused to join them. Overwhelmed by the visitors, Macklin had said. Peter could understand that.

On Macklin's other side sat Miss Harriet Finch,

who was the prettiest of the four, Peter decided. Her red-blond hair glinted in the candlelight. Green eyes and a pointed chin beneath a broad forehead graced a beautiful figure. If this had been a real choice, he'd have asked her to dance. She turned her head, found him looking, and raised her chin and her brows. Her gaze was cool. He dropped his own. He hadn't meant this as a challenge.

He shifted his attention to Miss Ada Grandison on his left side. Miss Ada, he corrected silently. Her aunt was enough Miss Grandison for anyone. He placed her at his other side because at least he'd met her before this visit.

It was too bad about the eyebrows, he thought. He'd noted them when he was first introduced to this girl by his sister. They were heavy, authoritative, hinting at a scowl even when Miss Ada was smiling, as she was now. They dominated the smooth brown hair, brown eyes, straight nose, and full lips that were rather too tempting for her schoolgirl's evening dress. Which was not a thing to be thinking. What was wrong with him? Peter turned away.

"This dinner is quite well cooked," said Miss Ada's aunt, sounding surprised. She poked at her roast beef as if it might yet reveal some shortcoming.

"Thank you, ma'am," replied Peter. "Mrs. Anselm will be pleased to hear that you think so."

"She is nearly up to town standards." Miss Grandison stirred a puree of potatoes with her fork. "You may tell her I said so," she added with gracious condescension.

Peter nodded and kept his smile to himself.

"I can't wait to look inside the ruined tower," said

Miss Moran on the large lady's other side. "It reminds me of an engraving of Tintagel."

"Tin-what?" asked Miss Deeping.

"Tintagel. The castle where King Arthur's mother lived."

"Wasn't she mythical?"

"Be very careful where you walk," said Peter. "There are places up the hill where you could fall and be hurt."

And just like that, Delia's death entered the room and settled at the table with them, the specter at the feast.

Everyone went silent, no doubt remembering that Peter's sister had been told to avoid a dangerous cliff path. She'd ignored the warning, slipped, and fallen.

"In fact, please don't wander about alone," Peter added. "Or at all. Until I can show you where it's safe."

"You may consider that an order," said Miss Julia Grandison, scanning her charges.

She received a chorus of subdued agreements. Everyone returned to their dinners.

As the pain of his sister's death came flooding back, Peter wondered why they had come. He would never forget Delia, but the immediacy of loss had been fading before they arrived. Now, her absence loomed over this gathering of her friends.

Gradually, conversations revived. Macklin, clearly a master at smoothing over awkward moments, helped them along with kindly remarks. Miss Deeping and Miss Finch debated the merits of Chantilly cream versus apple pie. Their chaperone cast her vote for the latter.

"You *will* show us the house?" Miss Moran asked Peter after a bit. "I would so like to see the older bits. Where it's safe to walk, of course."

"Sarah is terribly studious," said Miss Ada from his left side. "I expect she's read tomes about old towers in Shropshire."

Miss Moran's flush confirmed this guess, though she corrected it to "towers on the Welsh Marches."

"She'll probably tell you all sorts of things you don't know about your own home," said Miss Deeping.

"Will you stop," said Miss Moran. "You make me sound like a dreadful bore."

"Never," replied Miss Finch. "You are always full of interesting tidbits."

These four had clearly been friends for a long time, Peter thought. Their exchanges had an easy rhythm that he envied. He agreed to take them around the house in the morning.

Macklin expressed his interest in coming along. Miss Julia Grandison did not. "You'll be covered in dust," she said.

"Very true," said Peter. "You must be prepared for rather a lot of it."

"But it will be *ancient* dust. Eh, Sarah?" said Miss Finch.

"Venerable dust," Miss Moran replied.

"Ducal dust," said Miss Deeping with a sidelong smile at Peter.

"They are only teasing," said Miss Ada at Peter's side.

"Yes, I see." He wasn't sure whether he minded. He hadn't really been teased before. His lost sister had been a serious girl. Not humorless. Precisely. But certainly no jokester. "What did you mean by Delia's last wishes?" he asked Miss Ada. He'd been thinking about this phrase since she first uttered it.

"We can't talk about that here," said the girl.

"Why not?"

She nodded toward her chaperone on Peter's other side and gave him a conspiratorial smile.

The result was astonishing. The curve of those full lips and the sparkle in her dark eyes counteracted the harsh effect of the eyebrows. She went from stern to stunning in a single instant. The smile seemed to literally warm him, like a crackling fire on a cold day. It was almost enough to make him forget his question. But not quite. "Whatever can you—" he began.

"Is that a bat?" asked Miss Deeping.

Naturally it was, Peter saw with a sinking feeling in the pit of his stomach, even though he'd shut every nearby door that would latch. The dining room had a stone arch and couldn't be entirely closed off.

The scrap of black dipped and fluttered above them. Miss Deeping threw her arms over her head. Miss Finch crouched in her chair. Miss Moran loosed a small shriek.

And a small whirlwind erupted from the vicinity of Miss Ada's feet. Her tiny dog, which had been silently well behaved up to now, went berserk. In a frenzy of barking, the little creature raced up and down the room, leaping for the bat as if its tiny legs had springs.

The bat looped lower. Miss Finch squeaked and also covered her head with her arms.

The dog jumped amazingly high for its size. Time

almost seemed to slow as it hurtled into the air. The bat veered downward. The two drew closer, nearly, nearly meeting. Then the dog fell back, and the bat flew on.

"Ella, no!" said Miss Ada.

Peter noticed Macklin. The earl was gazing at him with a cocked head and a half smile, almost as if he was enjoying this spectacle. Easy for him to do so. It wasn't his house infested with flying rodents. Were bats rodents? Obviously, that didn't matter. Whatever its species, the creature was frightening his guests and driving a pet dog mad. With a sigh, Peter bent and picked up the wooden paddle from the floor. Rising, he caught up his napkin in his other hand.

The frenzied dog raced around Peter's feet as he stalked the bat. Peter had to take care not to trip or kick the little animal as he tracked the bat's flight pattern. Cries from the table and Miss Julia Grandison's stentorian exclamations didn't help. But at last, he calculated the correct angle and administered the rap that knocked the bat from the air. Bending quickly, he scooped it up in his napkin, only just snatching it out of the tiny dog's reach. Ella reared against his leg, front paws scrabbling, demanding the prize with a fury of barking.

Peter held the bundled bat well out of the dog's reach. He handed the napkin off to Conway, who carried it from the room. Ella followed him, still in full doggy voice, her tiny body vibrating with emotion. Murderous outrage? Territorial indignation? Defensive loyalty?

Turning, Peter found his guests looking at him

with varying degrees of astonishment. Of course. He was certain they'd never seen anything like *that* before. He'd tried to appear conventional despite his surroundings, but now he'd established himself as the eccentric duke in the crumbling castle. A sigh escaped him. Alberdene certainly *was* crumbling, and he supposed he was a bit out of the ordinary. But he'd hoped to play down the latter.

Well, there was nothing to be done now except try to be charming. Surely he was capable of charm? It was difficult to say actually. He'd had almost no opportunities to gain or exercise such a skill.

He returned to his chair, setting the paddle back on the floor. Everyone's eyes followed his movements. He straightened, smiled, drank a little wine, and summoned his wits. "Your dog doesn't like bats," he said to Miss Ada, and immediately deplored his choice of remark.

"I don't think she's ever seen one before," the girl replied. "But apparently she does not."

Miss Moran began to giggle. Miss Finch took a deep breath. "I was afraid it would fly into my hair," said Miss Deeping.

"I've never known a bat to do that," said Peter. "Despite the stories. In fact, they seem uncannily able to avoid it."

"And you are an expert on bats, I suppose," said Miss Julia Grandison dryly.

One might as well embrace one's fate, Peter thought. What other choice was there? "I am rather. They're…indigenous." He blinked. Where had that word come from?

"Where has the footman taken it?" asked her niece.

"Out to the battlements. It will recover in a bit." He didn't want them to see him as a killer. The older woman raised her eyebrows. Now she would tell him that the bat would simply fly back inside, Peter thought. And that his efforts were futile if he did not kill them. But she didn't speak.

"Ella is usually such a good dog," said Miss Ada.

Her aunt's snort argued otherwise.

"The footman won't let her out, will he?" the girl added.

"I'm sure he'll take care not to. As should you. There are foxes and other beasts in the woods that would eat her." Which added to the general impression he was making by suggesting that his grounds were a roaring wilderness. Peter pressed his lips together to keep any further slips from escaping.

"Unless she drove them mad with barking first," said Miss Julia Grandison. "Really the most undisciplined animal."

"I don't see how I was to train her about bats," replied her niece. "We haven't any at home."

And there was his situation in a nutshell, thought Peter. A cracked and moldering nutshell. His visitors would most likely flee Alberdene at the first opportunity, which was a rather melancholy thought, he found.

❧

Late that evening, the four young ladies gathered in the bedchamber Ada and Sarah were sharing. Ada's aunt Julia had insisted that they sleep two to a room, so that, as she put it, "the men couldn't get at them."

With hair braided for sleep, in nightdresses and shawls, they looked as they used to do in similar sessions at school. They did have a fire here, as they had not then, and Ella was curled up on the hearthrug, exhausted after her exertions with the bat.

"How long are we staying here?" asked Charlotte, lounging in an armchair. "The piano is so out of tune that it sounded like a yowling cat. I think it's been warped by damp."

"I want to look over the house," replied Sarah from the bed. "Particularly the Norman tower on top of the hill."

"Fine," replied Charlotte. "That may be interesting for a day or two. But what then? Look, the stuffing is coming out of this chair." She pulled on a tuft. "The place is falling apart."

Harriet, sitting cross-legged at the foot of the bed, looked at Ada, propped up by pillows. "What is your deep secret, Ada? You insisted we had to come but never said why."

They all gazed at Ada, their faces showing varying degrees of concern. They'd been doing that throughout the journey, as if they somehow knew about her dreams. But they didn't. "I should tell the duke first."

"Tell him *what*?" asked Charlotte. "Something about Delia? What in the world did you mean about her last wishes?"

Like every mention of Lady Delia Rathbone, this brought solemnity down on them. They had known each other far longer than they'd been acquainted with her. But Delia had been part of their group for two years. Her death had shocked them all.

"You never told us anything about last wishes," said Sarah.

Ada wished they hadn't heard that phrase. She wished she hadn't said it. "It's not exactly that," she said. "Or it is, in a way. I think."

"What is?" Charlotte's dark eyes narrowed. "What are you plotting?"

"Nothing!"

"I don't see why you shouldn't tell us now," said Harriet. "We won't tattle, and you don't even know him."

"He was her brother." Ada tried to keep her tone emotionless and, from the changes in their expressions, clearly failed.

"You like him!" exclaimed Sarah. "You didn't say you liked him."

"Because that would have been…exaggerating," replied Ada. A good word for it, she decided. "As Harriet pointed out, I don't know him."

"That didn't stop you mooning over that actor in the play at Bath," said Charlotte.

Ada threw a pillow at her. "I was thirteen!"

Charlotte deflected the pillow, which fell on Ella. She jumped up with an indignant bark.

"Well, I think it's romantic," said Sarah, blinking her pale lashes.

"You think nearly everything is romantic," replied Charlotte. "You find ways to make the most mundane events into epics."

"No I don't. But this *is*. I think the duke must be very lonely, living in this great house all alone."

"Don't go Byronic on us," said Charlotte. "He

seemed to have a jolly time swatting bats out of the air. I didn't know whether to laugh or succumb to the vapors."

This last phrase drew derisive glances, as nothing could have been more unlikely.

"He looked haunted," said Sarah.

"He did not. Not in the least." Charlotte turned back to Ada. "And he is definitely *not* a good prospect."

"Prospect! What a word." Ada evaded her friend's sharp gaze.

"We're honest among ourselves, are we not? Haven't we agreed on that? Money is important in life, and he obviously has none." Charlotte pulled another tuft of stuffing from the armchair and held it up as a piece of evidence to prove her point.

Ada looked away.

"Unless you've suddenly become an heiress?" Charlotte continued. "Oh no, that's Harriet, not you."

"I'm not an heiress," said Harriet.

"Yes, you are. What are you intending with this duke, Ada?"

"Nothing! Don't be managing, Charlotte. You promised to stop *interrogating*. This visit isn't about that."

"What then? Tell or we won't believe you."

Ada shifted under her friends' eyes. The four of them usually told each other everything. But she just couldn't admit to the dreams. She was rather ashamed of them. They seemed the sort of thing she ought to be able to throw off on her own.

"What are you up to?" asked Harriet. "If this is one of your mad schemes…"

"I don't know what you mean," protested Ada. "When have I ever made mad schemes?"

Charlotte held up one finger as if about to tick off a list.

"Don't start," said Ada. She would tell them about everything else, she decided. It was time. "I have something of Delia's."

"I thought all her things were sent back." Harriet gestured at the house. "Here."

Ada nodded. "But I couldn't stop thinking about her," she admitted. "After." This trip must have made that obvious anyway. "I went to the room where she stayed at our house." Actually, she'd gotten into the habit of sitting there alone, but no need to mention that. "And looked around. And I found something under the mattress."

All three of her friends spoke at once.

"Under the—" began Harriet.

"Something? What?" asked Sarah.

"So you took it to your mother?" said Charlotte. Sarcastically, as if she was well aware that the answer was no.

"I was going to," replied Ada. She had thought of handing it over, for a fleeting moment.

"But you didn't," Charlotte said.

Ada shook her head.

"You didn't write to arrange this visit either, did you?" asked Harriet.

She hadn't written because she didn't want to be refused, Ada thought. And she hadn't exactly *said* she'd written. Not in so many words. Her friends were all looking at her. Oh very well, she'd practiced a small deception. They didn't understand how important this was. They weren't woken nearly every night by grim dreams. They hadn't seen Delia lying in the mud. She squashed that recollection.

"So what did you find?" asked Sarah again.

This was the thing, Ada thought. She must keep her focus on the present. "It's a sort of…document."

"Sort? What does it say?"

"I can't read it," replied Ada. "It's in a foreign language."

Charlotte perked up. "Which?"

"I can't tell." Ada slipped off the bed and went to her dressing case. She extracted a folded sheet of paper and brought it to show them. The four girls clustered together to read.

"Well, that's not French or German," said Charlotte.

"Or Italian," said Harriet. Unlike Ada, she had profited from lessons in this tongue.

"Are you sure it's not just gibberish?" Charlotte frowned, running a finger over the lines. "I've never seen anything like this."

"I don't think it can be," said Ada. "It was so carefully hidden away. But I don't know what it is. I thought I would show it to her brother and see if he knows what it means."

"I wouldn't tell *my* brother if I had secrets," said Sarah.

"Even if he was the only family you had?" asked Ada.

They all contemplated this sad fact.

"That must be strange," said Charlotte, who had a large and lively family.

Ada put the page aside. "The other thing is, Delia told me a few days before she…died that she'd solved a puzzle about her family. She said it would change everything."

Charlotte looked skeptical. "Delia did tend to talk that way. She was worse than Sarah for flowery language."

"I beg your pardon?" said Sarah.

"She seemed to really mean it," said Ada, though Charlotte was of course right. Delia had often spoken like a Shakespearean heroine. Ada hadn't paid a great deal of attention at the time, particularly when Delia refused to be more specific.

"Well, she generally did," replied Charlotte. "She specialized in *meaning*. But her…prognostications didn't always come true."

The others looked at the paper, then back at Ada.

"So you've brought us here to figure out what she meant?" asked Harriet. "A mystery? Why didn't you say so?"

"The Grandison team reunited," said Sarah.

"You make us sound like horses," said Harriet.

At Charlotte's raised eyebrows, Sarah added, "We did discover where Mary Yelton's purse had gone. And the ring taken by the crow."

"True." Charlotte's dark gaze grew speculative. "So we are to find out what this secret is about. I suppose we might do that." Her expression belied her bland words. She was thrilled at the prospect. So was Sarah.

Ada was filled with warmth for her friends. She might be plagued by dire dreams, but she had staunch companions.

"No sneaking though," said Harriet, their perennial voice of caution.

"Of course not." Ada considered. "Except around Aunt Julia."

No one argued with that.

❧

In the deeps of the night, Peter heard an unfamiliar noise from the lower floor of his house. His room was near the head of the stairs, and sound carried easily up the stairwell. As he hadn't been asleep, he heard it clearly. Something had fallen down below.

He reached for the woolen robe he kept near his bed and lit a candle by feel. He was often awake in the night. Indeed, his common pattern was to sleep for a time, wake to read or think or even walk a little, and then go to sleep a second time. He'd been this way since he was a child and never felt ill effects.

Stepping into leather slippers, he left his room and moved quietly down the steps, holding the candle high.

He saw no other light. Shadows loomed around him, shifting with the moving candle flame.

He passed through the lower hall, peered into the dining room and found it empty. The largest reception room was ahead, and he heard another soft sound from that direction.

The door was open on darkness. He strode forward with his light held before him, and started at a shimmer of white in the corner of his eye. There were no ghosts at Alberdene. Delia had longed for them and searched for them and never found any. Peter turned toward the pale spot.

Miss Ada Grandison stood there, clad in only her thin nightdress. Her dark eyes were enormous. Her lips were parted. She looked bewildered and afraid. "Miss Ada?" he said. "What are you doing here?"

"I don't know." Her voice quavered. "It was so dark. I didn't know where I was." She swayed, putting out a hand as if to steady herself.

Peter stepped forward. Setting the candlestick on a table, he put an arm around the girl and led her to a chair. She half fell into it. He knelt beside her. "I don't understand. Why did you come downstairs?" he asked. Indeed, he wondered how she'd gotten here without any light.

"I didn't!"

He looked around the room and then back at her face.

She followed his gaze, her formidable brows drawn together in a bewildered frown. "I went to sleep," she said. Her voice sounded distant, as if she was still half there. "Just as usual. I did have a dream." She clasped her forearms as if for comfort. "I've had it before." She swallowed.

He gave her a little time. But when she didn't speak, he said, "And then?"

"There was a sound, I think, and I woke up in the dark." She shuddered. "I had no idea where I was!"

Peter had already noticed a vase lying on the floor in pieces. She must have brushed against the stand it had sat on and knocked it off. "You were sleepwalking?"

"What? No, of course I wasn't."

"But if you woke up here, you must have been."

She gazed at him, her eyes wide and frightened again.

"I've heard of sleepwalking but never seen it," Peter commented.

This was clearly the wrong thing to say. "Sleepwalking," she repeated as if the word was a curse. She clutched her arms tighter.

The movement drew her thin nightdress tight against her body, leaving very little to the imagination. Peter couldn't help noticing. Such a lovely sight compelled attention. He could stop staring, however. He raised his eyes to her face. "I beg your pardon." Whether this applied to his awkward remark or to noticing her unclad state, he could not have said. Both, probably.

She scarcely seemed to hear him. "I've never done *that* before," she said. A tear slid down her cheek. With a soft moan she buried her face in her hands. "You must think I'm mad."

"Not remotely," said Peter.

Miss Ada looked up. Her dark eyes swam with tears. "You don't?"

"Obviously you aren't."

She blinked, gazing at him. "You're so calm."

He wasn't certain whether this was a compliment or a criticism. Her tone was a mystery.

"Drawing-room conversation seems to unsettle you. But you're perfectly at ease with this." She gestured at their eerie surroundings.

The movement pulled at her nightdress in a way that sent Peter's pulse racing. *At ease* did not describe his state just now. And her opinion of his manners didn't help. He looked away. "I suppose I'm more accustomed to shadowy solitude than to drawing rooms." He realized the truth of this as he spoke, while wishing that it hadn't sounded so stilted.

Miss Ada appeared to consider this. She looked calmer, which was good. "Did I break the vase? Oh dear."

"A matter of no consequence. I've always thought the thing quite ugly."

This won him a fleeting smile. Then her formidable eyebrows came together again. "But why did I sleepwalk?"

Peter had no idea. He was moved to help her, however. "Perhaps the influence of a strange place?" He attempted a joke. "Alberdene must be unlike any other house you've visited."

"Delia said it was mystical," she replied in a strained voice.

He wanted her to find comfort. More than he could offer as a stranger. "I should fetch one of your friends," he began.

She straightened, suddenly fierce, and gripped his hands. "Promise you won't tell anyone about this!"

"You're freezing," he exclaimed at the touch of her fingers.

"Promise!"

"Wouldn't it be better if someone knows? Your aunt or—"

"I'm not a child!"

"No, but—"

"You couldn't be so low as to betray me."

Under the intensity of her gaze, it seemed he couldn't. And yet help wasn't a betrayal. Was it?

"This has never happened to me before. I daresay

it never will again. I can't bear to be watched as if I might go off at any moment. Or pitied for being odd."

Peter certainly understood that. "All right," he said. "I won't mention this. But if it *should* happen again—"

"It won't!"

She sounded certain enough to make it so. "Let me take you back to your room now," he answered. "You are cold."

Miss Ada rose, rubbing her hands together. Her nightdress billowed about her, to Peter's rueful relief. "I am," she said as if just noticing.

Retrieving his candle, Peter led the way to the stair. Behind him, she spoke very softly. "Sorry?" he replied. "I didn't hear you."

"You don't think it was Delia, do you?" she said.

"What?" He turned. The candle flame pulsed between them, gilding her face.

"Delia," she repeated. "Leading me? Somewhere?"

Instinctively, he rejected the idea. "No. No, I don't."

"It's just… This was her home."

Regret and remorse filled him. "It was. But she is no longer here."

"No. Of course not. There was nothing like that in the dream."

"Dream?" They stood very close together. The candlelight practically shone through the thin cloth of her nightdress. He could see contours that he… shouldn't be seeing. He felt his face flush.

"I dream of Delia. Sometimes."

"She was your friend," Peter managed. His throat was constricted. "She wouldn't hurt you."

Miss Ada's dark eyes widened. She stood a step below him—barefoot, her hair escaping its braid in dark, tousled curls, her nearly transparent nightdress gathered up in one hand for walking. Her lips parted in apparent astonishment. She stared at him, through him. "She…she wouldn't, would she?"

Peter was struck speechless. As if the power of speech hadn't yet been invented. He fought to tear his eyes from her. "Up," he said, and nearly choked on the quite unintended implications of that word. "Upstairs," he managed. "Must go." He turned and moved away.

Her footsteps were silent behind him. He wanted to turn and look, but he denied that inner request, told himself to concentrate on the stairs.

"What is that you're wearing?" Miss Ada asked then. "You look like an Arab in an adventurous novel."

Peter looked down at the robe he wore, with its wide stripes of buff and brown. He used it because it was warm and practical. And he couldn't waste his slender resources on a fashionable silk dressing gown. He half turned, his gaze firmly downcast. "My father found it in the attic. He thought it came from Egypt."

"Egypt?"

"My great-grandfather went there on the grand tour."

"Oh. How interesting."

Interesting was what kind people said when they meant odd, Peter thought. She sounded as if she'd recovered from her nighttime adventure. They were back in the realm of polite society, where he was a foreigner.

"My toes feel like blocks of ice."

"We must get you back to bed." He felt his flush deepen. Stop talking, Peter thought. Don't think of beds. Escort her back, leave her. He turned and hurried up the stairs.

"Thankfully, Sarah is a heavy sleeper," Miss Ada murmured as they reached the upper corridor. "She probably doesn't even know I was gone." They came to her room. She put a hand on the doorknob. "Thank you," she added, and smiled.

Peter nodded, and kept on nodding. As at dinner, her smile transformed her.

"You should take the light away before I go in. In case Sarah wakes."

He started and backed away, nearly stumbling on the hem of his robe. She seemed wholly recovered. Peter wasn't so sure about himself.

Three

PETER MADE HIS WAY TO THE KITCHEN EARLY THE NEXT day to speak to Mrs. Anselm. "I believe we need to hire more help," he said to the cook. "We can't take proper care of so many visitors." He'd seen Conway hauling a great load of wood and Evan staggering under a large can of hot water. That wouldn't do. The unexpected influx of visitors was asking too much of his aged staff. Yet he didn't want the newcomers to go. It had been pleasant to have Macklin's company. The arrival of the ladies had raised his spirits even farther. He disliked the thought of returning to emptiness and silence. He would have to use the small store of funds he'd been setting aside, for as long as it would last.

"I suppose this would be temporary?" the cook said. "Conway and Evan will worry you mean to turn them off unless we say so."

"How could I ever?" He'd known the two footmen longer than anyone else in his life.

"The maids are run off their feet as well," Mrs. Anselm continued.

"I'm sure they are."

"Young Tom has pitched in, but there's just too much to do. And he shouldn't have to, by rights."

Peter nodded. "Can you find some local helpers?"

"I expect I can."

"Thank you, Mrs. Anselm, for all your efforts."

"Provision bills will be up," she replied.

"I know." How he hated the pinching and scraping, Peter thought as he left the kitchen. He didn't want to spend lavishly or haunt the gaming tables. But what sort of duke couldn't even entertain a few guests? It was humiliating. And of course they'd noticed the truth of his situation. How could they miss it, what with the fraying draperies and sofa cushions? Not to mention the bat. Was it possible to be entertaining enough to compensate for dilapidation? How, precisely? Among all the things he'd been taught, there had been no lessons in that. What had Miss Ada said last night? That drawing-room conversation seemed to unsettle him. It wasn't the conversation so much as the fear of not being able to come up with any, he thought.

Most of his visitors were waiting for him in the drawing room, ready for the tour of the house he'd promised. Macklin and Tom flanked the four girls. Peter's gaze skimmed over Miss Ada. She looked prim and smooth this morning, not adorably disheveled as she had on the stairs. He glanced at her face for signs that she was thinking of last night and found none. Her little dog sat at her feet. "Are you sure you want to bring your dog?" he asked.

"I can't leave Ella alone in our bedchamber. She mopes dreadfully."

Peter thought of suggesting that Ella stay in the kitchen, but he didn't think Mrs. Anselm, or her cat, would appreciate the addition. He examined the dog. Bulging bright eyes in a tiny triangular face stared back at him. The creature seemed a mere puff of cinnamon fur. Her panting tongue was very like a grin. "You should put her on a lead then," he said. "There are places where she shouldn't run about. Most of them, really."

Miss Ada went to fetch the leash.

"Are you bringing your bat catcher?" asked Miss Deeping. Her dark eyes glinted satirically.

"I don't bother with it except in the dining room."

"You give the bats free rein?"

She made it sound as if his home was teeming with bats. Peter decided that Miss Deeping was his least favorite of the younger visitors. "There aren't so very many," he said.

"Perhaps there's only the one," suggested Miss Finch. "The same bat rendered mindless by repeated blows, so that it comes to the dining room over and over."

A smile softened this jest. Miss Finch really was lovely, Peter thought. That red hair combined with those green eyes was striking.

"Oh no," said Miss Moran.

"Or it's simply enjoying the game?" asked Miss Deeping. "Hide and smash?"

"Charlotte!" said Miss Moran.

Tom burst out laughing. This caused the three young ladies to look at him. He stepped behind the earl, who had been observing the conversation with silent interest. Almost as if they were all in a play that Macklin had come to see, Peter thought. He appeared to be enjoying it.

Miss Ada returned and fastened a lead to her dog's collar. Peter distributed unlit candlesticks.

"Are we venturing into darkness?" asked Macklin mildly.

"Ivy has grown over quite a few windows," Peter replied. "We can't keep up with it. It makes the rooms dim." He lit his candle at a lamp that had been left burning.

"Are there dungeons?" asked Miss Moran.

"No. Unless under the tower at the top. The rocks are too tumbled to tell what might be below."

"Were you hoping for a skeleton still locked in ancient shackles?" Miss Deeping asked her friend.

Miss Moran denied it. But her round face showed disappointment, as if she might have been.

"Shall I carry a poker from the fireplace?" asked Miss Deeping.

"Why would you wish to?" Did she imagine his home harbored bandits?

"In case of rats," she replied. The other girls looked anxious.

"There are no rats," Peter assured them.

"Of course there aren't," said Miss Ada. "You're being tiresome, Charlotte."

"I am not," replied the spiky, angular girl. "Only realistic."

"My father established a troop of cats in the tower block years ago," Peter said. "He made an entry for them in the oldest part of the house. They control rodents quite well." The stares of his guests made Peter realize that this was another oddity not encountered at the typical house party. At least, he expected it wasn't. He'd never been to one. His father had called the cats a troop, as if they were a military installation. He ought to find another word.

"I love cats," said Miss Moran.

"Ella mostly doesn't," said Miss Ada.

"We're not likely to see any of them. They're quite shy." Still another reason for the dog to be leashed, Peter thought. The cats that patrolled the uninhabited parts of his house probably outweighed the little creature. If any of them caught her alone, they might choose to punish her trespass on their territory.

"How can you keep such a large house clean?" asked Miss Finch.

"We don't try," Peter said. "I told you there would be dust." And they'd laughed at him as if it was a joke. Had they forgotten that?

"Of course there will be," said Miss Ada. "We are quite prepared."

Miss Deeping and Miss Finch exchanged uncertain glances. Miss Moran, on the other hand, seemed to brim with enthusiasm.

Among the many entertainments offered at fashionable gatherings, coating the guests with dust must rank near the bottom, Peter thought. Or…what nonsense. It wasn't on the list at all. He hoped Mrs. Anselm had recruited some stalwart helpers to carry hot water later. "You've seen this wing, which is much like any other house." Except for the general decrepitude. But he needn't mention that. "So we'll move on to the next oldest part and work our way up to the Norman tower." He started off, noticing that young Tom had fallen in beside Miss Deeping. Macklin took a position at the back, like a rear guard.

Peter unlocked a stout door and let them into the largest part of the house. This rambling seventeenth-century stretch was in poor repair but still livable. There was just no reason to use cramped rooms with low ceilings and warped paneling. Ushering his group in, Peter marshaled his facts. His father had made him memorize a condensed family history as a boy. Could he make it interesting to his guests? "The first Rathbone in this country arrived with William the Conqueror in 1066, though the name was a bit different then," he began. "He tagged along to the Welsh Marches with the first Earl of Shrewsbury, one of the Conqueror's chief henchmen. That Rathbone married a Welsh girl with some property and managed to establish himself before a later Shrewsbury rebelled and got his title abolished."

"But there is an Earl of Shrewsbury," said Miss Moran. "My father knows him."

"Yes, the earldom was revived later." Peter forgot why. Some service to the crown, he supposed. "After a few centuries of lying low, the Rathbones threw in their lot with the Tudors, as they were so near Wales here. Which was risky at first but advantageous later. The third Baron Rathbone was killed fighting at Bosworth Field."

"Fourteen eighty-five," said Miss Moran. "The last stand of Richard the Third."

"Yes." Peter smiled at her. She, at least, was

interested. It was a relief to have an appreciative audience. "His grandson was a friend of Henry the Eighth and benefited from that connection, moving up in the ranks over the years." He had in fact played tennis with that quixotic monarch, using the paddle Peter now applied to the bats. He debated whether to mention that and decided not to remind them. "No one knows why Queen Elizabeth granted the dukedom not long before her death."

"A romance?" asked Miss Moran, brightly hopeful.

"Well, the queen was seventy and the new duke nineteen." Peter made an equivocal gesture. Who knew what those ancient types got up to? He led his group out into a cavernous space. "This is the great hall which was once the main entrance to the house." The space was designed to intimidate. There had been banners hanging from the ceiling when he was a boy. Peter couldn't see any now. Perhaps they'd fallen to pieces. "We'd best light your candles here," he added. The ivy took over in the next section, and the medieval floors after that were uneven. "And look out for loose tiles. It's easy to trip."

Peter set his candle flame to their wicks and led them on through the dim, silent house. Gradually, his guests grew subdued. Even Miss Moran, who had started out wishing to peer inside every chamber and examine every ornament, began to look daunted. He knew the feeling. The dusty, empty spaces dampened one's mood. "Perhaps you've had enough for today?" he asked. He received a chorus of denials, and he couldn't tell whether they were sincere or mere politeness. So they pressed on. Peter searched his memory for entertaining anecdotes about his feckless ancestors.

Ada stepped over a broken bit of tile and moved past Charlotte, wondering how she was ever going to speak to the duke alone. Her friends had agreed to help her manage this, and Aunt Julia's absence was a definite advantage. But so far they'd all moved along in a clump. She couldn't say anything important in front of everyone. And after last night, more than ever, she longed to talk to him. She'd wakened lost in the dark, alone and frightened. Then Peter Rathbone had come along and comforted her. He'd accepted her bizarre situation as if she had done nothing wrong. She'd felt cheered rather than ashamed. And on the way upstairs he'd spoken the phrases that still rang in her mind. Delia had been her friend; she wouldn't hurt her.

The group paused to look at a huge painting of a battle. In the wavering light of their candles the mounted troopers seemed to lunge at each other. "Is that meant to be Bosworth Field?" asked Sarah.

"Yes," replied Compton. "That's supposed to be John Rathbone, the third baron, in the center."

"The one with his eyes nearly closed?" asked Charlotte.

The duke nodded. "He looks the same in his portrait in the gallery. Half-asleep."

Sleepwalking, thought Ada. She'd never done anything like that before. It worried her. Well, she never would again, she vowed, pushing the subject from her thoughts. One could refuse to think about distressing topics. That mostly worked.

"Not too smart for fighting," said Tom. "I'd think you'd want to keep your eyes open for that."

"Indeed," said Macklin.

At Ada's feet, Ella sneezed. She looked down and saw that her little dog's fur was coated with dust. She bent to brush her off as the others moved on and was surprised by a low growl. "I'm only cleaning you, Ella," she said. Then she realized that Ella wasn't looking at her. Following the dog's gaze, Ada discovered a pair of glowing green eyes staring from under a chest in the corner. "Oh!" she cried.

"What is it?" The duke was beside her. Ada pointed. The eyes disappeared and reappeared, as if something had slowly blinked.

"Just one of the cats," said Compton. "I expect we've passed several by this time."

"But Ella didn't bark." Her dog's growl was more a felt vibration than a sound.

"A mark of wisdom," he replied. "These cats are larger than she is and more than half wild."

"Oh." Ada decided to carry her dog. That fact that Ella didn't object to being picked up, as she usually would have, said much.

"Are you completely recovered?" Compton added. "I was concerned last night—"

"I am," she interrupted.

He stepped back, looking daunted. Which Ada regretted, but she didn't want anyone to overhear and ask what he was talking about. He'd promised not to tell.

They passed through another locked door into a section of the house with bare stone walls and no furnishings. Ada felt a breath of air against her cheek. She set Ella and her candle down, put on the shawl she'd been carrying over her arm, and retrieved the dog and the light. Moving forward, Ada stumbled over an uneven spot in the tiles. "Broken flooring along here," warned the duke. "Tread carefully."

"You could play hide-and-seek forever in this place," said Charlotte.

"'Forever' is the word," replied Compton. "There was no way to check all the possible hiding places."

It sounded as if he spoke from experience. Ada could imagine Delia hiding so well she couldn't be found. And then popping out in triumph when everyone had given up. Except there had only been the two of them in this great pile—no *everyone*. That seemed sad.

They emerged from a sizable room at a spot where the outer wall had fallen away. The opening showed a wide view of the valley below. Everyone set their candlesticks on a stone ledge. With a glance at Ada, Charlotte herded the others over to look out. "Stay back from the edge," Compton said. He started toward the group.

It was now or never. Ada spoke before he could move away. "Where was Delia's room?"

He stopped and looked down at her.

"She said not to call her Lady Delia. I hope you don't mind."

"I?" He gestured at the ruined wall. "I'm in no position to stand on ceremony."

When she'd first seen this man last year, Ada had been surprised by the idea that she would like to kiss him. After last night, the thought was back, much stronger. Nearly irresistible. Which made normal conversation difficult. "Delia used to talk about her turret," Ada said. His dark eyes and the shape of his lips were so distracting. The word *spellbound* floated through Ada's consciousness. "It sounded like an amazing place."

"We've passed that stair," he said. "It's just as you leave the modern wing."

"Delia lived in the old part of the house?" It seemed an odd quirk. Then, when she thought of her lost friend, it fit. She'd been unusual. As was her brother. Living here at Alberdene, both Rathbones had become rather like legendary figures in their crumbling castle, Ada thought.

"Yes. My father let my sister do as she pleased in many ways. They were kindred spirits." His tone was flat.

"Do you mind me asking about her?" Ada gazed up at him. "People go all stiff when I mention Delia. They think I should have forgotten her by now." As if a girl so fierce and vital one morning and then stiff and cold at the foot of a cliff a few hours later could be simply dismissed. She pushed away the image of Delia dead. Such people were idiots.

"I don't mind," he replied slowly, as if just now realizing this. "I've had no one to talk to about her death."

"Or her life," said Ada. "The way she died was terrible, but it didn't wipe out her existence! We ought to be able to speak of her."

Compton looked much struck by this observation. He nodded.

"She was such an original. Of course you knew her better than I." He would tell her pleasant things about his sister, Ada thought. Memories that would outweigh Delia's sad end. She would remember her *friend*, who would never hurt her, and that would replace the dreams.

"I doubt it," he replied. "She was five years younger. I was sent off to school when she was scarcely more than a toddler. Our mother had fallen ill and—"

"Your papa could think of nothing but her," said Ada. "He put everyone else out of the way." At his look of surprise, she added. "That's what Delia told me."

"Did she?"

Ada nodded. "She said it felt as if the whole world went off and left her."

He looked concerned. "I didn't want to go. Particularly to…"

When he said no more, Ada asked, "To?"

"A somewhat strange school," he answered in a distant tone.

"Well, you didn't have any choice, I suppose." Ella wriggled in her arms. Ada looked at the little dog. "If I set you down, will you go to Sarah?"

Ella's tongue lolled, her eyes bright.

Ada put her on the floor, keeping hold of her lead. With a few quick steps, she handed the lead to Sarah and returned.

Compton was gazing at her as if he found her puzzling. Ada spoke quickly, before he could say that they should rejoin the others. "Partly it was just Delia being dramatic, I think, about the turret," she said, picking up the conversation a few steps back from where they'd left off. "She loved living in this house. She made it sound like a fairy-tale castle."

"An exaggeration," said Compton, encompassing the ruins with a gesture.

"That depends on the fairy tale, I suppose."

The duke looked startled. He examined her as if he wondered whether she was joking, and then he smiled.

A smile couldn't actually warm you, Ada thought. Except this one did. It sent a wave of heat rushing through her and left her a bit breathless. "Delia couldn't help embroidering, I think," she managed. "She described the house as like a dragon lying over the ridge, with the tower as its head."

"That was my idea! A blatant appropriation." His smile faded. "I thought they didn't like it."

"They?"

"Delia and my father." He looked out through the opening in the wall. "They preferred their own forms of language."

"Forms? I don't understand."

"That was the point." He appeared to be seeing something other than the valley view. "They seemed more alike every time I came home from school. They had private jokes and wild theories that went on and on until I was quite bewildered. After a while, it felt as if they were the Alberdene family and I was an interloper."

"I'm sure they didn't mean that," said Ada.

"Are you? Why?"

He turned, and his dark gaze transfixed her. Ada

didn't know how to answer. She'd spoken without thinking, out of an impulse to comfort.

After what seemed like a long time, but wasn't, he went on. "I don't know. I only had one school holiday a year, so I scarcely saw them. And then Papa died, and I was expected to take charge. I think Delia resented that a good deal."

Ada could imagine this. Her friend had been very proprietary about her home. But these weren't the carefree childish memories she'd been expecting. More of a sad fairy tale of young people shut up in towers, she thought.

"And of course she missed Papa more than I did," he continued. "She hardly spoke. She seemed so isolated. That's why I sent her to school. To make friends. A respected school with pupils from good families. Though she didn't want to go. Which is a mild way of describing—" Compton blinked. He looked down at Ada. "I beg your pardon. I can't think what made me run on like that."

"Being allowed to talk about Delia suddenly," she answered. "I've done the same. It makes some people uncomfortable."

"Does it?" He seemed to be one of them.

"But not me."

The duke examined her, then smiled again. "Delia did make friends, as I'd hoped. I'm glad. And perhaps you knew my sister better than I ever did."

His smile could melt hearts, Ada thought. Those that weren't already molten. "I cared about her," she managed. "Would you show me her room?"

"Oh, I—"

"She called it her aerie."

He nodded. "I suppose your friends would like to see it as well." He looked over at the group.

"Oh no, it should be just the two of us."

The duke blinked.

As well he might. That had come out rather more forcefully than Ada intended. And the request—demand?—was not precisely proper. Indeed, it might be considered *improper*. But she had a mission to accomplish and no time to spare. Her aunt wouldn't let her stay at Alberdene long. "Tomorrow morning," she declared. She would find him before the others were up.

"Yes, I think that *is* a rowan tree," said Charlotte loudly.

It was a clear signal that the other conversation was limping badly.

Compton turned to his other guests. "We should move on."

Ada couldn't deny it. She could regret it, though. And she did. He hadn't actually promised to show her Delia's room. She hadn't told him about the paper she'd found. Or asked him what he thought it might mean. Remembering things like facts was next to impossible when he was gazing at her.

"Leave the candles," said Compton, moving toward an archway further along. "We'll get them when we come back this way." He gestured at Tom, who snuffed the flames.

As she took Ella back from Sarah, Ada began to plan. She needed to see where Delia had nested in this rambling building. For a whole variety of reasons.

There would be much to learn there. And then she had a great many things to say to Delia's brother. More occurred to her with every moment now that he was a little distance away. She simply needed to remember them when he was nearby. Perhaps she should make notes?

The duke led them on through an increasingly ruined building. The path turned from tiles to broken fragments and then to dirt as the walls grew lower around them. Occasionally, a short run of stairs took them higher. One had a missing tread they had to step carefully over. Finally, they passed under a stone arch and came to the remains of the tower on the top of the ridge. Stone steps brought them to a broken platform that had once been a floor. Ada pulled her shawl closer in the crisp breeze.

A panorama spread out around them. The ridge dropped away from the tower on all sides. Behind them, the house rambled downward. It did look rather like an ungainly animal sprawled over the hill, Ada thought. Ahead was a valley with a small river at the bottom. Hills rolled away at the sides, splashed with autumn colors. Ella strained at the end of her leash, sniffing.

Charlotte and Tom went to examine a ruined stairwell in the middle of the tower. The opening was choked with rubble. Harriet and Sarah flanked Lord Macklin and drew him over to point out features in the valley. Ada took advantage. "So we will go to see Delia's room tomorrow morning. After breakfast." She made these statements rather than questions. Her aunt didn't leave her room until noon. There would be time.

"Umm," said the duke, sounding distracted. He moved toward the group standing with the earl. "Don't go too close to that large rock, Miss Finch," he said. "It isn't stable."

His voice was filled with concern. Any chance of a tête-à-tête was over for now, Ada thought. But it was all right. She'd wait for tomorrow.

Ella backed away from one jumble of stones, her hackles raised.

"That leads to the cats' main den," said Compton. "Best keep her away. That footing isn't safe, Miss Moran. Do step back."

He was sounding more and more uneasy. Most likely their perch reminded him of Delia's fall. It rather did Ada. "The wind is chilly, isn't it?" she said. "We should go back."

Sarah's reproachful look crossed the duke's grateful one, and Ada basked a bit in the latter. She'd make it up to Sarah later, Ada thought. That, and the rest. She suspected that she would owe her friends a number of favors before this visit ended.

A mocking look from Charlotte assured her that she was right. Comradely accounts were being tallied. Reciprocation would be required.

Peter was glad to usher his guests away from the tower ruins. He knew that Miss Moran, at least, wanted to stay, but his mind was full of potential accidents—a young lady stepping wrong and breaking an ankle or, worse, falling as Delia had. He could almost see a slender figure stumbling and disappearing over a bit of broken parapet. Foolish, perhaps, but it seemed impossible to watch over them all.

Particularly with Miss Ada at his elbow. She occupied his attention in a way no one had before in his life. And she was certainly more forthright than any young lady he'd ever talked with. Not that there'd been very many. Were fashionable girls usually so outspoken? Was the *haut ton* not at all like his imaginings?

Peter glanced at her and took in those fearsome eyebrows, recalling that the formidable Miss Julia Grandison was her aunt. Perhaps that was it—a tendency to give orders ran in Miss Ada's family. She'd nearly snapped his nose off when he'd started to inquire about the sleepwalking. And yet last night, she'd been a creature of fathomless gazes and soft curves. Altogether a confusing situation. It seemed all too likely he'd make a misstep.

She'd been a good friend to his sister. He knew that. Exactly the sort of connection he'd hoped for when he sent Delia away. If he hadn't known that already, he would have heard it in the way Miss Ada spoke of her today.

Her words had touched something long hidden and neglected. Was he glad or sorry to have his sister so vividly evoked? Peter wasn't sure. Now, he almost expected to round a corner and find her here, digging through some ancient cabinet, hands filthy, a smudge of dust on her nose. She'd always been doing things like that. No one had known Alberdene better than Delia. And vice versa, in a way. Sometimes one of the cats would come out and sit at her feet, and they would stare at each other, silently passing arcane knowledge. They did for no one else. Certainly not him.

Must he think of that?

Ahead, Miss Finch threw back her head and laughed at some remark Tom had made. She looked carefree and extremely pretty. Peter decided he would seat her on his left side at dinner tonight. It made sense to shift the young ladies about after all, so as not to single out any one in the group. And if pleasure came into it, well, that was a bonus. He would enjoy becoming better acquainted with a girl who laughed so happily.

This appealing idea lasted just moments before reality rushed in. He had nothing to offer any lady, Peter thought—a title as threadbare as his tattered sofa cushions, manners wholly without town polish, a creaking estate that was certainly nothing to laugh about. What had he been thinking? Flirtation could only lead to disappointment, if not worse.

He walked faster, moving ahead of the ladies. Directing them to retrieve the candlesticks, he took them back by a different route. They went up a set of stairs in the seventeenth-century section and across the upper floor of cramped, mostly empty bedchambers. He ignored the swag of tapestry that covered one entry to Delia's old quarters. Of course he couldn't take Miss Ada up there alone. No doubt she had already realized that.

"Are you all right?" asked Macklin, who had come up beside him.

Behind them, Miss Ada's dog sneezed three times in quick succession.

"Spirits dampened by the decay of my domain," Peter said, attempting lightness.

"The years have certainly taken their toll," replied the older man.

This was one of the things Peter liked most about Macklin. The earl didn't offer empty platitudes. Yet there had been no disparagement in his tone either. He simply said the thing that others might have evaded or glossed over. It was curiously relaxing.

They came down at a different door into the modern wing. Peter unlocked it and ushered his group out into a corridor near the kitchen. As he was relocking the entry, he was surprised to hear Miss Julia Grandison's voice booming nearby. Concerned that she had some complaint, he turned in that direction, hardly aware that the others were following.

He found a considerable crowd in the kitchen. On one side, along with all of the current staff, stood Macklin's valet and Miss Grandison's formidable dresser. On the other milled a group of four young people, two male and two female. They looked familiar. Peter had seen them in the nearby village, though he didn't immediately recall their names.

Miss Julia Grandison faced them all at the end of the room, her stance effortlessly authoritative. "Good," she said. One of the new girls started at the boom of her voice. "Now we shall see." She pointed at the two young men and beckoned.

Conway and Evan bristled at the newcomers as they stepped forward. Like the Alberdene maids, they looked more jealous than relieved at the idea of help. Fortunately, Mrs. Anselm seemed amused.

"What are your names?" asked Miss Grandison.

"Jem Bailey," said one young man.

"William Williams," said the other.

Miss Grandison raised her eyebrows, but said only,

"Very well, William and James. The Alberdene foot-men will explain your duties. I hope you are ready to work hard."

"Yes, ma'am," the two answered in unison.

"Bumpkins," muttered Conway, just at the thresh-old of hearing.

"Perhaps," said Miss Grandison, clearly surprising Conway by replying to him. "That is why they will require your guidance." She turned to the Alberdene housemaids. "As the girls will need yours."

Rose and Tess dropped nervous curtsies.

"I can do hair," said one of the young women. "I'm always fixing my sister's." She nudged her com-panion, who flinched at the attention this brought her.

Peter expected Miss Grandison to reprimand the speaker, but instead that lady exchanged a glance with her dresser, who nodded once. "Those who desire training will find opportunities, if they show them-selves diligent," Miss Grandison said then. "What is your name?" she asked the newcomer.

"Marged Jones," she replied, her voice a Welsh lilt. "And my sister here is Una." The second girl half hid behind her braver sibling.

"Indeed. And *will* you be diligent?"

"Yes, ma'am!"

Satisfied, Miss Grandison turned and eyed Peter's group. "Good gracious, look at the dust on your gowns!"

Her four charges looked down. Their skirts were indeed coated inches above the hems.

"I told you how it would be," said Miss Grandison.

"Go outside and shake it off. There is no need to make unnecessary work for our new servitors."

Miss Ada set her dog at Peter's feet and followed her friends out the back door. Macklin exchanged a quizzical look with his valet.

Miss Grandison turned to Peter. "I have a good deal of experience running a household, Compton. Mrs. Anselm and I have agreed that since we are here, I may as well use it. I assume you have no objection."

What would she do if he did, Peter wondered. What would he? But in fact, he was grateful. "None." Perhaps they would all learn something.

The older woman accepted this as the queen might have acknowledged the natural deference of a subject. "It will give Ada and her friends an instructional opportunity as well."

"Splendid," said Peter.

This earned him a sharp glance from Miss Grandison and a raised eyebrow from Macklin. Peter expected to be accused of inappropriate raillery, but the kitchen cat chose that moment to rise with the majesty of many years' dominance, walk over to Ella, and extend her neck to touch noses. The little dog stood rigid, ready to erupt and yet clearly anxious.

The calico cat was a diplomat of long standing, however. She'd forged an alliance with the wild felines who patrolled the empty parts of the house, and even produced a litter that resembled one of the largest toms. Those kittens had gone off to join the wild side of their family when they were half-grown. Now the cat drew back, then extended the nose of acquaintanceship again. Ella accepted with a nervous obeisance, her tail and hindquarters depressed.

The young ladies returned with most of the dust shaken from their skirts. Miss Grandison surveyed them like a general reviewing her troops. "One should never neglect opportunities, whatever the situation," she said. "You will all attend me each day at noon, and we will review the tasks required to run a household efficiently, performing those that are properly the duty of the lady of the house."

This fiat was received with varying degrees of enthusiasm. Or perhaps lack of enthusiasm would describe it better, Peter thought. There were no overt objections, however. He imagined that very few people argued with Miss Julia Grandison. For his part, though he was embarrassed at the state of his home, he was also glad they were staying a bit longer.

Four

Arthur watched Miss Julia Grandison add a drop more milk to her cup of tea. He had come upon her, alone, in the Alberdene drawing room and thought it only polite to join her. Guests were not usually left solitary at the house parties he frequented. She'd accepted his company with an equitable nod, seeming neither glad nor sorry to see him. When he declined tea, she went back to her own.

Seeming satisfied with the mixture, she sipped. Golden afternoon sun slanted through the windows. The house was very quiet. It was large enough to absorb the small number of guests and the staff and still feel empty. "My young friend Tom has gone for a tramp around the countryside," said Arthur. "He's rather like a cat in that. He likes to explore any new place thoroughly before he settles."

"I don't believe in the idea of much younger friends," Miss Grandison replied. She set down her cup, added a bit more milk, tasted, nodded in appreciation. "The connection is bound to be unequal."

He'd expected some remark about the weather

or the local scenery. At most a complaint about Alberdene's limitations from a visitor's point of view. The sort of innocuous exchange that oiled the wheels of society, which he could produce automatically and at great length. Now he remembered that Miss Julia Grandison had never dealt in that sort of chitchat, not even when she was seventeen.

"What commonality can there be between the Earl of Macklin and a lad who, pardon me, seems to have no antecedents whatsoever?" she added.

"You feel he is beneath me?" He had no patience with such attitudes.

She gazed at him over the rim of her teacup as if he'd insulted her. "Nothing so petty," she said. "The differences are simply too large."

Arthur was intrigued. His slight acquaintance with this lady seemed worth pursuing, another point of interest in his final visit to the young men he'd singled out in London. This was easily accomplished. As the two oldest members of the Alberdene party, they would naturally be thrown together. "You only have friends who are like yourself?" he asked.

Her eyes were sharp, her posture imposing. She was actually quite attractive, but the chief impression she gave was of massive dignity, not the least daunted by his rank. "The term 'friend' is used far too loosely, in my opinion," she replied. "People employ it for a wide variety of social connections. Some of which have nothing to do with the others."

Arthur sat back, prepared to enjoy this conversation. "What do you mean?"

Miss Grandison put down her cup. The click on the

saucer was like a crisp reprimand. "I do not know you well enough to judge whether you are being satirical. Which proves my point, actually."

"I am not," Arthur said. "I'm quite interested."

She accepted this with a nod that seemed to make him responsible for whatever followed. "Some people name everyone they meet at an evening party their friends. For them, it's enough to have been introduced and exchange empty greetings."

"But not for you."

"I don't call that friendship," she acknowledged. "Those would be mere acquaintances. Distant." She spread one hand as if to establish a surface. "Some become close acquaintances," she continued, indicating a layer above her hand. "When I know their circumstances well enough to ask about their families, that sort of thing."

"But they are not your friends?"

"This is my own way of looking at the matter," she answered, as if he was arguing with her.

"And I find it most enlightening."

She sniffed as if she didn't quite believe him. But she went on. "Some of these people may become friends, over time, if we find we have common beliefs and experiences. Spend time together. And then develop bonds based on these things. This does not happen in a few evenings of idle chatter."

"It is a matter of effort and interest and goodwill on both sides."

"Precisely." For the first time in the conversation she looked approving.

"But don't you wish to have a variety of friends, of

different ages and experience? To add a bit of spice to the social mixture?"

"I find it tiresome if there are too many adjustments to make."

"That seems sadly limited to me," Arthur said.

"Well, I do not believe we really understand those who have had lives wholly unlike our own. They may tell us. We can listen. But that is never the same."

Arthur didn't like this idea. "We can sympathize."

"Of course. But that very act is…a kind of patronage. Even condescension."

"It isn't!"

His vehemence didn't appear to affect her. "Wide differences in situation mean differences in social position and power," she added. "Whether we are speaking of fortune or age or rank. You, who have all of those, must realize that they weigh in the balance."

He did, but he took great care not to let them upset it.

"I do not doubt your good intentions," said Miss Grandison kindly. "But neither do I believe in lasting friendships at such a great remove. Sooner or later, interests will diverge, and friction will arise."

"Perhaps." Arthur didn't like the idea, but he couldn't refute it. "In the meantime, there are new things to learn. Insights to offer."

"And if your suggestions are rejected?"

He'd thought something like this before, Arthur realized. How did you help others without imposing your own preconceptions upon them? Could he aid a young friend along a path he felt quite wrong for him, for example? He wasn't certain he could. And then there might well be friction.

He put this uncomfortable idea aside. "Have your young ladies gone out as well?"

"Yes, they expressed a desire to explore the gardens. Which are little better than a wilderness as far as I can see. In reality, of course, they wanted to get out from under my eye so they can chatter nonsense."

Arthur thought that was a fair assessment. Except perhaps the nonsense. "How do you come to be chaperoning them?"

"Ada wished to make this journey, and my brother was against it." Miss Grandison showed a thin smile. "I like to thwart him when I can. If it isn't too much bother."

"You do?"

"I'm not above a bit of revenge."

Searching his memory, Arthur wasn't able to recall Mr. Grandison or why he might deserve retribution.

"You don't remember the Collingford ball? It *has* been quite a few years now."

"Ah," said Arthur.

"Ah indeed." She gave him a sardonic glance.

At that long-ago event the youthful Miss Grandison had been drenched by an upended punch bowl. She'd been left sitting on the floor in the supper room soaked, dazed, and dripping on the carpet. Sticky as well, Arthur supposed. "That was unfortunate," he said.

"Indeed." Her tone was desert dry. "Afterward, my brother approached me. Not to deplore my plight or help me up, as one might have thought. But merely to say, 'You are always so clumsy, Julia.'" Miss Grandison bared her teeth like an extremely civilized lioness. "I learned later that he stood by when he heard that Trask and Quigley were plotting to humiliate me. As if it was my fault that Trask was a little shrimp of a man. You'd think he might have wanted to know that he had a bald spot on top of his head." She sniffed. "And it wasn't only that. John found it difficult to endure the come-out of his bumptious sister. He often pretended not to be acquainted with me when we were at parties together."

"Surely not." Arthur was shocked at the notion.

"You don't know him."

"It's true I can't bring him to mind."

Miss Grandison gave a bark of laughter. "Oh, splendid. He would be so mortified. I shall be sure to tell him." She fortified herself with tea. "Heavens, I haven't thought of that ball in years."

"Only when you've been thwarting your brother?" Arthur was unsettled by the idea that she'd held onto a grudge so long.

His companion waved this remark aside. "A side benefit. I wouldn't have put myself out, but the thing is…" She examined him as if wondering how much to say.

The scrutiny was quite thorough. Arthur endured it.

Seeming to come to a decision, Miss Grandison added, "Ada hasn't really recovered from the death of her friend."

"A terrible tragedy." It seemed that Miss Ada was as affected as Compton, Arthur thought.

Miss Grandison nodded. "I believe she thinks people haven't noticed, but of course they have. Her mother in particular. It has been quite a time since the accident. One must let these things go. I thought she should be helped to do so. Life will offer other trials soon enough."

There could be no doubt of that. Arthur nodded. He was glad to see glimpses of a kind heart behind her brusque manner.

"Ada insisted on this journey, and so it has been allowed to her," his companion finished. "All the girls are to be presented in London next season. Ada must put this behind her before that. I shall see that she does."

Arthur wondered how she meant to manage that. She seemed to imagine it would be simple. A doubtful assumption. And yet, was his own mission here so different? They were on parallel courses, he realized.

"Ada's first idea was to come with just her friends. Propriety in numbers." She snorted. "She was soon set straight about that!"

"Not acceptable," he said.

"No. She was quite despondent. So in the end I agreed to watch over them. A pack of babes in the woods. They can't be meeting just anyone before they're even out. Their parents have more sensible plans for them. And on top of everything, Harriet Finch is a considerable heiress."

"Indeed?" Arthur absorbed this bit of interesting information.

"She's old Winstead's granddaughter."

This was wealth indeed. "I wasn't aware that he had any heirs."

Miss Grandison gestured airily. "There was some

unpleasantness in the family, but it has been made up. It's settled that all will come to Miss Finch. As the world will discover next season. Should be quite the sensation, I would think."

Arthur nodded.

Sounds in the hallway heralded the return of the young ladies. They burst in with red cheeks from the crisp outdoors and a babble of conversation. Arthur examined Miss Finch—a pretty, lively young lady. Of course he would not interfere, but there could be no harm in creating a few opportunities. And then they would see. An heiress was certainly the traditional answer to Compton's aristocratic penury.

⁘

Ada felt a dizzy sense of anticipation as she slipped out of her room early the next morning to take Ella outside. When she returned to leave her with Sarah, despite the little dog's objections, Sarah merely turned over in bed and murmured a farewell, only half-awake, and thus not able to toss cautions in Ada's path. Ada had slept peacefully, too, with not so much as a dream, which was a true blessing.

Downstairs, she surprised one of the new young maids in the breakfast room, making her jump and tip a plate of scones onto the table. "Sorry, miss," the girl said as she gathered up the pastries and set them back on the plate. "Mrs. Anselm reckoned no one would be up just yet."

"I woke early."

"Shall I you bring anything?"

"Some tea, thank you, Una."

The duke appeared as Ada was sipping it. He paused in the doorway. "You're already up," he said.

"We agreed to meet." She'd put on her favorite blue gown for the occasion. It was a little more dashing than the rest of her wardrobe. Which wasn't saying much, she acknowledged silently.

"Would you call it an agreement?"

"You wouldn't go back on your word?" Disappointment loomed. "You're here," Ada pointed out, hoping he didn't mean to draw back.

"As I am each morning at this time."

"You promised I could see Delia's room."

"I'm certain I made no promises. You have no grounds for such a ferocious scowl."

"I'm not scowling."

Rather than reply, the duke indicated the large mirror that hung on the inner wall of the breakfast room. She was frowning, Ada noticed. And her eyebrows did accentuate that sort of expression. Other people had accused her of glowering when she wasn't doing anything of the kind. "I was only concerned," she explained.

"Then you should take more care with those brows."

Her breath caught in a gasp. This wasn't the sort of exchange Ada had imagined when she thought of seeing Delia's brother. Not in the least.

Compton looked chagrined. "I did not mean—"

Taking advantage of the awkward moment, Ada rose and headed for the door. She would push him along before he could go back to refusing. "Let's go." She walked out of the room, silently commanding him to follow.

After a moment, he did. Ada hurried to the first door they'd used yesterday to enter the older part of the house. Compton hesitated as if he didn't know what to do, but then he unlocked it and let her through, leaving it open behind them. "You could just tell me where Delia's room is—was," Ada said. And immediately regretted it. That wasn't what she wanted.

He considered the idea, then shook his head. "You mustn't go wandering about alone." He took candlesticks from the small table beside the door and lit them. "The first part is dim." He held his light high and led the way to a hidden corner. There was a spiral stair tucked away there, built of great blocks of stone. "Please walk very carefully. The steps can be treacherous." Ada took her candle and started up before he could change his mind.

The stair *was* a challenge. The inner sides of the steps were too narrow to stand on, and the passage was just wide enough for one person. Though tiny slits of windows added some illumination, there was no rail to cling to. Ada wondered that Delia had wanted to climb this corkscrew to her bedchamber. But then, Delia had not been a very practical person.

They walked around several turns in silence and came to a small landing. "That door leads to the upper floor," said Ada.

"Very observant," Compton replied. "It's covered by a tapestry. Delia liked secret entrances."

They moved on. "She climbed up here every day?" Ada had begun to feel oppressed by the stone walls. They were not closing in on her, of course. She knew that.

"More than once sometimes," he replied.

"And the servants. How did they ever carry wood and hot water all this way?" She didn't like to think of the old footmen toiling up this stair.

"They didn't have to. Delia discovered a pulley suspended outside one of the tower windows. She rigged up a rope for raising things."

"How clever."

"She was."

They hadn't passed a door for a long time. "We must be very high up by now," Ada said.

"Quite. This tower is one of the tallest parts of the house, though not the oldest. It was added fifty years ago by a forebear with a taste for the medieval." They came around a final turn, and he stopped before a low door. "Here we are."

They were crowded together on the small landing. Their shoulders touched. Ada waited, but he made no move to go in. She put a hand to the doorknob. It didn't turn. She looked at him. Candlelight flickered over his features.

"I came up here just after Delia died," he said, his voice gone distant. "I found the door locked. The key was with her things when they were returned to me, but I didn't try again."

"So you haven't been inside?"

"No."

"At all?"

He shook his head.

"You didn't want to come alone," said Ada, certain she was right.

Compton looked down at her. "Perhaps I didn't," he replied. "Can that have been it?" he murmured.

"Well, I am with you now."

"Yes."

He still didn't move. She couldn't be sure of his expression in the dimness. There was sadness, certainly, and perhaps discomfort. "So you haven't been in her room since…a while ago."

"Or ever?" he replied, as if asking himself. "I must have looked in when I was a boy. I was all over the house. But I've not been to this chamber since Delia moved in when she was fourteen."

"Not at all?"

"She wouldn't tolerate *invaders*. She called this tower her bastion."

Ada was amazed that she'd been allowed to do so. *Her* parents would never tolerate that kind of behavior. "So it's just as she left it."

The duke nodded. His face seemed full of doubt.

"I don't think she'd mind if we went in. Now." She *needed* to enter.

"Don't you?" He gazed at the door. "*I* think she would have wanted the room sealed, like a forbidden chamber in a fairy tale." As soon as the words escaped him, Peter wished them unsaid. Not that they were untrue. He could easily imagine Delia expressing such a wish. But they sounded daft.

Miss Ada cocked her head. "Perhaps," she said. "For a while. A year and a day, like in a story."

It had been almost that, Peter realized. Time passed so swiftly. When it didn't crawl.

"But then she would have expected someone to come and break the spell," the girl added.

She had taken up his idea as if it wasn't the least

odd. Peter felt an uncomfortable mixture of gratitude and remorse. He'd been rude about her eyebrows. He shouldn't have said what he did. Awkward remarks just popped out sometimes. Far too often really.

"And we were the ones closest to her."

"You were, perhaps," Peter replied. He'd never felt more distant from his sister than at this moment. He could almost imagine Delia's ghost swooping down to warn them off.

"She worried about you."

He blinked in surprise. "Me?"

"She said so. She wanted to help you."

"With what?"

"Well." Miss Ada gestured at their surroundings. "Everything."

Did she mean the house? The dearth of money to keep it up? The slow crumbling of a noble heritage? Or the darkness pressing close upon them? None of those bore thinking of.

"All your efforts to maintain the estate," she added.

In the glow of candlelight, Peter saw admiration in her eyes. There was no mistaking it. He'd been admired before, by a few younger boys in his last year at school, by tenants he strove to help. He knew the expression. But to see it on the face of a young lady was quite different. Peter enjoyed the sensation. His impulse to turn tail and retreat died.

He reached out and unlocked the door with the key that had been returned from this girl's house in his dead sister's luggage. He ducked under the low lintel and stepped into the circular room beyond. Miss Ada Grandison followed him.

Space opened out around them. The slender tower bulged at the top, Peter remembered, like an upended onion. It looked incongruous from the outside, stuck onto the corner of an English house, another sign of the Rathbones' eccentricity. But from the inside it was roomy, nearly twenty feet across. He found no memory of being in this room before, certainly not since it had become his sister's fantastical nest.

Four tall casement windows were hung with billows of brocade. The colors didn't match, but they harmonized somehow—deep blue and scarlet and yellow. Miss Ada went over to touch one of them. "How beautiful," she said.

"I believe they're made from the gowns of some Rathbone ancestor. Delia was always foraging in the attics and storerooms. She found them in a trunk." He did remember her delight in that. Delia was never happier than when she enthused over some ancient *treasure* she'd discovered. The room was cluttered with such objects, some whole, some broken by the centuries.

"It makes me feel small," said Miss Ada.

Following her gaze, he looked up. The ceiling was open to the pointed roof, creating a conical space. The fireplace looked far too small to heat it. "I believe my great-grandmother, who ordered this tower built, was inspired by *The Castle of Otranto*."

"Is that in Italy?"

"It's a novel by Horace Walpole. Delia liked it too. I would think spiders might drop on you from that ceiling as you slept."

"Spiders?" She scanned the beams apprehensively.

"No they wouldn't," said Peter. "There's a canopy over the bed."

Miss Ada walked over to the large four-poster. "However did they get this up the stairs?"

"They didn't," he answered. "Impossible. It must have been built here." He eyed the tall posts. "It would have to be taken apart to be moved. And even then—"

"Lowered with the rope," Miss Ada finished. "These posts wouldn't fit down the stair. They'd get stuck."

"Yes." This girl kept revealing new facets, Peter thought. She was quite intelligent.

She gazed around the room. "It's beautiful, but I think I'd be lonely, so far from the rest of the house."

"Delia loved solitude. She was like my father in that. Both of them could spend whole days reading and studying alone." The house could feel empty even when they were in it, he remembered. "And they were equally irritated if one interrupted them. They had much to say when they met for dinner, however." Conversations full of obscure references that he had rarely understood, as if they inhabited one world and he another.

Miss Ada moved over to the armchair in front of the small hearth. It was flanked by a table piled with books. She picked up one and read the spine. "*The Romance of the Forest*."

"Is that Mrs. Radcliffe?"

She nodded. "I remember that name. Our head-mistress at school was shocked when she found Delia reading one of her novels. And Delia told her there was much to be learned about the struggle between good and evil, hedonism and morality, in the story."

Peter smiled. "I can hear her saying it." His sister had been fond of her own opinions.

"She was never afraid to express her views. I admired that in her."

"Even when they were quite unusual," he agreed.

"Yes, but Delia didn't care," Miss Ada replied. "She didn't worry about whether people agreed with her."

"Very true." One didn't dispute with Delia, Peter thought. She simply didn't bother arguing. She might listen to an alternative explanation, sometimes with exaggerated patience, but he couldn't recall one instance when he'd convinced her. She'd found certainty at a very young age. Rather too much so, in the end. If she'd listened to advice, she might be alive now.

Miss Ada opened the massive carved wardrobe, another piece that must have been constructed up here. "Oh, I recognize that gown from school," she said. Tears welled up in her dark eyes. She blinked rapidly.

Peter felt an answering tremor of grief. He *might* have forged a closer bond with his sister, if she'd lived.

"She would have done such interesting things with her life," said the girl, closing the wardrobe. "I'm sure of it. It's so sad."

He nodded. Both were undoubtedly true. He met her gaze and was overtaken by a sense of shared melancholy, poignant and somehow comforting as well. It was a relief to speak of his sister, even as it hurt to acknowledge her loss. Miss Ada was right. Delia's name shouldn't be met by a stretch of awkward silence.

His companion swallowed back tears. Peter felt moved to comfort, an impulse to put an arm around her, draw her close against him. But of course he couldn't do that. Not here, alone together in a bed-chamber. Not anywhere, he reminded himself. Her family wouldn't approve of even a mild flirtation with him, circumstanced as he was. He ought to get them out of here. She'd seen the room now. Yet somehow he didn't speak.

"We should tell happy stories about her," Miss Ada said. "There's so much more to remember than just her death. Years of things. Tell me something good you recall."

Peter's mind was blank at first. "I don't know what to say."

"What's your first memory of Delia?"

"She was the fiercest child," he said immediately. "As soon as she could walk, she started stumping around the house. And then running when she could. If you tried to stop her, her eyes would just *blaze* with rage. That glare made you take a step back, I can tell you." Details of the memory unfolded as he spoke. "Our parents set me to chasing her once. I'd forgotten that I made her a kind of leash."

"You didn't!"

"She wouldn't slow down or watch where she was going," Peter said. "I was afraid she'd trip. So I tied a rope around her waist. Quite loosely. And she didn't seem to mind. It made her laugh. She pretended to be a pony." He smiled at the remembered image of the tiny girl pawing the air and neighing. "She pranced."

"She loved animals," said Miss Ada.

"They seemed to know it somehow, too."

"And learning. Delia loved learning."

She smiled rather as he had, Peter thought, at a pleasant recollection. He felt a pulse of connection with this increasingly interesting young lady.

"Girls at school often didn't, you know," she went on. "Some found it difficult, and some were lazy. Quite a few thought the only reason to be there was to gain accomplishments, so that they could draw attention to themselves and be admired. But Delia wanted to *know*."

"Yes, she did." She'd shared that temperament with their father. Or absorbed it from him? Peter didn't know. But the need to learn had certainly drawn them together.

"I didn't understand at first. How she could be so...enraptured by facts. Greedy for them, like girls who stuffed themselves with sweets. I suspected her of affectation."

"That is one thing my sister was never guilty of," Peter replied.

"No." Miss Ada shook her head, smiling again. "She was the most unaffected person. But not like an innocent."

"Delia was aggressively unaffected," suggested Peter. "She presented herself without subtlety. If you didn't like it, you could...go hang."

Miss Ada burst out laughing. Peter felt a surge of triumph. He had made her laugh.

"A little like my aunt, really. I just thought of that. Her approach, I mean. They were very different in the...details."

Peter considered. "I see what you mean."

"Delia thought everyone should be that way," said Miss Ada. "Express their true feelings and original thoughts. She encouraged people to do so. When girls worried that they weren't like the others and that they would be mocked, she told them to 'defy the small-minded.'"

"That sounds like Delia." It might have been a motto for her personal crest.

"And of course she stood with them when they did. If they did."

"Of course." His sister would have waved a flag on the barricades in the French Revolution had she believed in the cause.

"There was even one of the teachers. Miss Rahm. The girls thought her odd. Well, she *is* rather odd. She gets agitated if different sorts of food touch on her plate. And she can't bear open windows, no matter how hot the weather. But she knows six languages!"

"Delia would have admired that." Peter was admiring his animated companion.

"She did. And she told the girls who laughed at Miss Rahm that they might have opinions when *they* could speak and write as many. And then Delia began talking to them only in Italian. She could speak it very quickly. Mostly they couldn't puzzle out what she meant. Though they could certainly *suspect* it was satirical. We couldn't believe Miss Rahm would have taught her some of the gruesome words she used. And yet where else would she have found them?"

"Dante?" said Peter.

Miss Ada stared at him. "Of course! Oh, Delia."

"I would think such twitting might cause resentment," said Peter.

"Well, yes, it did," Miss Ada admitted. "But Delia didn't care. She really didn't. She just dismissed them."

He believed it. "Do you see that as a happy memory of my sister?" asked Peter. "Delia could be quite rigid in her…judgments. And she didn't understand that not everyone is capable of original thought. Or that other talents might be just as…worthy of respect." He had felt the weight of her disapproval himself. Now and then.

"That's true," she admitted. "It isn't a completely happy memory, I suppose. But very real."

Peter nodded. Miss Ada Grandison seemed a thoughtful person. More than one expected at her age. With her striking appearance and lively sympathies, it was a potent combination. A kind of inner warning bell told him to watch what he was about.

"And not sad," she added. "Not about the…end." Her expression shifted, as if the circumstances of Delia's death had come rushing back.

It was hard to long to comfort when one couldn't, Peter thought. He felt another pang at the ending of their confidences.

Miss Ada drifted over to the writing desk. Like the rest of the room, it held a collection of odd little keepsakes—a tiny figurine of a rearing horse, a crystal bud vase, a furled fan. "Have you looked at her papers? No, you said you hadn't come in here."

Even now it felt like prying. Could a solitary person leave an imprint behind, discouraging intrusion? The threat of Delia's outrage seemed to hover over Peter.

Then an irregular shape caught his eye. A small ring of keys sat on the desktop—a tumble of metal, familiar, but half-forgotten. A wordless exclamation escaped him.

"What is it?" she asked.

He stepped over and picked up the keys. There were only three on the ring. "These were my father's. He kept them with him always. I wondered where they'd gone after he died." Had he asked Delia? He couldn't remember. Conversation hadn't been easy then.

"What do they unlock?"

"I don't know."

"That could be important."

"For what?" Peter shrugged as he put the keys in his pocket. All he could see was another sign of the closeness his father and sister had shared. Neither had thought to include him.

"To figure things out," said Miss Ada. She stood straighter, arms at her sides, chin up. "I came here to tell you something," she said. "A few days before she…fell, Delia told me that she'd uncovered a secret that would change everything for your family. She was terribly excited."

"A secret?"

The girl nodded. She waited, vividly expectant.

"What sort of secret?"

"I don't know. I thought you might."

"I? Why would I?"

"I supposed she might have talked about it. Whatever it was." Miss Ada faltered, and Peter realized he was scowling at her. He tried to stop. But he was overwhelmed by melancholy. He was a Rathbone, the last of his name, but he'd never been told any family secrets. He hadn't been given his father's keys. This near-stranger apparently knew more than he did.

"I had the sense that she'd been working on it for a long time."

"It?"

"Whatever the secret was."

Peter flicked a folded page on the desk. It fell open—a perfumer's bill. Small, not portentous. Another meaningless remnant. "I have no idea."

"The answer might be in this paper of hers," Miss Ada continued. "I think it is."

"Paper? What are you talking about?"

Ada fumbled a little as she took the folded page from her pocket. They had been speaking so openly. She'd felt very close to the duke. But now he'd gone gruff. His frown made her clumsy. "I found this under the mattress in her room. I brought it to you." There was no need to discuss why she hadn't simply sent the document. She'd wanted to see him, and she was glad she'd dared to come. Delia would have approved, she thought. Of her determination, at least. What she would have thought about Ada's interest in her brother, she didn't know.

"Then you must know more about this secret than I do," he said. "I assume you've read it."

"You think I'm a snoop?"

"I don't see how anyone could resist."

Ada ducked her head, wishing he sounded less angry. "I did try. But Delia wrote it in some other language." She unfolded it to show him. He bent closer to look. Ada took a careful breath. Being so near him fogged her brain. With his hair nearly brushing her shoulder it would be all too easy to babble. But she wasn't going to do that. She'd made a vow not to be a silly chit. Now or ever.

"That's not French or German," he said.

He sounded less irritated. Ada sent up a silent thanks. "That's just what Charlotte said."

"It's not Italian or Spanish either."

"You can read all those?"

"No, but I have seen examples. This looks completely unfamiliar."

"What can it be? And how did Delia know it?"

"I have no notion." Compton stared at the page. "Or…wait. Miss…Miss…what was her name?"

"Who?"

"For a while, Delia had a governess from…Russia? Sweden?" He looked at the writing with narrowed eyes. "I don't think this can be Russian. Their lettering looks different, doesn't it?"

"You think it's Swedish then? Did Delia really learn Swedish?"

"I was at school when Miss…whatever her name was…worked here. I was never really acquainted with her. Delia loved languages though. As your story proved."

"Yes. Languages were like games to her."

The duke frowned. "But isn't Swedish a little like German? Distantly related at least? This isn't. I've never seen anything like this. *Koska.* What can that be? *Tuuma. Vastaus.*"

"We should find the old governess and get her to

read it to us." Ada wanted to run out right now and search for the woman. She also wanted to stay exactly where she was, with her shoulder almost touching his and the clean scent of him around her.

"I don't even remember her name," replied Compton.

"There must be a record of her employment."

"Such details were not my father's strong point, Miss Grandison."

"But Delia wrote down the secret." She tapped the paper. "At least, it's very likely she did, right here."

"I very much doubt—"

"I *feel* she did!"

He fell silent. Ada waited, her heart sinking. He was going to dismiss her ideas. He thought she was a fool.

He looked at her, his face quite close to hers. The smallest movement would have brought their lips together. Ada's pulse accelerated. At the same moment, his expression shifted.

"I suppose we could look around," he said. He moved back a step. "See if my father kept any receipts."

"Oh yes! And we should find out where those keys fit as well."

He touched his pocket as if he'd forgotten them. "Do you have any notion how many locks there are in this house?"

"Charlotte will make a list. She's terribly organized."

"Is she?" He looked down at her.

Ada nodded. "And Sarah can find the governess in your record books. She adores that sort of thing."

"Indeed. And what does Miss Finch adore?"

A pang of apprehension went through Ada. Harriet had sat beside Compton at dinner last night. She hadn't been able to hear all they talked of. But she refused to show agitation. "Any number of things," she declared airily. "As do you, I'm sure."

"More each day," he answered.

After all that had passed between them in this room, she decided to place herself among these items. She only hoped that she rightfully could.

Five

DINNER THAT EVENING BEGAN SMOOTHLY. MACKLIN had encouraged Peter to seat Miss Harriet Finch on his left, even though he'd done so the previous night as well. He didn't mind doing so. Miss Finch was a lovely, restful young lady. She kept the conversation flowing so that he didn't have to worry about finding new topics. And she received his responses with calm equanimity, almost making him feel socially adept.

Unlike Miss Ada, who gazed at him from the other side of the table with dark eyes that seemed to burn under those authoritative brows. He ought not to have mentioned her eyebrows. He knew that. He'd apologized. Hadn't he? He'd meant to. Under the weight of her gaze he couldn't quite remember. Was she reproaching him? Was he mistaking her expression again? He couldn't tell. Miss Ada didn't make him feel adept. Surprised, moved, intrigued, heated, but not deft. She was complicated, and somehow far more compelling than her friends.

All through the meal, his eyes kept being drawn back to her. It was as if she was trying to convey some secret message, rather like the mysterious bit of paper she'd brought along. Delia's last words, as it turned out. Typical of his sister that they were a mystery.

Their time together in Delia's room remained with him—the stories Miss Ada had told, but more her quick, ardent response to him. She roused a confusion of dreams and desires. Which he, in his position, should resist, Peter thought. He would. He was. No, he was staring at her again.

He turned away, and encountered the censorious gaze of her aunt on his right side. A different sort of look, but just as powerful. He could certainly see a family resemblance between Miss Ada and Miss Julia Grandison. The older woman seemed continually disapproving, however. Peter had even caught her casting hard looks in Macklin's direction. He couldn't imagine a reason for that. If there was anyone here that Miss Grandison should admire it was the earl.

Peter returned his attention to Miss Finch, who made some comment about the herbed sauce. Was it possible that she was a trifle boring? No, of course she wasn't. This was the way of society—cordial, reassuringly predictable. And so he was enjoying his orderly dinner. Of course he was. Thankfully not interrupted by bats.

He did notice afterward that he couldn't remember anything he and Miss Finch had talked about, while he remembered every word that Miss Ada had said to him about his sister. But that just showed that sad thoughts could overwhelm happy ones. Hadn't the poet Milton said so? Or someone said it about *Paradise Lost*? Peter shook his head. First Dante and now Milton? Why the deuce was he thinking about them?

⁓

That night, at last, Ada had a different dream. It was just as vivid as the disturbing ones, but the mood was something else entirely. She was at a wedding. She knew that's what it was, even though she was alone at first. The knowledge was simply there. Then her friends appeared—Charlotte and Harriet and Sarah in bright dresses—and others as well. Her family sat in a church pew. She walked by them.

That was when Ada realized that this was *her* wedding. She was pacing down the church aisle alone. Where were her attendants? Why wasn't her father at her side? She felt her gown frothing around her feet and wondered about the flowers on her bonnet. She'd always meant to have roses when she married. Were they there? Her hands were empty.

The aisle seemed very long. She walked and walked without seeming to make progress. And she couldn't see who waited for her at the altar. Which was the most important part, wasn't it?

She walked faster. The place must be the size of a cathedral. And who were all the shadowy figures filling it, stretching out on either side? She didn't have nearly that many acquaintances, let alone friends. Multitudes watched her pass. She felt the weight of their attention and wished for a supporting arm. But there was only herself and the endless aisle.

Finally, finally, she reached the front of the church. But the two who waited there—the groom and the vicar presiding—remained vague, mere outlines. "Who are you?" she asked the former. It wasn't fair. A dream shouldn't leave out the crucial piece.

Her question had no effect. Though she peered and peered, she couldn't see. The ceremony took place. Or maybe it didn't. There were gestures and perhaps words, but Ada couldn't hear them. She wasn't certain whether she spoke. Her throat felt tight. The guests had vanished. Most of the church had as well. The edges of her view had gone misty. "Why can't I see?" she complained.

In response, the two indistinct figures at the altar gradually faded.

Ada turned in a circle, searching, but they were gone. Everyone was. She was alone again. And so very tired. She lay down on the first pew, which was now empty. She folded her hands, closed her eyes. A little rest and then she would...

"Miss Ada?"

She wasn't Miss anymore. Possibly. Or not.

There was a touch on her shoulder. Ada stirred. Ah, there was a gentleman kneeling beside her. Surely this was her bridegroom, solid at last. She reached out and laced her arms around his neck and pulled him close and kissed him. It was her very first kiss, though she wouldn't have admitted that to anyone.

She touched his lips with hers, tender, experimental. More of an imagined kiss at first. She raised up a little, pressed closer.

For one startled instant, there was no response. Then his lips softened under hers. His arms came around her and pulled her against him. He was very strong! The kiss deepened. A bolt of arousal shot through her. Passion, she thought. This was what people meant by it. Ada felt as if she was melting, and yet also newly vibrant. Her arms tightened around his neck. She clung to him and to the kiss.

And then he pulled away with a jerk and a wild look. He put his fingers to his lips as if hers had burnt him.

The Duke of Compton pushed Ada back onto a sofa in the Alberdene drawing room. On which she lay instead of her bed. And she had no memory at all of getting here.

Ada blinked, shaking off sleep and the lingering wisps of her dream. She'd kissed Delia's brother. She'd often wondered during this last year what it would be like to kiss him. She'd imagined scenes where a kiss might happen. Nothing like this one, of course. But now she knew that it was lovely. The sort of thing one would like to try again, when more than half-awake. She sat up. A candle burned on a low table nearby.

"What are you doing?" he asked. "Here."

Was that one query or two? Ada looked around. The corners of the room faded into dimness—rather like, and unlike, her dream. "I suppose I was sleepwalking again?" The words were half a question. "I don't remember." She shook her head. The sleepwalking was a worry. "I dreamed of—" No, she wasn't going to tell him about the wedding. The thin folds of her nightdress shifted around her, translucent in the light of the candle. She could see her knees through the cloth. One couldn't get more improper than this. She ought to be mortified, but she felt curiously elated instead. In fact, a bubble of rapturous excitement rose in her chest.

"We must tell someone," he said.

"That we kissed?"

"No! The sleepwalking. As for the other—"

"The kiss?"

"I didn't mean… I had no notion—"

"I believe I kissed you," Ada said. She savored the word. She liked saying *kiss*, the effect it had on him. She enjoyed flustering the duke, she realized. It was fun. Clearly he had no idea what to say next. "I won't kiss you again if you don't want me to."

"It's not a case of wanting." He sounded hoarse.

"So you *do* want me to?" She longed to hear him say so.

His eyes burned into hers. The desire in them made her breath catch. "You know we can't," he said.

It was difficult to know anything at that moment. Ada felt like a child who'd inadvertently teased a tiger.

"This." His gesture encompassed the dark, silent room, their nightclothes, the mere inches that separated them. "Is so far beyond the line."

Ada knew the situation was scandalous, but she was still glad she'd kissed him. "You *seemed* to like it," she couldn't help saying.

He stood and stepped away from her. "What I like and what I can offer as a man of honor may not be the same. Most often they are not. I've known that since I was fifteen." He picked up the candlestick. "You must take more care, Miss Ada."

Care not to push him too far? Or was he speaking of the proprieties? His expression was unreadable.

Had she offended him? Ada had a sudden quiver of concern. She wanted him to think well of her. "I've never done anything like this before, of course. I was dreaming, and the dream kept going and…shifted into something else."

"Nothing to do with me, you mean."

That was *not* what she'd meant. She searched for the right phrase. She couldn't say she'd imagined kissing him since they first met. She might be daring, but she wasn't *brazen*. "It was the sleepwalking," she said, and thought herself the lamest creature in nature.

"Indeed." He looked stern in the dancing light of one candle. "And that is a problem. You can't wander the house at night. It's dangerous."

"I only seem to come here." Now Ada indicated the room around them.

Compton shook his head. "We must ask your aunt what to do. That is, you must. Best not to mention me."

"If I say anything, Aunt will take us away at once."

"Perhaps that would be best."

He didn't look at her. Had he sounded the least bit forlorn? Or did she only wish it? "You want me to go?"

"What I may want…is irrelevant. There's no point in you staying."

"Yes there is! I don't want to go until we solve Delia's mystery."

At last he turned, his face despondent. "You know it's very likely that there's nothing to find," he replied.

"No, I don't. I think there certainly is."

"Miss Ada."

"I'll lock the bedroom door," she interrupted. She'd have to think of something to tell Sarah. Well, she would. Not about the sleepwalking, though, unless she had to. Her friends already thought she was not acting like herself. Charlotte had said so. "I'll hide the key so I can't find it when I'm asleep."

"I'm not sure—"

"Or I'll have Sarah hide it."

"You'll tell her then?" Compton looked relieved.

She would tell her *something*, Ada repeated to herself. "And then we can work together to discover what Delia meant. We'll begin tomorrow morning."

He looked uncertain.

She must end this before he made some irrevocable pronouncement, Ada thought. "I should get back to my room."

"Yes, of course."

Ada's nightdress pulled taut as she stood. The duke looked away, the perfect gentleman. She hadn't understood until tonight that one might sometimes wish a man *not* to be a gentleman.

She walked at his side toward the stair. He wore his odd Egyptian robe again. Her aunt would deliver a scold of epic proportions if she happened to open her bedchamber door and see them, Ada thought. Once she got over her utter stupefaction. Ada walked faster.

❧

Ada gathered her friends the following morning right after breakfast, well before her Aunt Julia would be downstairs. A sense of urgency drove her. She didn't know how long she had at Alberdene and felt there was no time to lose in figuring out what Delia had meant.

She'd found a room in the modern wing of the house that didn't look much used. The furnishings were a hodgepodge, and the draperies even more frayed than in other places. She didn't think anyone would object to a bit of rearrangement, or perhaps even notice that she'd pulled a large table away from the wall and set chairs around it.

Harriet had brought along pencils and paper. Charlotte had drawn up the grid they always created, with each girl's name at the top of a column, into which would be entered the tasks they agreed to take on. Sarah had a book. It would be some useful history or reference to suggest how they should proceed. That could be counted upon.

The sight of their faces around the table warmed Ada's heart. She'd known these three since their first year at school, when their troop of gangling fourteen-year-olds had united to defend a housemaid accused of stealing a ruby ring. Ada had been convinced by the maid's tearful denials and determined to help. But without Charlotte's methodical systems, Sarah's head full of odd facts, and Harriet's practical sense, she would have failed. Together, they'd discovered that the ring had been snatched by a teacher's pet crow and hidden in the bird's cage, along with a number of other small lost treasures. That revelation had been the greatest triumph of her young life up to then, Ada remembered with a smile. They'd all nearly burst with pride. She hadn't understood then that their burgeoning friendships were the real boon.

She did now, and she couldn't imagine the last four years without these three. They'd grown from girls into young ladies together. They'd shared victories and tragedies. They'd learned that different temperaments could be something to celebrate, and disagreements could be quite useful things. It was a measure of Delia Rathbone's quality that she'd been welcomed into their tight-knit group. The shock of her death could still be felt in the fabric of their connection.

"Are we going to begin?" asked Charlotte. "Why are you standing there staring at us?"

Harriet straightened the pile of paper that sat before her. She didn't look up, and Ada wondered if this had to do with Harriet's place next to the duke at dinner for two nights in a row. It didn't matter now, of course. Harriet hadn't kissed him. The tactile memory of that kiss flamed through her. She had to shake her head to clear her mind. "There's just one more thing," said Ada. Under her friends' eyes, she hesitated. "I invited Compton to help us."

"A stranger?" said Charlotte.

"A man?" said Sarah at the same time.

"Ada," said Harriet.

Ada resisted the impulse to take a step back. "This is his house, after all, and we are looking for a secret about his family."

"But when we've helped people before—" began Sarah.

"You just want to flirt with him," interrupted Charlotte.

"No, I don't. That is…" She did, Ada admitted silently. Not flirt, but spend time with him. Learn about the man whose kiss could linger in her mind and heart and right down to the tips of her fingers. But that wasn't her only motive. There could be two quite different reasons for doing a thing, she thought. Equally strong. Or three, even. This was for Delia, too. She wanted to…complete her dead friend's mission. "He knows all about this place. And Delia was his sister."

"Haven't we made a vow that no gentleman will ever come between us?" asked Sarah.

"No," replied Charlotte. "We decided that was very silly."

"Decided when?" Sarah's round face wasn't well suited to annoyance.

"It was more dispute than decision," said Harriet. "And not resolved."

"Ha," said Sarah.

"We are *not* going to start one of Sarah's endless debates," replied Charlotte. "We have planning to do." She tapped the page in front of her.

"Mine?" Sarah sat straighter and glared at Charlotte. "You made us talk about different kind of charts for *hours*."

"That was important!"

"He's going to meet us here," said Ada.

Silence fell over the group.

"Shouldn't you have consulted us?" asked Harriet. Her reasonable tone was almost worse than Charlotte's outrage or Sarah's wounded gaze.

"You never look before you leap," said Sarah.

Charlotte stood. "Well, I'm not going to—"

The door opened, and the young duke walked in.

Peter's experience with groups of young ladies was

sparse. Indeed, if he was honest, it was nonexistent. But there was no mistaking the uneasy atmosphere in the room. He'd felt the same awkwardness in the past, when he'd intruded on his father and his sister bent over some shared project. They too had looked at him as if he was an unwelcome diversion. He hadn't cared for the experience then, and it was worse now, when one added illicit kisses to the equation. He nearly turned and walked out again.

"Come in," said Miss Ada.

He looked at her, and then he couldn't look away. "Am I interrupting?" he asked.

"Of course not."

The warmth in her voice brought back other sorts of heat—the sight of her in a nearly transparent night-dress, the soft languor of her lips, the feel of her in his arms. Peter grew almost dizzy with it.

"What sort of neckcloth is *that*?" asked Miss Deeping.

He put his hand to his throat. He hadn't been able to unearth a proper neckcloth this morning in the jumble that was his wardrobe. He'd tied on a spotted scarf, meaning to change, and then forgotten about it. Living alone, he wore whatever was nearest to hand. But he wasn't living alone now. He needed to remember that. Peter tugged at the cloth, as if he could make it fashionable by adjustment. It was sometimes difficult to know you'd done something eccentric until you did it and saw the result. Miss Charlotte Deeping's mocking smile, for example. How was he to make improvements in his wardrobe?

"It's rather like a Belcher neckerchief," said Miss Ada.

"Oh, is there going to be boxing?" replied Miss Deeping. "If I'd known we'd planned a bare-knuckles bout—"

"Charlotte!" said the other three young ladies in unison.

"She has brothers," added Miss Ada, as if this explained something.

Peter had no idea what they were talking about.

"And you know very well you've seen them wearing odder things," Miss Ada said to her friend.

"Is that meant to be a recommendation?" asked Miss Deeping. "Because I must tell you it is not."

Peter decided to ignore the whole exchange. That worked sometimes. "You did say ten o'clock."

"Ha," said Miss Deeping, as if this was an admission of guilt.

"Did you bring the keys?" replied Miss Ada.

He pulled the small ring from his pocket. "Yes."

"Charlotte will take charge of finding where they fit."

Miss Deeping scowled. Clearly she didn't like being given orders. And yet she reached out, as if she couldn't help it. Peter let her take the keys. "That will be a monumental task," he said. "I don't know how you will—"

"I shall divide the house into sections and eliminate them one by one," she interrupted. "Crossing them off on a grid I assemble. I assume you have architectural plans?"

She seemed to imagine she was another Julia Grandison, Peter thought. But he refused to be intimidated. "For the modern wing, yes," he answered. "The older ones were chewed up by rats."

"There are rats in your record room?" Miss Sarah Moran shuddered and held a book to her chest.

"No longer. My father saw to that, with the cats." He was fairly certain they'd swept out all the droppings as well. He had organized the family records, but he didn't spend much time reviewing that long, sad saga of spendthrifts and scoundrels.

"Sarah will look," said Miss Ada. She turned to her friend. "You won't have to go very far back to find Delia's governess. The one I told you about last night."

"Are you assigning our tasks then?" asked Miss Harriet Finch quietly.

For some reason Miss Ada winced.

"What about me?" added Miss Finch with raised eyebrows.

Her slender, auburn brows couldn't begin to compete with Miss Ada's, Peter thought.

"They're the sorts of things that Charlotte and Sarah always do." Miss Ada's voice had a pleading edge. "They like them."

Miss Finch made no reply.

"I suppose you know where to find the plans of this wing," said Miss Deeping to Peter.

"I do indeed."

"Then you can get them for me." She stood. "Which was your father's bedchamber?"

She seemed to think he was under her command. Outlandish neckcloth or not, Peter wouldn't be chivvied. "What?"

The dark, slender girl looked impatient. "That is the obvious place to begin with his keys."

"Ah." He hadn't thought this through, Peter realized. He'd been diverted by the prospect of seeing Miss Ada again. And then by sartorial embarrassment. He didn't want a stranger poking through his father's room, even though it had been cleared out after his death. "I will examine it," he declared. "If I find nothing, you can begin a wider search." He held out a hand.

Miss Deeping hesitated, obviously reluctant to return the keys. After a moment she did, however. Looking sulky, she started toward the door. Miss Ada's other friends joined her.

"Not a word to Aunt Julia," said Miss Ada.

They looked at her as if she'd said something very stupid and trooped out. The door closed behind them with a definitive click.

They left silence behind. And the aftermath of a torrid kiss, though they didn't know that. Did they? "I don't think your friends wanted me here," said Peter. "Did you tell them about…last night?"

"Of course not." She sounded annoyed.

"Well, girls confide all sorts of things, don't they?"

"Oh, are you an expert on girls?"

"Far from it. Quite otherwise. That's why I asked." He held up his hands in surrender. The ring of keys jingled.

"Charlotte would have enjoyed trying those keys."

"Of course her amusement is of paramount importance. But this is my house, and I do insist on being involved."

"Well, you are, aren't you?" Miss Ada often seemed older than her years. But this remark might have been tossed across a schoolyard.

"Why is this going so badly?" asked Peter. Last night she'd been eager and pliant in his arms.

She raised her formidable eyebrows.

"It is, isn't it?"

"Yes," she answered, her voice clipped.

"Well, why? Do *you* know?"

She seemed to search for words.

"I never understand why people don't just admit that a situation is awkward. Wouldn't it save a great deal of time?"

"That depends on what is behind the awkwardness, I suppose."

"Which is what I'm asking you," he pointed out.

Miss Ada frowned. "My friends are trying to help you," she replied. "And you were rude to them. Well, to Charlotte. You ought to be grateful."

"I don't agree."

"You don't think you should be grateful?" She looked shocked.

"That I was rude," Peter said. "I simply wished to be the one going through my father's bedchamber. It seems a reasonable desire. Wouldn't you feel the same?"

"You didn't say it that way."

"It seemed obvious."

"Well, it wasn't."

They faced each other across the table. He resented the change from last night, Peter realized. When his senses had swum with tenderness and desire. But they couldn't repeat that venture into temptation. It might be better to be at odds. "I wasn't the one ordering them about, which they didn't seem to like, if I'm any judge."

Miss Ada's face crumpled. She looked as if she might weep. "Sarah and Charlotte and Harriet are my best friends in the world. It feels as if I've known them all my life. I won't be set against them!"

"Of course not." Peter was shocked at the idea. And envious of the bond they shared. He had no such friends.

"I won't take your part over theirs."

Could he ever wish her to? Might there come a moment… No. Every feeling revolted at the thought of asking that. And in any case, such a moment would not arise. Because he had to keep away.

She gazed up at him, her dark eyes soft and pleading.

If he stayed in this room, he was going to take her in his arms, to comfort her and more. "We shouldn't remain alone together," he said.

Miss Ada stiffened. "Well, I suppose you should go then."

"And so I shall." With a bow, and many vain regrets, he left her.

Ada stood alone beside the long table. He'd actually gone! When he must have known that she meant just the opposite. It had been perfectly obvious. She sank into one of the chairs and rested her chin in her hands. Ella rose from her spot by the hearth and trotted over to paw at her skirts.

"There is no reason to feel abandoned," Ada said to her dog, reaching down to pat the little animal's head. Yet she did—quite pathetically abandoned. Her… host had walked out on her. She'd annoyed her best friends. Stepped on their toes. Ridden roughshod over them. Their investigations had always been mutual.

They tossed ideas back and forth. They rushed to volunteer for various tasks. They urged each other on. But not this time. She'd pushed forward without them, brought in a stranger. "He doesn't even understand what an…honor it was," she said to Ella. "'Insist on being involved,' he said. Does he know that he sounds like a schoolmaster?"

Ella offered a sharp bark of acknowledgment.

Ada sighed and turned to gaze out the window at the ruddy leaves of an oak tree. This morning had been such a prosaic contrast to their passionate encounter in the dark. A duke living in a ruined castle, with bats, ought to brood and simmer with passion, shouldn't he? He should growl and rant. Seize the object of his desire and press her against a wall, kissing her witless.

A small sound escaped Ada's lips. The picture brought back every delicious sensation of last night.

And then a memory of Compton tapping the bat out of the air at dinner rose in her mind, bringing a reluctant smile. He wasn't gloomy. He was… unique. And she was glad, actually. She didn't care for dour. And brooding quickly palled. Last year, one of Charlotte's brothers had decided that a touch of Byronic sulking would make him interesting. A dreadful, and rather amusing, mistake. No, she liked Compton just the way he was—except that he might have made more of the opportunity just past. How often could they be alone?

But she'd annoyed her friends. Which wasn't right. She must go and apologize to them. Ada pushed away from the table and headed for the stairs, Ella trotting at her heels.

Her own bedchamber was empty, but she found Harriet in the room she and Charlotte shared. "Don't scold me," Ada said before the redheaded girl could speak.

"Is that what you expect? What have you been up to since we left?"

"And please don't answer me with questions, the way you do."

"Do I?" Harriet flushed. "I do. Sorry."

"Well, it's very useful sometimes, when we're trying to work out a puzzle. But not now." Ada sat down, facing Harriet across the hearth. "I came to beg your pardon. Sarah's and Charlotte's, too. I didn't mean to…manage everyone. I was hurrying."

Harriet raised her eyebrows.

"And bringing in Compton without telling anyone," Ada added. "That wasn't right. I shouldn't act the leader."

"But you are."

"No I'm not," replied Ada, shocked.

"You're the one who begins things. We never would have come together in the first place without your conviction that Meg hadn't taken that ring."

"But you all joined right in," said Ada, startled.

"We did. Once you insisted. If you hadn't, I probably wouldn't have done anything. Mortifying, but true. I don't think Sarah or Charlotte would have either. We've never acknowledged this, but perhaps it's time."

Ada didn't know what to say.

"It's a good thing, Ada," said her friend. "Admirable. I'm so glad you goaded me." Harriet smiled.

"Well, but…bringing in Compton. Aren't you going to tell me that my friends are more important to me than any gentleman?"

"No."

"You aren't?" Ada was surprised.

"School is over," said Harriet slowly. "Things will never be the same for us."

A sinking feeling came over Ada. "Well, not exactly the same, but—"

"We aren't living in each other's pockets, knowing every detail of our lives. We won't be, ever again."

"But we'll always be friends!"

"Of course we will. And we were all delighted to come on this journey of yours. One last time."

"Last?" Ada didn't like the sound of that.

Harriet gave her a sweet smile. "Haven't you been thinking about the future? We're all going to London next season, Ada. I can hardly wait. I'm sure we'll see each other often in town. But we'll be living with our own families, going about with them. And then we'll marry and have families of our own. Perhaps it's time to become accustomed to others becoming…attached to our group. Gentlemen in particular."

This was unexpected. "I'm not sure Sarah would agree with you."

"Oh, she wouldn't. Now. But when it is *her* gentleman?" Harriet cocked her head, her smile broadening.

It was odd to think of her friends with husbands, probably quite varied sorts of men. Ada tried to picture them as eight rather than four, but the gentlemen remained as vague as the groom in her dream. "Charlotte swears she will never marry."

"I know," said Harriet.

"You think she doesn't mean it?"

"Oh, she does. Now. But I suspect she will change her mind. We're young. *I* intend to enjoy two seasons at least before I settle down."

"You don't seem young just now."

Harriet laughed.

"And you're an heiress. You'll have more choices than the rest of us."

"True."

Ada was surprised. Harriet usually evaded mention of her unexpected fortune. Her friends knew only that her inheritance would be very large.

"And more trouble determining whether men like me for myself," Harriet said. She hesitated, then added, "In fact, I've been wondering whether Compton may have heard how I'm placed."

Ada's mind went blank.

"He has shown a few hints of interest. Nothing marked, but—" Harriet fell silent, looking troubled.

It was possible to have too many feelings at once, Ada realized. They jostled in her throat, and she almost choked on a combination of jealousy, a fierce denial that the duke could be so mercenary, and the knowledge that Harriet's fortune would probably save his disintegrating estate. For the first time, Ada was envious of one of her friends. And she hated it. "How would he have heard about your inheritance?" she managed. "He doesn't seem to know anybody."

"True." Harriet looked relieved. "I mustn't imagine things." She grimaced. "My mother says word will spread like wildfire now that my grandfather has made his intentions known. And I must expect gossip and a great deal of attention. Some of it quite false. I don't wish to seem arrogant, but I truly dislike the idea."

She ought to be full of sympathy for her friend, Ada noted, not thinking of herself. If they'd been speaking of any other young man she would have been.

"I'm not interested in Compton," Harriet added. "I mean to stay out of his way."

And so now she was an object for Harriet's charity. Immediately, Ada felt dreadful. Where had that idea come from? And should she be trying to make a match between her wealthy friend and Delia's brother in some saintly act of self-sacrifice? Like the heroine of a pious tract? A hot surge of denial told Ada that this would always be beyond her. She was no pattern card of goodness. Quite the opposite, apparently.

"Charlotte is right, you know," Harriet added. "He isn't a good prospect."

She couldn't talk about this now. "I should find her, and Sarah, and beg their pardons." She rose.

"Ada."

"Charlotte was angry. She'll want me to crawl a bit."

"*You're* angry with me."

"I'm not."

Harriet shook her head, clearly skeptical. "You see how things are changing between us already."

"We won't let them!" declared Ada. And then, like a coward, she fled.

Six

PETER FOUND IT STRANGE TO BE IN HIS FATHER'S OLD
bedchamber. He hadn't come in often when Papa was
alive, and he'd had no reason to be here since they'd
cleared out his clothing and personal items after his
death.

The furnishings were the same, the dark-blue
draperies and coverlet familiar. His father had admired
the large painting over the fireplace, a Dutch still life
of fruits and vegetables. Peter found it gloomy and
oppressive. He'd tried to sell the piece a few years after
his father's death, and been told the artist was third
rate. A smaller study of his mother had been moved to
the gallery with the other ancestral portraits.

He walked about the room. There was little left of
his father's presence. Except an atmosphere. A wisp
of memory perhaps, or an imprint of seven decades of
living. Peter didn't feel as if his father was looking over
his shoulder exactly. But he didn't feel completely at
ease either.

None of the three keys on Papa's old ring fit the
door lock. Peter had known they wouldn't. They

didn't look right. He was familiar with a variety of keys from his repair work about the house. There was a whole drawer full of unidentified keys in the study. Yet his father had valued these three in particular.

The largest one on the ring might work in a door in the older part of the house, he thought, though it was a bit small. Another seemed more suited to a cupboard or chest. The third, the smallest, might fit a box or casket. It was too large for a pocket watch.

Peter tried them all in the wardrobe lock. Without success. He checked inside, and found the shelves empty, as they'd left them. He went to the writing desk, which had two rows of small compartments. He had the keys to several of those, and none on the ring fitted any of the locks.

He moved around the room, looking for chests or boxes. As he'd recalled, there were none. Finally, he searched the walls and floorboards for hidden spaces. His father had loved that sort of thing. Peter remembered his delight at finding a secret priest hole in the older part of the house.

But there was nothing. Just a rather shabby bedchamber and a growing sense of melancholy. Peter gave up and left the room, closing the door with a sense of finality. His father was gone and would not be suddenly dropping hints in his ear from the beyond.

Peter headed for the stairs only to encounter Miss Ada surging up them, her little dog trotting hard to keep up. She looked as gloomy as he felt. "I've been apologizing to Charlotte and Sarah," she said. "Charlotte enjoyed it a bit too much."

"Apologizing for what?"

"Never mind."

"Ah, bringing me into your golden circle."

"Golden." The word seemed to trouble her. "Would you call it that?"

He didn't like to see her downcast. That was his arena. "I would, with my acute sensitivity to atmosphere," Peter said.

This won him a dubious glance.

"A joke," he added. "Actually, I have very little. Delia found my lack of…er, subtle awareness inexplicable, as she was brimming with it. She called me a changeling once. But we made up after that quarrel."

"Oh, good." Miss Ada smiled at him, almost as if his shortcomings were charming rather than deplorable.

Peter felt as if he was expanding under her warm gaze. "Are they reconciled to my presence in your midst?"

"Well—"

Of course they weren't, any more than Papa and Delia had ever been. "It doesn't matter. I'm used to that." He brushed his feelings aside. "There was nothing to find in my father's old room. Nor was there when we cleared it out, if I remember correctly. And I do."

She looked uncertain, as if he'd confused her. "Oh well, there are many other places to try."

"Far *too* many, I fear. There are dozens of locks at Alberdene." He dangled the keys from one finger. Ella came alert at the jingling sound. She set her paws on Peter's leg and barked. When he stuck the key ring in his waistcoat pocket, the dog looked reproachful. She went to sniff at the fraying hall carpet.

"Charlotte won't care," replied Miss Ada. "She loves laying out charts and ticking off the boxes. She'll be delighted to get the keys back."

"I have no doubt. It was all she could do to return them to me."

"So, you see, you do notice things."

Her smile was back, even sweeter. She was teasing him, Peter realized. And it was nothing like mockery. Mockery stung. Made one want to raise one's fists or to slink away. This was…appreciative not cutting, alluring not contemptuous. He knew this from the lovely way her dark eyes danced. He couldn't look away.

Ada wondered what she'd been saying. She'd lost track. Indeed, she'd lost more than that. She was very much afraid that she'd lost her heart to this endearing man. She had to speak or she was going to step into his arms right here on the staircase. No doubt Aunt Julia would appear then. And chaos would ensue. What had they been talking about? Charts! "Charlotte is very methodical. She gets great satisfaction from her grids." Ada's cheeks flamed. Why had that sounded improper? It had nothing to do with midnight kisses. Say something else, she told herself. "Like your papa. When he made a list of every bottle of wine in the Alberdene cellars."

"What?"

"And then drew up a plan to rearrange them by vintage." What had become of her determination not to babble?

"I never heard anything about that. How do you know?"

"Delia told me."

"Of course." He looked piqued. "Since Delia knew my father much better than I."

"I suppose that happens in all families."

Her response appeared to surprise him. Indeed, Ada was rather surprised herself. She hadn't known she was about to say that. It was odd to be curious about where a conversation was going when you were the one speaking. An image popped into her head, of a performer she'd seen at a village fair, walking on a rope stretched between two poles. Which had nothing to do with anything! "My sister Lily—she's fourteen—is much closer to my mother than I am," she went on.

"Ah." He looked sympathetic.

"Which only makes sense," Ada said. "They're so alike, you see. If pressed, Mama *will* go out to evening parties and neighborhood assemblies. But she'd much rather stay home with her family and her embroidery. And Lily is just the same. They always have their heads together over some new pattern or shade of thread. They make the most beautiful pieces. They're artistic."

"One can feel quite left out," he said.

He wasn't getting it. And Ada hadn't quite realized the truth of this herself until she had to explain. "No, when Lily first showed her talents I was *delighted*."

"You were?" It seemed that she'd startled him again.

Ada nodded. "I always hated fancywork. And I was dreadful at it. I don't know if I hated it because I was so clumsy, or was clumsy because I hated it. But my family jokes that if I am given a needle and just one strand of thread, I somehow create a snarl as large as my fist." She held out her hands to show the span.

"And your mother was disappointed by this." His tone suggested that he was familiar with this sort of reaction.

"She was, a bit, and *sad*. That was difficult. But Lily makes her happy."

"And you are shut out of their…magic circle."

He still didn't seem to see her point. "Mama and I were never going to be similar," Ada said. "She is positively *dreading* going to London next season. Can you imagine?"

"I can, rather."

She made a face at him. "And Lily begged not to be sent away to school. When I was her age, I begged to go. I couldn't wait to see new things and people. They don't understand me in the least."

The duke frowned at her. "No?"

Ada shook her head. "But that doesn't matter."

"It did to my father," he answered. "He found me quite disappointing." Compton put a hand to his waistcoat pocket where the key ring lay. "Papa believed that formulating theories and testing them was the highest use of the mind. He could debate a single step in a chain of logic for hours. Then, when he was finally satisfied, he would simply move on to the next point. He never seemed to *conclude*. It drove me half-mad."

Ada nodded to show that she was listening.

"I remember sitting with him in his study, at an age when my feet barely reached the edge of the chair, and being asked, 'What do you think comes next, Peter?'

My mind always felt as empty as a dry well when he posed that question." He shrugged. "I *had* thoughts, but with him standing over me—"

"The thread snarled."

He gazed down at her. The sudden spark in his dark eyes was dizzying. He smiled. "Yes, I suppose so. And then came Delia, who bubbled with ideas from the time she could talk. She never minded when Papa said one was foolish either. I hated that, but she just brushed it aside and plowed on. She was the most indomitable child." He shook his head as if mystified still.

"They were made from the same mold," said Ada. "As you were not."

"Yes." His smile died.

"Wasn't that a relief?"

"A...?"

"Your father had someone to his taste," Ada explained. "And you didn't have to try to be something you weren't. As I don't have to embroider. Ever." She added a comic shudder for effect.

"Yes, but...don't you feel...judged? Belittled?"

Ada shook her head. "Mama loves me just the same as Lily. I know that. I'm sure your father did, too."

"Did what?"

"Loved you."

Compton went very still, as if he'd heard a threatening sound in the distance.

If only she could take his hand, Ada thought. She so much wanted to. She glanced down the stairs. There was no one about. Ella sat on the top step looking bored. She dared, folding her fingers over his. "Delia certainly did," she added.

He gazed down at her, a picture of vulnerability. Ada felt as if all the layers of social convention had been stripped away and she was seeing right into him. It was the strangest sensation—a swooping fall that went on and on.

"Delia told you—?" He couldn't seem to finish the question.

"It was obvious. Just as it is with Sarah or Charlotte or Harriet and their families. Delia didn't need to say so."

"For some reason I believe you." He sounded puzzled by the idea.

"Why shouldn't you?" Ada asked.

"You're hardly more than a schoolgirl."

"And that means I'm witless?"

"No, of course not. But one doesn't expect... wisdom. You must admit it's unusual."

"I'm not fond of the word *must*."

Compton surprised her by laughing. His clasp on her hand tightened. "I never would have guessed. But how can you be so sure you're right?"

"I observe, and I pay attention to what I see."

"That sounds too simple."

Ada started to object. But he spoke again before she could.

"And yet isn't."

"Most people miss half of what goes on around them," she replied. This fact continually puzzled her. "Three-quarters. It's as if they *prefer* to be ignorant."

"As you never would."

"No! Why would anyone?"

"So what do you observe about me?" he asked.

The words that had been coming so easily dried up. Or crowded forward so thickly that they stuck in her throat. "I...I don't—"

A silence fell and stretched.

Compton looked disappointed. "There's been very little time, of course."

"You're—"

Ella gave a welcoming bark. Ada pulled her hand free just before Charlotte appeared at the turn of the stair. "Did you discover anything?" she asked the duke.

Ada took a step back. So did Compton, as if this had been a clandestine meeting. Charlotte clearly noticed. "Quiet, Ella," Ada said, even though her little dog had stopped barking already.

"There's nothing in my father's old bedchamber," Compton said.

"Right. Shall I take the keys then?" Charlotte came closer and held out her hand.

The duke took them from his pocket and gave them to her. "That larger one is probably for a door in the older part of the house. From its looks."

Charlotte nodded. "Do you have the plans for this wing?"

"I was just on my way to get them."

"Shall we go then?"

Ada wasn't surprised when Compton raised an eyebrow. Charlotte sounded more like a sergeant major than ever. "I'll come along and see so I can show Sarah the records room," Ada said. And to keep Charlotte from quarreling with the duke. Had Harriet meant that their lives would become far more complicated when she spoke of change? "You're sure there are no rats?"

"Utterly," he replied, leading the way.

He took them to a room not far from the stair that led up to Delia's chamber. It held shelves of bound volumes and piles of documents, and smelled a bit musty. Ada saw no sign of rodents, however. The duke found the roll of plans and gave it to Charlotte. She hurried away as if it was a prize she'd won and meant to keep all for herself.

"I'll bring Sarah here to look for mentions of the foreign governess," said Ada.

"It occurs to me there might be another source of information," Compton replied. "The servants—the original ones, I mean—were all here when that woman was employed. They might know something about her."

"Oh, that's good idea."

"I should have thought of it sooner. Let's go ask."

But before they reached the kitchen, Ada received a peremptory summons from her aunt Julia. There could be no question of evading it. Her aunt's stentorian voice could be heard through two closed doors.

"I'll inquire," said Compton as she reluctantly turned away.

"And tell me."

"Of course."

Ada's eyes lingered on him as he turned away. Then she heard her aunt again and rushed toward the sound, Ella right behind her.

She found her three friends gathered around Aunt Julia in the drawing room. Ada's tardy arrival earned her a sharp glance, which proceeded to rake the other girls, compelling their attention one by one. "There is more to managing a household than being handed a bunch of keys and called chatelaine," said her aunt then.

Charlotte started and shoved the keys Compton had given her into a pocket of her gown. The move was so obvious that Ada expected her aunt to remark on it. But she was apparently too involved with her subject.

"One must first know what needs to be done," she went on. "Second, one must have some notion of how best to do it. A lady needn't possess every skill, but she should understand enough to direct others. Finally, an air of calm authority is desirable." She stopped and frowned at something over Ada's shoulder. "What are you doing here?"

Ada turned to find the lad Tom in the doorway. He didn't cringe under her aunt's glare. Indeed, he smiled, which made his homely, round face quite engaging despite the prominent front teeth. His blue eyes were open and friendly, and Ada thought his appearance would probably improve when he grew into his features and the large bones that showed in his hands and wrists. "I like to learn things," he said.

"You are proposing to join us?" Aunt Julia looked startled.

"If I might, your ladyship."

"I am not a ladyship. Why should you wish to know about household management?"

Tom spread his hands. "I like knowing all manner of things. I make a study whenever I can. When I come across a new bit of knowledge, like."

"Do you?" Ada's aunt eyed him as if probing for weaknesses. "Give me an example."

The lad nodded as if the demand was only natural. "I know a bit of blacksmithing and how a dame school is run and the best way to pickle eels. I can cook a bit, and I learnt summat about the theater when I was in London. That was right interesting."

"You know we are going to be engaged in what is called women's work?"

Tom shrugged. "I reckon everything comes in useful. And even if it ai—isn't, it's better to know than not, eh?"

Aunt Julia continued to examine him. It seemed she found no flaws because she said, "Very well. But if you lose interest and wander off, do not expect to return. I am not providing *entertainment*."

Tom nodded as if confirming a bargain.

Ada's aunt accepted his gesture and turned back to her charges. "We will begin with linens. Ada, please ask the housemaids to join us. And bring along writing materials." She looked down. "*Must* your dog come?" she asked.

"She doesn't like being left alone. She'll be good."

Aunt Julia stared at Ella. Ada was surprised when her little dog stared right back. For a moment, it appeared that they were locked in a battle of wills.

"Pfft," said Aunt Julia then. "Keep the creature out of my way."

Ella couldn't really look smug, Ada thought as she went to fetch the housemaids. Except that it certainly seemed she did, just now.

Returning with the servants, Ada saw that Charlotte was wildly impatient. She wanted to be off poring over the house plans, Ada knew, and trying keys in locks. Sarah appeared merely resigned. Harriet gave Ada a sharp glance, which she evaded.

"Take us to your linen store," commanded Aunt Julia.

Rose and Tess, the two older maids, led the way upstairs to a small room, or very large closet, with shelves on three sides piled with folded bedding and toweling.

"We cannot all fit in here." Aunt Julia shooed them back into the corridor. "We will take one shelf at a time." She pointed at the younger maids. "Bring out the contents of the highest on the left."

"I could help reach things down," said Tom. Despite his youth, he was the tallest of the younger set.

Aunt Julia nodded, and the lad began handing linens to Marged and Una.

The first piece, a bedsheet, was unfolded in the hallway, held up, and evaluated. Rose wrung her hands over the patches. "We've done our best to keep things up, ma'am."

"The mending isn't bad," Aunt Julia pronounced. "Neatly done, in fact. I commend you. And the cloth hasn't yellowed." Rose and Tess looked startled, then pleased.

Ada's thoughts drifted off to the feel of the duke's fingers warm on hers. Or his lips, deliriously rousing.

"Ada," said her aunt. "Ada!" She started, brought back to the present moment with a thud. Aunt Julia sighed. "You are keeping the list. Note, one bedsheet with three large repairs. Write it down. No woolgathering!"

"I'll do it," said Sarah, taking the paper and pencil. "My handwriting is much better than Ada's." Sarah clearly wanted more to occupy her mind as well.

It seemed Aunt Julia might object. But then she gave in with a wave of her hand. "Fold that up again and place it there," she told the maids, indicating an open space by the door to the cupboard. "We will establish categories and reorganize the shelves."

Rose started to speak. Possibly to mention that they had a system already, Ada thought. But then she caught her remark behind tightly pressed lips.

"Next piece," said Aunt Julia. Another bedsheet was brought out, unfolded, and held up.

This was going to take a long time, Ada realized. All afternoon, perhaps. She met Charlotte's burning gaze and wondered how she might rescue her friend from a task that was obviously driving her mad. After all, Ada had brought her here, and into the clutches of her dictatorial aunt.

"I need to write to my parents," said Charlotte. "Perhaps I might be ex—"

"Commendable," interrupted Ada's aunt. "You may do so before dinner."

Charlotte growled, but too softly to be heard by their chaperone. Ella's ears perked up, however, and the dog came over to sit at Charlotte's feet. Harriet hid a smile. Sarah attended to her list.

And so they looked at linens—large sheets and small, pillowcases, toweling, tablecloths and napkins. Some pieces were set aside for mending. A few were consigned to the rag bin. It seemed a long age of the world before they had seen them all and returned them to the shelves in the order Aunt Julia decreed. "Good," she said then. "A job well done."

Ada could feel the others come alert, poised to flee,

like a herd of deer when some sound disturbed the forest.

"The room needs better airing, however," her aunt went on. "You should keep those windows open." They followed Aunt Julia's pointing finger to the small two-pane windows near the ceiling.

"We was worried the bats would fly in," said Tess. Marged stifled a giggle, Rose a shudder.

"Ah. Well, I suggest you arrange for wire screens to exclude them. Surely there is someone about the estate who could produce such things."

"The duke could do it," said Rose, then flushed as if she'd said something shocking. Ada wondered what that might be.

Tom stepped in front of the maid, a touch of kindly shielding, Ada thought. "I reckon I could make up something," he said. "If they have the materials about."

"Good," said Aunt Julia. "Find them and do so."

Charlotte was already turning away. She'd taken several steps along the corridor when Ada's aunt spoke again.

"The linens would benefit from some sprigs of lavender or perhaps rose petals. We will go out to the garden and see what we can find. Though from what I've seen out the windows, I am not optimistic."

Charlotte groaned. She didn't even bother to keep it quiet this time. Ada's aunt either didn't hear or chose to ignore the protest. Instead, she pointed at Una. "You will accompany us. Find a good-sized basket and meet us in the front hall."

The youngest maid gulped. Her dark eyes were wide as she nodded.

"The rest of you can be about your duties," Aunt Julia said to the other servants, waving them off. "You girls, go and put on your hats. And if you have any sturdy gloves, you will likely be glad of them."

"I'll get Ella's lead," said Ada.

"Splendid," answered her aunt, her tone desert dry.

"I hereby consign all linens to the nether regions," muttered Charlotte. "And their sprigs of lavender may go with them."

"Did you say something, Miss Deeping?"

Charlotte was apparently too irritated to be cowed. "I don't think I have the patience to be a proper chatelaine," she replied.

"In fact, you see tasks such as the one we just completed as a waste of time."

Ada's friend half shrugged. She looked sulky as a child.

"And yet you expect to be comfortable in houses you visit, and in your own home, presumably. *Someone* sees to that. Your mother, I suppose. Do you think yourself above the work she does?"

"No!" Charlotte shook her head. "Not above. Only that my...skills lie in a different direction."

"And what would that be?"

Ada would have subsided at this crisp question, but her friend was made of sterner stuff. "I like solving problems," said Charlotte. "Through observation and analysis."

"Well, if you think that managing a large household is not solving problems, you are a sillier girl than you appear." Ada's aunt pointed down the corridor. "Hats. And gloves."

A few minutes later, their party walked out into Alberdene's gardens. Ada's aunt tsked at the state of them. "What a shame. I hate to see such neglect. Overgrown flower beds. Shrubbery run rampant. Compton ought to see to this."

Ada was moved to defend him, but she knew this would be a mistake. Aunt Julia would not be convinced. And she didn't want to draw her aunt's attention to her…keen interest in their host.

Tom, tagging along at the rear of their group, pointed. "There's an herb garden over there."

"Indeed? How would you know that?"

"I like to walk about a place when I arrive, get to know it, like."

"And you can recognize herbs?" asked Ada's aunt.

"Yes, your…ma'am. The lady at a dame school where I lived for a bit grew all sorts."

"Show me."

Tom led them to the proper section of garden. A row of raspberry bushes had sent thorny canes twisting across it. "Lavender there," said Ada's aunt. "We must have that. There are even a few flowers left. Cut all of these stalks, Una. And orris root. Splendid! We may hope that whoever planted this dried some. That takes a long time."

"My head is going to explode from sheer frustration," hissed Charlotte.

"I think it's interesting," said Sarah.

"You would."

"So do I," said Harriet.

"Don't tell me that you agree," Charlotte said to Ada. "I do not *care*."

Ada caught movement in the corner of her eye.
Looking up, she saw the duke standing at a window,
looking down at them. He raised a hand in greeting.
Ada felt a flush of delight. She waved and turned
back to find all three of her friends watching her.
Fortunately, her aunt was bent over a row of plants.
"Did you notice any roses in your rambles?" she asked
Tom.

"Yes, ma'am. There's an avenue of 'em over that
way." He pointed.

"Splendid! Do you know, girls, I think we may be
able to assemble a potpourri." Enthusiasm lit the older
woman's face. Ada had never seen her so pleasantly
animated. "With this garden, I believe someone here
was doing that once," she continued. "Depending
on what we find in the kitchen, I can teach you my
special method."

"Now?" The word burst from Charlotte.

"No, Miss Deeping, not now. The process will
require preparation. You may go and write your
letters."

Charlotte didn't wait for further permission. She
rushed away.

"I'd like to learn how to make it," said Sarah.
Harriet nodded agreement. "Do you use rose petals
and lavender?"

"I do," said Ada's aunt. "There are many recipes,
some of them quite ancient."

"They used potpourri in medieval castles," said
Sarah. "Some scents ward off insects, I think."

"Lavender, lemon, and cinnamon," replied Aunt
Julia. "Well dried. All the plant material must be dried

before you add spices and the ground orris root to fix it. Then you place the mixture in a dark, dry place for a month or two, to form a mature fragrance. Shaking the container daily for the first week."

"We won't be here that long," said Harriet. She sounded firm.

"No, but we can instruct the servants in my method."

"Will the duke even want it?" wondered Sarah.

Ada's aunt waved the question away. "That is not my concern. I am teaching you."

"We could leave it like a gift," said Ada.

"Indeed. The fragrance will continue to strengthen if left in a sealed container."

Sarah and Harriet nodded. Ada said nothing more. She was lost in the idea that they would soon be gone from Alberdene, and she might never see the duke again.

༄

Ada lay in bed staring at the dim ceiling. Sarah slept peacefully on the other side of the big bed, a champion sleeper. Waking Sarah in the morning had been a sort of game at school. She'd had to be dragged, and not always metaphorically, from her slumbers.

Ada had locked the bedchamber door as she'd promised, but she hadn't given Sarah the key. She wasn't ready to explain about the sleepwalking. She'd put it on a high shelf instead. If she could climb up on a chair and reach above her head in her sleep… Well, she didn't think she could do that.

Of course she hadn't known she could prowl

through a house in darkness, while sleeping, either. Sleepwalking was such an odd thing. Almost a kind of magic. As if strange powers wafted one from place to place. And then one woke and found the fairy-tale prince and kissed him and all difficulties disappeared. Ada sighed. She hadn't quite managed that last part. But she had the aid of her friends instead of a magic wand.

She turned over, too restless to sleep. She must stop sleepwalking, of course. Compton was right; it could be dangerous. And she didn't want to feel quite so out of control. She would stop. She already had, she vowed. She'd commanded her dreaming self to stay in bed. Otherwise she would have to confess to Sarah and endure her friends' anxious pity. More of it; she'd seen signs of worry in their eyes already. As for Aunt Julia, she would have her in a chaise going home before Ada could even try to explain.

A longer sigh escaped Ada. This determination put an end to her secret rendezvous with the duke. There would be no other opportunity to see him in such thrilling circumstances. He thought clandestine meetings improper, and of course he was right. Why must he be? They would be limited to the snatches of private conversation allowed by polite society. And she would have to watch him talk to her friends as well. Tonight at dinner he'd burst out laughing at something Harriet said, and he'd sung a duet with Sarah in the drawing room afterward. She'd barely spoken to him all evening.

Ada squirmed into a more comfortable position under the bedclothes. She'd never been jealous of her friends before. She wasn't now, exactly. They hadn't been setting their caps at the duke. Far from it. They'd behaved correctly, as they had innumerable times before. She was the difference, the turmoil inside her. Here was a sign of the change in their lives that Harriet had talked about. Harriet, who was a great heiress, which Compton might have heard.

With a tremor of chagrin, Ada faced the knowledge that she *was* fiercely jealous of her friend's money. If she had a fortune… Her dream of a wedding wavered in her mind. She'd thought Compton was the groom when she half woke from it. If she was an heiress, that might have been a prophecy. Those delirious kisses might have led to a real altar. A bolt of desire for him and for that future flashed through her.

But she had no fortune. Not to speak of. Her family was comfortable, not rich. The marital vision collapsed around her ears, a victim of the unfairness of the world.

Ada turned over again. She was never going to sleep now. How could Sarah be so oblivious? Not that she wanted her to wake. She *wanted* to see the duke. She needed to.

An outrageous idea bloomed in Ada's consciousness. Her face grew warm at the mere thought. Of course she couldn't go downstairs when she wasn't sleepwalking. All alone, in the middle of the night, looking for her host. Shockingly improper! The idea would never have occurred to her if she hadn't done it already.

But once planted, the thought would not go away. Compton had begun checking the house at night; she knew that. He would find her. They would find each other. Perhaps just one last time she *could* have this.

Ada slipped out of bed. Now she was sorry she'd put the key away so securely. Glancing at Sarah, she shielded a candlestick with her body and lit the candle. She would never be able to retrieve the key without light. Sarah didn't stir. Ella did, however, rising from her spot on the hearth with a curious little woof. "Guard," Ada whispered. It was one command her dog knew. She gave it every night. Ella would stay in place until released, as she had during the sleepwalking. Which just showed how wrong Aunt Julia was about her training, Ada thought.

Gathering her nightdress in one hand, Ada climbed up on the chair and groped for the key. Her fingers closed on the bit of metal and she stepped back down. She unlocked the door. But when she set her hand on the knob, she realized she couldn't take the lighted candle with her. It would be like a beacon pointing her out, and also prove that she wasn't sleepwalking after all. She'd have to move through the house in darkness, which was daunting. "Well, if I can do it in my sleep, I can do it awake," she murmured.

She put on her dressing gown and slippers, snuffed the candle, and left the room. Outside, she stood still for a bit, allowing her eyes to adjust. Glimmers of moonlight from the window at the end of the corridor outlined the hall. Slowly, she moved toward the stair.

It was both harder and easier than she'd expected to navigate to the drawing room. With a hand on the banister, carefully sliding her feet, she could feel her way without trouble. But the eerie emptiness of the house was oppressive, which she hadn't felt when sleepwalking, of course. Solitude seemed much... thicker now that she knew everyone else was asleep. She trailed a hand along the wall of the downstairs corridor as she walked, avoiding a small table that sat in the hall.

At last she reached her goal. Moonlight poured through the drawing-room windows, lighting her way to a sofa. Ada sat down, pushing aside the unsettling idea that something might look in through the panes from the darkness. She had only to wait for the duke now. And if he didn't appear soon, she would knock something over.

That ploy proved unnecessary. After a little time, light wavered in the doorway, and he came in carrying a lit candle. Ada rose. The duke started and strode toward her. "You promised this wouldn't happen again. We must tell your aunt as soon as she wakes—"

"I'm not sleepwalking tonight," Ada said. "I just came down."

"What?" He looked shocked.

He also looked like a Renaissance painting, with his dark hair tousled from sleep, in his strange Egyptian robe, candlelight shining down over his figure. This was probably her last chance ever. She couldn't let it pass. Ada stepped forward, slid her arms around his neck, and kissed him.

Peter's body responded like a racehorse at the gate. He could feel the lithe softness of her under his hand. He held her like a lifeline, her body a blazing benison against him, and kissed her with all his heart. Her eager response was sweeter, fierier, than anything he'd felt in his life before. He wanted it to go on forever.

Hot wax dripped onto his hand from the wavering candlestick, a burning reproach. He pulled away. "We can't do this." He heard anguish in his voice and knew it was perilous.

Miss Ada put fingertips to her lips as if feeling for the lost kiss.

The gesture nearly undid Peter. "I have nothing to offer but the scraps of a noble house going down into ruin. You see how impossible—"

"Nothing is impossible if you put all your heart into it," said Miss Ada.

"Nonsense."

She blinked as if he'd shouted at her.

"I beg your pardon, but that sort of sentiment sounds noble and isn't really true." Peter hated the way she was staring at him, as if he'd disappointed her. At least she'd put on her dressing gown this time. He wasn't driven distracted by the near-transparency of her nightdress.

"If one finds a way to fight for—"

This stung. She didn't understand. And how could she, with the life she'd led? Yet he wished she might. "I've been fighting for most of my life, a new disaster threatening nearly every hour. I've only just managed to hang onto the Rathbone lands. And that may not last much longer." He shoved this fear aside with a gesture. "Imagine trying to hold back the tide with a shovel. Believing in the impossible makes no difference at all when the waves are about to engulf you."

"You would give up?"

The hurt wonderment in her tone overset him. Must he escort her back to her bedchamber? No, that was too much to ask of a man. Leaving her the candle, like a coward, he ran.

Seven

THE FOLLOWING MORNING, PETER FOUND THE FOUR young ladies in the parlor they'd taken over for their use. Or rather, the three young ladies and Miss Ada, as he thought of them now. She'd become a category of her own, unique in his experience and beginning to occupy all his attention. Peter had spent the second half of the night getting control of himself after that latest kiss, and mainly he had succeeded. He was accustomed to disappointment and not being able to have things he wanted. Ada was just the latest, though certainly the most searing, in a long line. Probably by this time she'd realized there was no future for them. How could she not?

He knew that he ought to avoid her, even tell his unexpected houseguests that it was time for them to depart. Why prolong a vain temptation? At the same time, he longed to see her. He could feel her presence in his house like a lodestone that draws a magnet. Once she left, he was unlikely ever to meet her again.

Full of this turmoil, he entered the parlor on a sigh. He had reason to be here this morning. He had news to bring them. Under Miss Deeping's stern gaze, he felt rather like a junior officer reporting to headquarters. An odd sort of headquarters, admittedly.

At this hour, before Miss Julia Grandison left her room, the young ladies sat at ease around the room. A colorful scatter of their possessions covered the long table. Chairs had been rearranged around the hearth, and Miss Ada's little dog was curled up before the fire. Ella seemed a placid creature, except around bats. In the short time they'd been here, they'd made this spot feel more homelike than any other room in his house. But he thought that was as much a function of their long-established friendships as of any particular talents. He wondered if they knew how fortunate they were to have such a connection.

Under scrutiny from four pairs of pretty eyes, only partly welcoming, he stood straighter. Perhaps more like an examination than a report. And naturally he'd spilled gravy on the lapel of his one good coat at dinner last night. While it was being cleaned, he wore a relic of his ancestral trunks, an old-fashioned garment that Miss Deeping clearly found amusing. He should find time to do something about his clothes.

"I asked the servants about Delia's foreign governess," he began. "It took a bit of time to catch up with them all. They remembered her, and that she was from some northern country, but no one knows where she is now."

"Do you think she went back to Sweden?" asked Miss Ada.

Peter shook his head. "Conway was certain she wasn't Swedish. She once told him that her country had been 'ground under the heel' of Sweden as much as of Russia."

Miss Sarah Moran raised her head like a hound catching an interesting scent. "Perhaps Finland? That would fit."

All of them looked at her.

"Finland was ruled by Sweden," she continued. "And then Sweden fought a war with Russia and lost it to them."

"You have an impressive knowledge of history, Miss Moran," Peter replied.

"You have no idea," said Miss Finch.

"Where is Finland?" asked Miss Ada.

"In the far northwest of the Russian empire. They speak quite a different language there. Perhaps that's why the words in Delia's message look strange."

"So far away," said Miss Harriet Finch. "I wonder how she ever came to be here?"

"Perhaps she grew tired of being in a place that was being ground under various heels," said Miss Deeping dryly.

Miss Finch nodded. "And perhaps she didn't wish to go back and stayed in England."

"I should look through the records room then," said Miss Moran. "To see if I can find any mention of her."

"Yes, I'm sorry." Peter didn't envy her the job.

"Oh, Sarah likes nothing better than a pile of dusty documents," said Miss Ada. "In complete disorder, preferably."

They all smiled, even Miss Moran. "Not preferably," she said. "I enjoy a tidy order as much as anyone."

"Oh, far more," said Miss Finch.

The obvious affection in the looks they exchanged revived his envy. But it also gratified him. "I'm glad I sent Delia to your school," he said. When they looked puzzled at his non sequitur, he added, "I wanted her to have good friends. I hoped she'd find them. You."

The young ladies' smiles turned pensive. "The connection didn't come easily," said Miss Ada.

"When she arrived at school, she was like a pot on the boil," said Miss Moran. "You almost expected steam to pour out of her ears."

To Peter's surprise, Miss Moran stood and began to stride back and forth across the room. She'd been the quietest of them so far, but now she stomped and scowled and swung her arms. Small and sturdy, she looked nothing like Delia, but still she evoked his sister's restless presence. Delia had tossed her head just like that when she was displeased.

"At first, Delia used to walk up and down in the garden and mutter complaints," said Miss Ada, as if narrating a legend.

Miss Moran made a low grumbling sound. "'The food is bland and monotonous,'" she murmured, pacing. She even sounded rather like Delia. "'The grounds are cramped and tame and *boring*.'" Miss Moran grimaced and gestured. "'The conversation is utterly insipid.'"

They all laughed again.

Peter thought he'd never seen a prettier picture. In their pastel gowns, they were a medley of feminine beauty, and gentle humor lit their faces. Miss Ada's smile had an impish charm as she continued. "Finally, one day, Charlotte stepped in front of Delia and stopped her pacing. She looked her straight in the eye. Charlotte was the only one of us tall enough to do that. And she told Delia that she couldn't know anything about our school conversations, because she hadn't had any."

"And then they had an argument," said Miss Finch.

"Discussion," said Miss Deeping. She stood and faced Miss Moran. They squared off like cats priming for a fight.

"A loud and lively discussion," said Miss Ada. "With rather a lot of arm waving."

The two young ladies demonstrated, each trying not to laugh.

"And then we all joined in," said Miss Ada.

"For a bit of…vigorous wrangling," said Miss Finch.

"Delia could curse in five languages." Miss Deeping clearly admired this ability and wished she could claim the same.

"And I think she was *longing* for an opportunity to shout at someone," said Miss Ada.

The other young ladies nodded. Peter didn't doubt this point. Delia had certainly shouted at *him* when he decreed that she was going off to school.

"And for signs of intelligence," added Miss Deeping. "A spirit of rebellion."

"So that's how we became friends," Miss Moran finished. "Or began to be, at least."

Which was why he couldn't regret his choice to send his sister away, Peter thought. Yet a pang of melancholy shot through him. She'd been such a lively spirit, obviously, and he'd missed the chance to know her well. The circumstances of his life, and of course her early death, had conspired to keep them apart. A shame, never to be mended. "Good," he managed.

Miss Ada's dark eyes warmed with sympathy, as if she'd followed his thoughts. "You went to an interesting school, I think. Delia told us about it."

Somehow, she made him feel better. How long had it been since someone cared how he felt? A man might lose himself in that gaze. If he allowed it.

"She called it a marvelous place," said Miss Moran.

It was odd to think of his sister talking about him. He would have said she had little interest in his life. "Did she? She was never there."

"It was in Wales, I believe?"

"Yes."

"Tell us about it," said Miss Ada. The others nodded.

He would never be able to resist those looks, Peter thought. He simply wanted to do whatever Miss Ada Grandison asked. Which was likely to get him into trouble. And then Peter remembered that he wouldn't have to worry about that. They'd soon be gone. The idea was so unpleasant that he rushed to speak. "The school is run by a man who was—is a noted scholar. He formed a theory—my father loved theories—that use of the hands stimulated and… informed use of the mind. Sharpened the faculties as one might hone an ax-head. So along with more common disciplines we learned practical skills. And no Greek. Mr. Griffiths took against Greek at an early age."

"Why would anyone reject a whole language?" Miss Moran shook her head.

"What sort of skills?" asked Miss Deeping.

"Simple carpentry," Peter replied. "And I can shoe a horse."

"You cannot," said Miss Moran.

"Oh yes. We became crude blacksmiths. I can milk a cow. I can pleach a hedge as well."

"What is *pleach*?" asked Miss Ada.

"Make a hedge. Create, you might say. One cuts through the stem of each hedging plant near the base, bends it over, and weaves it between wooden stakes." Peter realized that all four young ladies were staring at him.

"I never heard of a duke doing things like that," said Miss Finch.

Because no other duke ever did, Peter thought. Why had he told them so much? Now, they thought him even odder. Miss Finch in particular seemed to draw away.

"I suppose that's rather…useful," said Miss Moran.

Peter might have agreed, and pointed out that carpentry came in handy on his crumbling acres. But he didn't want them thinking of that. "We also studied Latin and philosophy and poetics. We put on Shakespeare's history plays." He definitely wouldn't mention Mr. Griffiths's interest in more arcane subjects. The man hadn't *really* believed that he was a magician. Only that some of the effects could be duplicated. He'd been spectacularly unsuccessful in that arena. The young ladies were gazing at him. "We had to calculate the height of every tree on the property using mathematics."

"How do you do that?" asked Miss Deeping, looking interested for the first time.

"With shadows," replied Peter. "You need a sunny day, and a measuring stick. With the sun at your back, you measure your shadow on the ground. Then you do the same for the tree's shadow, including half the width of the trunk. Shadow lengths are proportional, you see. So with those three figures you can calculate the tree's height."

"Or any other object," said Miss Deeping. She jotted notes on the sheet of paper before her.

He'd finally impressed her, Peter thought. That was something. He would have preferred it to be for different reasons, of course. For the thousandth time, he noted that his education had *not* included the social graces.

"I'm sure you made good friends at your school," Miss Ada said. "Just as we did." She looked at the other young ladies.

The truth was he had not. His title had intimidated most of the boys. He had disliked the place. And unlike his sister later on, he'd never found kindred spirits. His schooling had been one long endurance test.

Something of this must have shown in his face, because Miss Ada added, "You learned interesting things."

Had she begun to pity him? The idea was insupportable.

"But you know, young men are supposed to make important connections at school," said Miss Finch.

She echoed complaints Peter had made in his youth. He ought to have gone to Eton or Harrow and woven himself into the fabric of society. He'd argued with his father over this. Without success. But he wouldn't say so. It was not for a stranger to judge Papa.

"My brothers say Harrow set them on the right track," said Miss Deeping.

Peter felt a surge of annoyance. No doubt these brothers were the sort of young men he'd seen at White's. With clothes and manners more polished than his, and far fatter purses. Easy for them to speak about *right tracks*.

"It's good to know practical things," said Miss Ada.

"But he won't be shoeing horses or laying hedges or milking cows," replied Miss Finch.

Would he not? Who knew what he might come to? Let her try to manage a large estate with no money. "You know nothing about it," he said.

Miss Finch bridled at his tone. "I believe I *do* know—"

Miss Ada stepped between them like the monitor at a boxing match. "Charlotte has made progress with the keys," she said.

There was a moment of silence. Though no one moved, their positions in the room seemed to reshuffle. Finally, Miss Deeping spoke. "Not nearly as much as I *would* have if I weren't forced to waste time on stupidities like potpourri." She said the last word as if it was a curse.

"But still a great deal," replied Miss Ada.

The taller girl went to stand beside the long table. She picked up a pointer, apparently made from a tree branch, and set the end on a sheet of drawing paper inscribed with a grid. "I've tried all the doors in the modern wing."

"*We* have," said Miss Finch, looking even more irritated. "I fetched and carried for you."

Miss Deeping nodded. "More than that," she answered, showing more tact than Peter would have expected of her. She turned back to him. "You were right that the keys didn't work in those. So we're about to move on." She flipped over the grid, revealing another page which showed very creditable sketches of the next oldest part of the house.

"Those are well done," said Peter.

"Harriet drew them," said Miss Deeping.

He gave Miss Finch a bow. She deigned to nod in response.

"We'll start in as soon as we get free from our *household management* lessons." Miss Deeping grimaced.

"You might be doing it now," said Peter.

The thin, dark girl gave him an incredulous stare, as if she'd extended herself for him and he'd spurned her efforts.

"I only *just* finished the sketches," said Miss Finch. "They were a good deal of work, you know."

"Of course we do, Harriet," said Miss Ada.

"Perhaps you could tell your aunt I'm ill," said Miss Deeping. "Then I could—"

"Aunt Julia would come and check on you, Charlotte, or send Tate."

"I can do it," said Peter.

He'd meant it as a service, but Miss Deeping looked even more reproachful. Peter understood the reaction. She wanted to find the solution herself. He realized that he felt the same. And this was, after all, *his* house. He held out his hand for the keys.

"You can't just walk off with my drawings," said Miss Finch.

"I'm familiar with my own home. I can do without them." His hand was still. He did not beckon impatiently. Not quite. "We have established that I have practical skills."

With patent reluctance, Miss Deeping handed over the keys.

He received them with a disproportionate sense of triumph. The young ladies were a happy addition to Alberdene society. But they didn't rule the roost. A man's home was his castle, wasn't it? Quite literally in his case. It might be falling to pieces, but it was still indubitably his. As were his father's keys. And what he lacked in savoir faire he might make up in native ingenuity, he thought as he left the room.

He wanted to impress his feminine visitors. All of them, he realized, but one in particular. He needed Miss Ada to think well of him. When she thought of him. When she was gone from here. He wanted a favorable place in her memory.

Peter's sense of triumph dissipated. When she looked back, what would she think of him? Would he dwindle into a motley figure of fun?

Instead of going directly to try the keys, he passed through the kitchen, snagging two lanterns from a side table, and headed for the back staircase. On his way up, he passed one of the new footmen hauling a load of wood to the bedchambers and nodded a greeting as he continued to ascend.

Living alone, one didn't have conversations, Peter thought. One had thoughts, which might be quite interesting and could be recorded or even spoken aloud. "Though best not to do that," he said to the empty stairs.

He heard a scrabbling sound behind him and paused to listen. Had the young footman overheard? No talking to yourself, he warned silently, and moved on.

His young lady guests had endless conversations, he thought. Words flew back and forth between them like a tennis ball in the matches his ancestor had enjoyed with the old Tudor king. It was fascinating, the process as much as the subject matter. He'd never seen anything like it. His talks with his family had been halting and awkward. And yet. He suddenly felt that he could talk to Miss Ada forever.

Peter reached the attics and lit his lanterns, carrying one in each hand along a familiar route through the boxes and discarded furnishings. He came to the area his father had established years ago when he realized that there was a hoard of stored clothing at Alberdene. Certain of the Rathbone ancestors had apparently been fashion plates. Some of their lost fortune had clearly gone to expensive tailors and dressmakers, Peter thought. And those past family members had splashed out for many more ensembles than they could ever wear out.

As soon as he realized this, his father had declared that their clothing would come from this source, saving untold sums by his reckoning. Papa had discovered that the castoffs of one particular forebear fit him perfectly, and *he* didn't care a whit that no one wore full-skirted satin coats anymore. He'd used a long brocade robe from even earlier times as a dressing gown, pacing the corridors like a medieval grandee. And of course there was the Egyptian garment as well. Delia had fallen in line, refashioning sweeping skirts of silk and satin into more up-to-date styles with every appearance of delight. Of course, she'd been taught to sew.

Peter had never had as much luck. Taller and lankier than his father, he hadn't found clothes that fit well. He'd hated it when he was sent off to school with his wrists protruding from the sleeves of outmoded shirts and smelling of camphor, which had not contributed to his success, even among the boys of his unusual school. He'd made certain Delia had more fashionable garb before he sent her off to hers.

In adulthood, Peter had found a seamstress in Wrexham who could alter the old garments. But the truth was, he didn't always bother. There was no society in the neighborhood to exchange visits or give balls. Alberdene had been established to hold the Welsh Marches against attack, not entertain. His ancestors might have wasted the ready on building a cavernous house here, but he had no reason to spend time or money on clothes.

Except, now he did. He'd had his fill of Miss Charlotte Deeping's sidelong glances and sour smiles at the clothes he wore. And Miss Moran's understanding sympathy. And Miss Finch's raised eyebrows, as if she couldn't see why he made so little effort. But most of all he wanted Miss Ada to admire him. Yes, he did, even though he knew he should not.

He placed the lanterns on small tables set up to receive them, on either side of a cheval glass. They cast a pool of light that was reflected in the mirror. Darkness spread around this island of brightness into the corners of the attic.

Peter stripped off his coat and shirt and began a systematic search for better clothes, pulling out anything that looked as if it might do, trying it, and setting the most suitable aside to bundle off to Wrexham for tailoring. He'd ask the seamstress to be as quick as she could. He had to have more than one good coat. The black made for his father's funeral, and then used at his sister's as well, cast a pall of melancholy over every occasion.

As he straightened from bending over an open trunk, Peter caught a stealthy movement in the dark. Peering out of the circle of light he spotted one of the cats who roamed the older parts of the house, watching him from under a broken chair in the corner. "Hello," he said to the animal. "I shan't be much longer. Very good work keeping down the mice up here. I haven't seen any signs of rodents."

"Who are you talking to?" asked a female voice.

Peter started and dropped the filmy undergarment he'd been about to set aside. The gossamer set of drawers floated down to settle over the toes of his boots as he turned to find Miss Ada standing in the open doorway. She glanced at the unmentionables and away. Her small dog trotted over to sniff at them. "Ella, no!" she added.

"Cat," Peter replied before he could think. Which was just the icing on the cake for a man standing bare-chested, apparently fingering an ancient undergarment.

"What?"

"I was talking to one of the cats." He glanced at the corner. Of course it was empty. How could it be otherwise? With an effort at nonchalance, he fetched his shirt and put it on. He picked up the underdrawers and threw them back into the trunk. "What are you doing in the attic?" he asked.

Miss Ada came one step closer. She looked like a visitation from the bright world outside this shadowed space. "Ella ran up here."

Peter suspected that this wasn't true. He thought perhaps she'd followed him, an idea that filled him with elation and regret. "Indeed?"

"Also Charlotte thinks we should make a catalog of the whole house. We're each taking a part."

"For what purpose?" Peter closed the trunk he'd been rooting in. There was nothing to be done about the pile of clothes he'd chosen. He would ignore them.

"In case Delia's note points us in a particular direction," she said.

"Ah, yes, my sister's mysterious last words."

"Must you be sarcastic about it?"

"I wasn't." He hadn't meant to be. He'd been thinking how foolish he must look. And wishing to be otherwise. Like the polished young men she would meet in London next season. One of whom would undoubtedly carry her off into marital bliss. Peter felt a quick hot flash of hatred for this imagined gentleman.

"You certainly sounded it."

"It's difficult to judge one's tone sometimes. Don't you find?"

Miss Ada gazed at him from under her formidable eyebrows.

"The simplest phrase can have a wildly unintended effect," Peter added.

"Wildly?" she echoed.

And just like that, wildness swirled to life between them, like a vortex of autumn leaves suddenly raised by the wind. Peter felt it as an urgent invitation from desire. Passion would certainly have been part of their life, if they could have had a life together. Peter was tight and breathless. He curled his hands into fists, restraining his impulses, remembering his limitations.

Miss Ada's dog sniffed at the corner where the cat had been sitting. Ella snorted with disapproval at the scent. Peter almost remarked that it was easy to be disdainful now that the cat was gone. He just managed to keep those words from escaping.

Miss Ada crossed her arms over her chest, and then seemed surprised to see that she held a pad of paper in one hand and a yard-long measuring stick marked out in inches and feet in the other.

"Where did you get that?" Peter asked about the latter.

"Charlotte made it." She sounded shaken. Peter couldn't help but be glad.

"She's extremely enterprising, isn't she?" At the girl's raised brows, he added, "That wasn't meant to be sarcastic." He laid a hand over his heart, and only then remembered that he hadn't put on his coat. He hastened to do so. When he turned back he noticed a smile tugging at Miss Ada's lips. Appreciation or ridicule? Always so hard to tell. "Are you actually going to measure the attic? There's nothing up here but discarded things."

"Charlotte thinks we should check everywhere."

"And she gives the orders?"

"No. We each have our areas of…proficiency."

"Proficiency." He repeated the word because he liked it. She frowned at him. That hadn't been sarcastic either. Should he say so?

"Charlotte says the inner dimensions of the house must match the outer ones." She looked around the attic. "If the inside is shorter, then there is a hidden space."

"I understand the concept." His father and sister had undoubtedly found any such hideaways that existed in the house, Peter thought. But he didn't want her to go. "I'll help you."

She looked pleased, which made him glad. Peter threw caution to the winds as he took the stick and applied it to a stretch of wall.

Her little dog ran around smelling boxes and corners as they moved about measuring. Miss Ada noted the results on her pad.

They came to one of a line of stone pillars set into the wall that supported the roof. Peter held the stick up to the column. "No way to measure this," he said. "We'll have to estimate."

Miss Ada took a ribbon from her hair, stretched it around the half circle of stone, then laid the resulting length onto the measuring stick. "Fifteen inches," she said.

"How very clever," said Peter. Indeed, he admired her quickness very much.

She looked gratified.

At the far end of the attic, Ella exploded in a frenzy of barking. Peter could just see her small cinnamon-colored form bouncing in the dimness.

A bat swooped out of the dark corner, fluttered over Miss Ada's head, and veered up toward the roof peak, pausing to cling there upside down. Ella skidded to a stop below it, madly barking and jumping up and down like a mechanical toy with an overwound spring.

"Ella!" said her mistress, with no effect.

The bat shook itself and dove, swooping toward Ella as if it meant to hit her. Ella leapt and snapped her tiny jaws. At the last moment, the bat jerked away. And then it led the dog up and down the attic on what seemed like a teasing dance designed to wear her out. Peter chased after them, but he had nothing to bring the bat down, and he didn't quite want to grab it with his bare hands.

Finally, the small creature swooped back into the corner where it had emerged and disappeared. The dog went after it, barking.

Peter waited a moment, then followed Ella. She was pawing at something in the corner. He had to move a small chest, kneel, and then thrust his head into the narrow opening to see that there was a small jagged hole where the slant of the roof met the attic floor. "Good God, this is where the bats get in," he said. "We've searched for this for years."

"You see, we do solve mysteries," Miss Ada replied.

He turned his head to gaze up at her. Her dark eyes twinkled in the lantern light, full of warm amusement. Peter eased out of the corner and burst out laughing. She joined in. He couldn't remember when he'd last felt such free and easy merriment.

"I'm so glad to have made you happy," she said.

Her voice was like a warm fire on an icy night. Sitting on the dusty attic floor, with Ella trying to nose past him and hunt bats, Peter melted. "What makes you happy?" he asked.

"All sorts of things."

"Tell me some of them. Three things that make you happy."

Miss Ada smiled down at him. Peter grew warmer still. "I will, if you will do the same," she said.

He could only nod, speechless with longing. He wanted her with him always. He wanted to know all about her.

Her thick eyebrows came together in an adorable, considering frown. How had he ever thought them a flaw? He edged out of the corner and stood up.

"It's like being granted three wishes in a fairy tale," she said. "How to choose?"

"We didn't say there were *only* three," Peter answered.

"True. Very well. Dancing makes me happy. I love to dance."

"Ah." Peter's skills in this area were rudimentary. He could just about tramp his way through a country dance. He had heard of the quadrille. For the first time, he was almost glad of his isolated situation. He would never meet her in a ballroom, with boundless possibilities for humiliation.

"Now you choose one."

"Walking in the countryside. Except—" When he saw a tumbledown cottage where a tenant was trying to survive, this happiness was spoiled.

"Except what?"

"When I step into a bog and lose a boot to the mud," Peter said.

She laughed. "You should watch where you walk."

She was playing a game, Peter thought. While he was grasping at shreds of her company before she disappeared from his life. Being with her under any circumstances at all made him happy, he realized. Not that he could say this. "Always good advice in a pasture," he answered.

Miss Ada nodded. "Lemon tarts make me happy," she said. "Particularly when they're served at tea with my friends. Because not only are they delicious, but Sarah adores them, too. And so my enjoyment is compounded by hers. Oh." She looked thoughtful. "That's the real bit making me happy, sharing enjoyment with friends. Seeing them glad."

"Of course," said Peter.

She looked up at him, a soft silhouette in the dim lantern light. "Are you choosing the same thing? That's not fair. You must use your own."

As if happiness was to be found in many places. "Making something right," he said. "By my own efforts. Like repairing a broken floorboard or a cracked windowpane." As soon as he'd spoken, he worried that she would despise such endeavors, as his footman did. Yet he'd spoken the truth. It did make him happy.

Miss Ada showed no sign of judgment. "And my third thing," she said softly, her eyes fixed on his. "Is kisses in the night."

Desire shot through him, compelling, demanding. "You must allow me to agree on that one." His voice was thick with yearning.

"I will." She smiled and moved closer. Peter's arms reached for her.

Ella growled, the sound reverberating with an odd depth. Miss Ada's smile died. "Oh, don't let her go in there," she said.

Peter turned and found that the little dog had pushed her head into the hole where the bat had disappeared. She seemed bent on making her shoulders follow. "She wouldn't fit."

"Ella can wriggle into the smallest spaces."

Peter strode over and picked up the dog before she could try. He handed her to her mistress, then pushed the wooden chest snugly over the hole in the wall. "This should help until we can block the opening permanently," he said. He gazed at Ella, who had saved him from wild imprudence and deprived him of what he wanted most in the world right then. The dog stared back from slightly bulging brown eyes, looking as thwarted as Peter felt. With an annoyed yip, she squirmed out of Miss Ada's arms and returned to the corner to paw at the chest.

A call echoed up the stairwell.

Miss Ada stiffened. "Oh dear, what is the time?"

He took out his pocket watch and consulted it. "Twenty minutes past one."

"I'm dreadfully late for Aunt Julia's lesson! She'll

be so annoyed." Miss Ada thrust the pad of paper and measuring stick at him. "Come, Ella."

But the dog declined to leave her discovery. She sat as if she intended to contest the entry of any bat that tried to squirm through the reduced opening.

"Bring Ella down with you," said Miss Ada. She ran out.

The space felt so much emptier with her gone, Peter thought. Far more than before she'd come. A waft of her sweet floral scent lingered behind, like a taunt on his solitude.

He went over to the pile of clothes he'd picked out. Putting down Miss Ada's implements, he looked for a container and spotted a half-empty wooden box. He dumped out the contents—a clutter of mostly broken crockery—and filled it with the clothing. The pad of paper went on top, the measuring stick laid across it.

"I'm leaving," said Peter to Ella. "You don't really wish to stay here all alone."

Ella's resolve appeared unshaken.

"A cat will return once I'm gone. More than one perhaps."

The dog ignored him.

"Large, fierce cats," he added.

Peter made a sudden unexpected swoop on Ella, picking up the small animal and tucking her under his arm. Ignoring the dog's objections, he hefted the box and left the attic.

Eight

"Miss Julia Grandison knows a deal of things," Tom reported as the Earl of Macklin prepared to go down to dinner that evening. "She had us put together a load of this po-purry stuff. Turned out Cook had most of the ingredients on hand."

"My mother used to make that," said Arthur, settling the folds of his neckcloth before the long mirror in his bedchamber. "Quite a pleasant scent."

"Lasts for years, she says," replied Tom. "And fleas don't like it. Right clever. Then we put by bunches of herbs and petals to dry."

"She didn't mind your joining them?" Arthur had wondered how Miss Grandison would react to Tom.

"Not so long as I behaved proper."

"Which I'm sure you did." Tom grinned at him, and Arthur thought again how much he enjoyed the lad's lively company.

Clayton cleared his throat. Arthur raised an eyebrow. "You think this neckcloth is too wide?" He trusted his valet's taste above his own.

"No, my lord. Quite elegant. I was wondering—"

"When we are going back home?" Arthur supplied.

"If you please. There's his lordship Jocelyn's grouse hunt in November."

The baron's hunt was a much-anticipated feature of the autumn. His coveys were renowned, and a host of luminaries was invited. Arthur was expected to attend. Jocelyn, a neighbor and a friend, counted on him.

"And the family coming for Christmas," Clayton added.

"We have to be back by then, of course."

"Christmas," said Tom.

Had the lad ever had a proper Christmas? Because it was the way they dealt with each other, Arthur simply asked him.

"Not certain what you mean by proper, my lord," he answered. "The missus made a plum pudding when I was at her dame school. She roasted a goose as well. Right tasty, that was. I never turn down a good feed." His smile was sunny. "But mainly I ain't... Haven't had much to do with Christmas."

"Well, you will see a fine celebration at my home." Arthur wondered what his grown children would think of Tom.

The lad nodded, acknowledging this promised treat with less enthusiasm than Arthur had expected. "I wonder if there'll be a bat at dinner tonight?" he went on. "Conway said it was a rare sight to see. Miss Ada Grandison's little dog going mad trying to catch the creature."

"You won't know, because you refuse to sit down with us."

"Miss Grandison wouldn't like it, my lord." Before

Arthur could answer, Tom added, "Or I wouldn't. Too many finicking rules to remember. Not to mention trying to make po-lite conversation between bites." With another smile to show he was joking and a gesture like a salute, Tom went out.

Clayton busied himself tidying the room.

"You are still wondering when we will leave Alberdene," said Arthur. "As I have not answered you." After all their years together, he could practically divine the valet's thoughts.

"Yes, my lord."

"You are more than ready to return to a familiar household."

Clayton said nothing, but his agreement was obvious.

"We will have to go soon," Arthur acknowledged. "But I have an idea I wish to try first."

His valet waited.

For some reason, Arthur felt reluctant to say more. "It may well come to nothing. We'll have to wait and see."

∽

The young ladies took turns providing music after dinner, despite the dreadful state of Alberdene's piano. They played and sang partly for entertainment and partly to pass the time.

After she had sung several ballads, Ada retreated to a settee just down the room from the duke. From this vantage point, she could steal glances at him while seeming to watch the performance. His face was full of cleverness and character, she thought. He was not precisely handsome. More than that, he was very *interesting*. She hadn't realized, until she'd met Delia's brother, that she required the latter characteristic in a man. Interesting was exciting. A sense of depths was thrilling. Compared with Compton, other young gentlemen she'd met seemed shallow and dull.

Examining his profile, Ada sighed. Before long, her party would leave Alberdene. How was she ever to see him again? He'd made it clear he never went to London for the season or to country house parties. He was practically a recluse. There must be something she could do about that! Either the one thing or the other. And the proprieties could just…go hang!

Sarah rose from the piano, and Harriet replaced her. Ada took advantage of the movement to shift her seat and sit beside the duke.

She watched him watch Harriet as her friend began a sonata. He looked appreciative. Could Compton be thinking of Harriet's money? How was one to discover such a thing? And why must everything be such a muddle?

"I apologize for the pianoforte," he said. "It's a disgrace. I didn't realize. No one has played it since my mother died."

"Delia wasn't musical."

"No. She could never be bothered to practice."

He didn't look at her. Their time in the attic, and in other dim rooms, hovered between them. "Thank you for bringing Ella down," she said.

"I believe I've offended her beyond redemption."

"Oh, she's very forgiving." For some reason, this innocuous remark made Ada's cheeks redden.

Charlotte slipped around the back of the sofa like a spy on a clandestine mission. She sat on the duke's other side. "Have you tried the keys in all the remaining doors?" she asked.

"All the remaining...? I haven't had the time."

"What do you have but time?"

"I beg your pardon?"

"*You* don't have to look over piles of linens or grind up grubby roots. Potpourri! Was there ever such a foolish task?"

Ada glanced over to make certain her aunt hadn't heard. But Charlotte had enough sense to speak quietly about Aunt Julia's projects even when roused. "It does seem useful for—" she began.

But Compton interrupted her. "Of course I simply sit and stare at the surrounding decay," he said to Charlotte. "I don't try to do anything about it. I have no work."

"I could have tried the locks by now if I was allowed," Charlotte grumbled.

"Those keys belonged to my father. It is reasonable that I be the one to try them."

"Yes," put in Ada. She'd noticed that this word was a helpful way to insert oneself into discussions. Even when you meant to disagree. Especially then. People softened at the sound. In this case two people who weren't listening to each other. "Charlotte only wishes to help. As we all do."

"Really? It seemed to me that Miss Deeping thought I was usurping *her* prerogatives."

"Prerogatives," sniffed Charlotte. "I don't seem to *have* any." Her jaw tightened with irritation.

Two very touchy people, thought Ada. With Harriet thrown in, a girl who worked out her positions carefully and valued them. At least Sarah hated friction. But Ada had always relished the challenge of taming the prickly. Though she'd never before wished to kiss one of the combatants.

"You are officious," the duke said.

"And Harriet says you are maladroit," Charlotte replied.

He scowled. "Miss Finch is unreasonably opinionated."

Ada felt a sneaking gladness that he'd criticized Harriet. And then was shocked at herself. She stifled the thought and offered a defense of her friend instead. "She changes her mind when presented with clear facts," she said.

"I simply like to do a job quickly and thoroughly," said Charlotte, defending her own reputation.

"And I prefer to be clear," said Compton. "If that is maladroit, so be it!"

Nobody here was wrong, Ada thought. Charlotte often plowed ahead relentlessly in her enthusiasms. Harriet did make rash judgments now and then. The duke had somewhat odd manners on occasion. But it wouldn't do to say any of *that*. "Charlotte just loves solving puzzles. She can never resist a hidden corner."

"All very well," Compton began, and fell abruptly silent. "What did you say?" he asked then.

"Charlotte loves unraveling puzzles?"

"After that."

Ada didn't remember exactly.

"She said I can never resist a hidden corner," said Charlotte. "Which isn't *absolutely* correct. I can—"

"Corner," he repeated. "A hidden corner."

"Yes." Ada watched his expression go from dubious to speculative. "And that reminded you of something." It wasn't a question. The answer was obvious.

When he didn't go on, Charlotte shifted with impatience. "*What* did it remind you of?"

"A corner that I'd nearly forgotten. There are quite a few of those at Alberdene." He took the ring of three keys from his waistcoat pocket and looked at them.

"Are you being mysterious just to tease us?" asked Charlotte. "Because I must tell you that is vastly provoking."

Compton blinked, startled. "No. I wouldn't do that."

"But you *are* being mysterious," Ada pointed out.

He had a smile for her. "There's a cul-de-sac near the tower stair, caused by its construction. No one goes down that stub of corridor, because it leads nowhere."

"So a prime spot for a locked room?" Charlotte said, catching his drift at once.

He nodded, looking as if he'd like to race off and examine it immediately.

"You can't go now," said Ada.

"I suppose it would be rude to walk out on my guests," he acknowledged.

"And if you wait until we've gone to bed and sneak off to look, I will murder you," said Charlotte.

His expression gave him away. "I have no need to sneak in my own home. I can go where I like."

"You must take us along," said Ada. "All of us. I inspired you to find the answer after all."

"To consider a possibility," he replied.

"But you think it's the place."

He nodded slowly.

"And you wouldn't have thought of it without me."

"I would have...eventually."

"I don't know why you say so," replied Charlotte. "When you admit you've forgotten all sorts of places in your house."

"It's only fair that we come," said Ada. "Surely you see that?"

"Yes. All right. Bring everyone. The more the merrier."

Charlotte sniffed, still annoyed.

"Not Aunt Julia," said Ada quickly.

"You think your aunt would have some objections?"

"Well, she so often does, you know," said Charlotte.

"Let us see what we find first." Ada smiled at him. "Tomorrow after breakfast?"

"As long as it is an early one. I won't wait past nine."

"Oh certainly, *Your Grace*," said Charlotte. "Does my lord have any other orders?"

Her voice dripped with sarcasm, but this time the duke seemed amused by it, which was a relief. He smiled at Ada. She smiled back, warmed by their shared secrets. And then even more by a hint of promise for the future.

❧

Peter was unsurprised to find that all four of his young lady guests were there before him at the breakfast table the next morning. He was a bit taken aback by a row of militant looks. He got the sense that they all felt he'd usurped their proper roles in this drama, even Miss Ada, a bit. Indeed, Miss Deeping looked positively predatory behind her buttered muffin, poised to leap if he tried to steal a march on her. Possibly she suspected him of having already done so, but Peter had kept this word and not gone looking without them.

Miss Finch appeared to be…not quite sulking, but not as calm as usual either. He wondered if her friends had reported the conversation about her opinions? Miss Moran looked determined as a hunting dog who has caught a strong scent and is longing to be set loose.

He was startled when Tom arrived. The lad took his meals in the kitchen. In fact, Peter hadn't seen much of him during the earl's visit. "I heard you were going off to solve a mystery," Tom said. "I'd like to see that, if there's no objection."

Peter wondered how he had heard. Seeing the young ladies exchange glances, he doubted the lad was in their confidence. They seemed to view him a bit as they did Miss Ada's little dog, who thankfully wasn't one of their party this morning. Not a position Peter would have relished, though Tom didn't seem bothered. The boy was likable, but he had no clear social context. As a duke without a penny, Peter understood that sort of awkwardness.

"How do you know that?" asked Miss Deeping, echoing Peter's thought.

"Una told me," Tom replied. "Was it a secret? I

reckon she didn't know that. Or she wouldn't have said a word."

For a moment, Peter couldn't place the name. Then he remembered Una was one of the new housemaids.

"Una is so quiet, one forgets she's in a room," said Miss Finch.

"Shall we go?" asked Miss Deeping. "I really can't bear to dawdle any longer. And if we sit here all morning Ada's aunt will catch us."

"I will just eat something," replied Peter.

"Must you?"

The few minutes it would take hardly mattered, but Peter didn't say so. He simply turned and led his trail of young ladies in bright gowns, and one gangling youth, into the older part of the building. He distributed candlesticks and lit them. "As you've seen, most of the rooms aren't locked," he said as he ushered them along. "One can walk through the house and see all they contain."

"Not necessarily," replied Miss Deeping.

At this point, she was ready to dispute anything he said, Peter suspected. But he had an irresistible urge to assert his leadership in his own home. "My father, and sister, wouldn't have taken such care of a key to an unlocked room."

Miss Deeping's expression suggested he was being obvious.

"Obviously," said Peter to goad her a little. "I couldn't think where that would be until last night." At a sharp glance from Miss Ada, he added, "During a conversation with Miss Ada and Miss Deeping, I realized that there was a place I'd forgotten."

"It's difficult to see how you could have," said Miss Deeping.

"I have a good many things on my mind," Peter shot back. *She* didn't have to juggle an endless list of needs and nearly empty accounts, he thought. Deciding which critical service or repair could be managed and which must wait occupied much of his attention. "And this place has gone entirely out of use because of the awkward rebuilding."

He led them past the entry to the spiral stair that went up Delia's tower. A section of the house had been cut off when the tower was added, leaving a short stub of corridor that ended in three doors, left, right, and straight ahead. His group crowded into it. The doors to the sides were ajar, and revealed only dusty floorboards when pushed open. But the one at the end proved to be locked.

"A secret room," said Miss Moran in a thrilled tone.

Not precisely, Peter thought but didn't say. The small hallway was full of sweet scents and bright eyes. Miss Ada's shoulder was pressed against his.

"Are you going to try the key?" asked Miss Deeping. Her fingers twitched, as if she wanted to rip it away from him and do it herself.

Peter inserted the key in the lock. He couldn't resist a dramatic pause. Miss Deeping made an impatient sound. Peter twisted the key. It turned. The lock clicked. He removed the key and opened the door, raising his candle to illuminate whatever lay ahead.

The room was dark. There were no windows; the tower had cut them off. The furnishings consisted of a desk with an unlit oil lamp and a candelabra atop it and two chairs. But that wasn't what drew the eye. As the others pushed in behind him, holding up their candles in turn, Peter took in the tumultuous decor. Aside from the doorway and a small hearth, all four walls were covered, from about knee high to well above his head, with a dizzying mélange of paper. And other bits of things as well. Documents and pages of notes and small objects were pinned to the plaster, solidly, with no spaces between. Here an old-fashioned broad-brimmed hat with a feather was stuck beside an aged deed, there the snake of a leather belt with a chunky silver clasp flanked a list of some kind. Beyond that a series of drawings seemed to tell a tale. There was some sort of accounting next to those. Words and images and numbers clamored for attention all around him, making his head spin. It was bewildering, made worse by a web of string that overlaid the walls, pinned from one spot to another, as if a literary spider had run amok.

"Lordy," said Tom.

"I knew my father was eccentric, but I didn't think him mad," Peter said.

Some of the pages had obviously been in place for a long time. Their edges curled up. Others looked more recent.

"It seems like some kind of research project?" suggested Miss Moran uncertainly.

"Like a grid, perhaps," said Miss Deeping. "Only more complicated."

"You may say so," replied Miss Finch. She sounded daunted.

Raising her candle, Miss Moran walked along the

back wall. "The strings might show a relationship between the two things at the ends." She leaned closer. "See, here, this one connects the bill for an emerald necklace and a garden plan."

"What would those have to do with each other?" asked Miss Ada.

"Well, we don't know yet, do we?" answered Miss Deeping. She stepped over to join Miss Moran and traced the string with a finger. "They are from the same year, 1594. That is a start."

The group stood near the center of the room, slowly rotating to absorb the whole. Demented, Peter thought again.

"Perhaps this…organization starts at the right-hand side of the door," said Miss Moran, walking to that spot. "And then goes clockwise, as one logically would."

"Logically!" said Peter. He could see no logic to this display.

Miss Moran held her candle higher. "Yes, there's a note here, right at the edge." She leaned forward. "Listen to this." She read aloud. "In the year 1643, being a time of civil turmoil in England, the wife of Thaddeus Rathbone, the third duke, determined to hide away what she could of the family fortune. Knowing well that Thaddeus had no knack for politics, always seeming to end up on the losing side, even though his loyalties were remarkably flexible." Miss Moran laughed. "I think Delia wrote this. It sounds like her."

"It does," said Miss Ada.

Miss Moran returned to the page. "She gathered

every item of value she could put her hands on and secreted them, to save them from being taken should the battles between the king's men and the parliamentarians reach Alberdene."

"Which they never did," said Peter.

"So she buried the plate and jewels," said Miss Moran.

"It doesn't say buried," said Miss Finch.

"Right," said Miss Deeping. "*Secreted* might mean any number of things."

"There's a bit more," said Miss Moran. She returned to the page. "Unfortunately, in 1645, as the war raged on, a virulent illness swept through Alberdene. It is thought by some to have been the plague. The duchess and many of the servants and tenants died of it. Two of her children survived, but they were young, and she had not told them of her hiding place. Or left any clue. And so the Rathbone fortune was lost."

"Well, what an utter ninny!" exclaimed Miss Finch. "Who would hide a fortune away and leave no way to retrieve it?" Tom nodded as if he agreed.

"I wonder how Delia and her father found out about it if no one knew," said Miss Ada.

"They did not," replied Peter. His voice sounded hard in his own ears, but he couldn't help it. "This is a fantasy they concocted. They told me once." He had mocked the idea, rather impatiently. They hadn't mentioned it again. Instead, apparently, they'd retreated to this…den and encouraged each other's delusions.

"But." Miss Moran turned, gesturing at the mass of papers and objects. "There's all this."

"And what is *this*? A…clutter of paper and moldering junk."

"A great deal of *work*," said Miss Deeping. "Do you imagine they did it for nothing?"

They didn't understand, Peter thought. They hadn't seen his father try scheme after scheme and fail. *He* hadn't known that those years of futility had culminated in this…stationary whirlwind. His companions were gazing at him with varying degrees of reproach. "How would a duchess hide a fortune without help?" Peter asked them. "Do you imagine her carting piles of plate down dark corridors, digging in the gardens with her fingernails? Someone would have had to aid her, and thus know how and where it was done. And if this ever happened—doubtful—those helpers stole everything the moment she was gone."

"Unless the servants who helped her died as well," said Tom. He nodded at the explanation.

Peter made an impatient gesture.

"The plague did take whole households," Miss Deeping said.

He sighed. How many times had he told himself that his father might be right this time?

"Was there less money after her time?" asked Miss Ada.

"Many great families were ruined by the civil war," said Peter.

"So there was?"

"I suppose so, but…" He gestured at the walls, the layers of muddled papers gathering dust. "This is a forlorn dream. My ancestors spent their fortune." He was very conscious of their stares, but these young ladies didn't understand the peril of hope. Each time one yearned and dared to believe—over and over again—the disappointment grew more crushing. It accumulated, like a further weight added to an inevitable burden. For his father, the process had apparently edged into a sort of madness.

Miss Ada walked along one wall, examining the bits and pieces. "When she was visiting me, Delia seemed so certain she'd discovered something new. She was terribly excited. She could think of nothing else."

"Leaving her so distracted that she walked off a cliff path," said Peter. His intemperate remark was met with gasps and silence.

The air in the room seemed even more stuffy suddenly. He felt as if the cluttered walls were closing in on him.

"She wasn't mad," Miss Ada said. "Delia had all her wits about her."

"Far more than most people," said Miss Finch.

"She had prodigious powers of concentration," said Miss Moran. "I envied them."

"This here took a mort of hard work," added Tom, waving an arm at the exhibits.

Peter threw up his hands. If they wanted to believe in a lost treasure, he couldn't stop them. But none of them would be actually pinning their future to a chimera. When they grew bored, they would go away, leaving him right where he was on his wreck of an estate. Only more lonely, he thought, with Miss Ada's bright presence removed.

Miss Deeping sat down in one of the chairs and

tugged at a desk drawer. "Locked," she said. "Let's see if one of the other keys fits this."

Her peremptory tone almost made Peter wish for failure. But she turned out to be correct. One of the smaller keys opened the drawer. Inside they found a stack of notebooks, a stoppered bottle of ink and some quills, and a palm-sized wooden box.

"Records of their researches," said Miss Deeping, leafing through one of the former. With a pointed glance, she handed the box to Peter. He tried the smallest key on the ring, which opened it. Within, on a bed of white silk, lay a ruby as broad as his thumb and half as long.

The gem sparkled in the candlelight. The young ladies bent over it with oohs and ahhs. "That's pretty," said Tom.

If the jewel was real, it was probably worth a good deal of money, Peter thought. Even so, the sum would be a drop in the bucket compared with what was needed to restore his patrimony. And he suspected it was the last dregs of the Rathbone fortune.

"Light the lamp and the other candles," said Miss Deeping. She suited her action to her words. The rest of them set their candles beside hers. They made a pool of light on the desk. "We will make a thorough examination of this room and the notebooks. We could use a fire, assuming that chimney draws."

"There are ashes in the grate," said Miss Finch.

"I'll fetch some wood," said Tom, leaving the room.

The others bustled about to do Miss Deeping's bidding.

Peter relocked the little box and put it in his coat pocket. He felt as if he couldn't get enough air into his lungs in this closed room. Abandoning his guests to their explorations, he strode out.

Ada watched him go. Worried by the expression on his face, she followed him down the short hall and past the stair to Delia's retreat. She caught up to him by the door to the modern wing, snuffing his candle and setting the holder on the table there. She could see that he was unhappy, though she didn't understand why. Their discovery was thrilling. "What's wrong?"

"I can't bear to watch," he answered.

"Watch Charlotte and the others look over those papers? Because they're intruding into your affairs?" Charlotte was quite unlikely to stop unless she was thrown out of Alberdene, Ada thought.

He shook his head, half turning away. "Do you know how many times I heard my father claim that this or that stratagem would restore our fortune?"

He waited for an answer, still not looking at her. "No," said Ada quietly.

"I don't either." The duke turned back to her, his hazel eyes stormy. "I lost count. But I know it was many. From the time I was very small. And each one was a disaster. This person disappointed, that plan didn't pan out. The vein of coal or lead turned out to be nothing. The canal investment was a cheat. More money was lost than he put in." He let out a long breath. "So in the end he settled on a hidden treasure, it seems. Which does have the advantage of not relying on other people to make the business a success."

Ada didn't know what to say. She wanted to comfort him.

"One cannot keep believing!" he continued. "The strain is too great. The discouragement grows each time until it becomes too much. You have to give up. Unless you go mad." He gestured toward the room they'd left.

"Delia wasn't mad," Ada said again. She was very sure of this. They'd had many intimate talks near the end of her friend's life, and she'd seen no sign of derangement.

Compton sighed again. "No, she was young. She hadn't experienced so many defeats. Papa kept most of them from her, you see, because her good opinion was so important to him."

"As was yours," Ada said. How could it have been otherwise?

The duke shrugged.

She so wanted to help him. "Delia wasn't defeated. I know it. If we can just find out what that paper she left says."

"Don't!" He turned his back, reaching for the door latch.

Tom came through the entry with an armload of firewood. They stepped back to let him pass. The lad carried it onward with a grin.

Ada tugged at the duke's sleeve. He allowed her to pull him into an empty, dusty chamber opposite Delia's tower stair.

"I beg your pardon," he said. "I didn't mean to shout at you. I shouldn't speak this way. I never have to anyone. I loved my father."

Ada moved her hand to his shoulder.

For a moment, they stood perfectly still. Then she moved around to face him. His dark eyes were bright with unshed tears.

"He tried so very hard," Compton said. "And yet he could never make any of his ideas succeed. I see now that it broke him. I hadn't realized."

Ada didn't know how to answer that. She'd never met the elder Rathbone. "Delia missed him terribly," she replied, and immediately wished the words unsaid.

"I know. They were…comrades. At least he didn't have to endure her death. It would have destroyed him."

He labored under such a burden of melancholy. Ada moved her hand to his cheek.

Compton gazed down into her eyes. "What do you do, to make me talk this way? Why do I simply trust you?"

Ada thought she knew, because she felt the same herself, but she couldn't quite say it just yet. Nonetheless, her spirits soared at the tenderness in his gaze. "With this new discovery—"

"There has been no discovery," he interrupted, his voice gone hard. He stepped away, and Ada let her hand drop. "I'm sorry, Miss Ada. I don't mean to be sharp with you, but that is the truth of the matter."

He couldn't see it now. She'd have to show him. But at last she had a way to change everything, to make the future she wished for. She'd recover his fortune, with the help of her friends. And then she and the duke—Peter—would say all the other things that hovered in the air between them.

"Have you heard what I said?" he asked. "Have you really looked at Alberdene?" He gestured at the paneled wall. A streak of mold ran down the wood. "I don't think you have. You or your friends." He gave a short laugh. "Unlike your aunt, who seems well aware."

She started to answer, but he went on before she could.

"How could I ask any woman to come here? To be mistress of a ruin?"

"Restoring it to its former glory could be wonderful. A task for the ages."

He grimaced. "Oh yes, I've had that dream. Castles, so to speak, in the air. When I was a boy."

Ada could see him as an ardent youth. She wanted to reach out to him again, but he stood stiff and distant.

"And then I woke to the reality."

"I do see how hard that has been. I… We want to help."

His face twisted. "No, don't say any more. Please. I can't bear to think of your hopes slowly subsiding into defeat. You mustn't endure that."

"But if we find the lost treasure, everything will be changed."

"Don't you understand? I have no luck." His face set in harsh lines. "Or nothing but bad luck, I should say. I have a surfeit of *that*."

"Even if that was true, perhaps your luck turned when you met me. I'll be your good luck." She smiled up at him.

"You would be any man's great good fortune." But his eyes were bleak. He turned and left the room. Ada heard the door to the modern wing open and close. She stood in the dilapidated chamber alone. Squaring her shoulders, she headed back to her friends and the most important task of her life so far.

Nine

"AND THERE WAS A WHACKING GREAT JEWEL IN THE little box," Tom told the earl later that day, finishing his report of the morning's activities.

"Fascinating." Arthur had pushed aside the letters he'd been writing to hear the tale. "I'm sorry I missed that unveiling."

Tom nodded. "Those young ladies are right smart. I didn't know their sort would pitch in like that. But they work together like they done it before."

"Along with Compton."

Tom shook his head. "He didn't seem best pleased. Said the papers and all were a load of…nonsense. Thought his dad had gone mad."

Arthur frowned. "I must go and see this mysterious room," he said, standing.

"Shouldn't be anyone there now. Miss Grandison just sent for the young ladies. For their daily lessons. Miss Deeping had some choice words to say about that." Tom's eyes twinkled at the memory.

"Why not tell Miss Grandison about their new project?" Arthur asked.

"They didn't seem to want her to find out."

"Thinking she wouldn't approve?"

"Seemed so," answered Tom.

The earl thought about that, then shrugged. "Let us go and look. Unless…perhaps the room is locked up again."

"His Grace went off with the key. Didn't see him come back." Tom turned to lead the way.

As they descended the stair, they heard feminine voices in the hall behind them. Arthur walked faster, not wanting his visit to the secret room interrupted.

Sarah, Charlotte, and Harriet didn't see them. They walked on along the corridor. "I don't see why we are obliged to obey Ada's aunt," Charlotte was saying as they reached the steps.

"She is our chaperone," replied Harriet.

"And arbiter in matters of propriety. That doesn't mean we must let ourselves be *enslaved*."

"Oh, Charlotte."

"I want to talk to you about Ada," said Sarah in a low voice. She checked the stairwell to make certain they were alone. "You know how different she's been since she…found Delia."

"Yes, yes," said Charlotte. "Which of us wouldn't be?"

"But it has been such a long time now. And you know her mother is worried about how Ada broods."

"It was strange to have Mrs. Grandison ask for our help," said Harriet.

They exchanged uneasy glances. In their lives up to now, parents had been figures who gave, not required, aid.

"I suppose that's part of growing up," said Harriet with a wry expression.

"About Ada," said Sarah, bringing them back to her point. "She's *too* excited about this idea of a treasure. Which may or may not exist, you know. We have only piles of paper so far. But when I said that in our bedchamber just now she practically bit my nose off."

"She's excited about solving such an important puzzle," said Charlotte. "So am I."

"Is she?" asked Sarah.

"What do you mean?" said Harriet.

"I don't think it's the solving. I think she's more interested in what it would mean for the duke. She seemed almost feverish about that."

The three of them looked at each other.

"Because she likes him," said Harriet slowly.

"Or more than likes," said Sarah.

"And if he had money," Charlotte added.

"His situation would be altered," finished Sarah.

"Radically," said Harriet.

"But…" Charlotte began, and stopped.

"How likely is it that we will find a fortune?" asked Harriet. "Really."

"We might," replied Charlotte.

They looked at each other. "We've never taken on a puzzle this large or this…portentous before," said Harriet.

Even Charlotte looked daunted.

Sarah held up a hand. "We must look out for Ada," she said, with the air of one reverting to the crux of the matter. "Our friend."

"Of course," said Charlotte.

"But what does that mean?" asked Harriet. "Might it be best to leave here?"

"Without even trying to discover the truth?" objected Charlotte.

"But if we don't? Or if the truth is not what we would wish it to be? This isn't a game. We are talking of Ada's future happiness."

"You've changed since you became an heiress, Harriet," said Charlotte.

"I have not!"

There was the sound of high-pitched barking from the corridor behind them. "Ada's coming," said Sarah. She lowered her voice further. "We must watch over her. Help her."

"But what exactly does that entail?" murmured Harriet.

"Find the treasure and let her like Compton as much as she wants," said Charlotte.

"Delia was smarter than we are, and she didn't find it," replied Harriet.

"She was not smarter!" said Charlotte.

Sarah and Harriet exchanged a long look.

"And does Compton like Ada?" said Sarah.

"Are you there?" called Ada from upstairs.

This brought their whispered conversation to a halt.

Ada descended with her dog on a lead. "Ella did *not* want to wear her leash. She ran me round and round the room. What does Aunt have us doing today, do you know?"

The other three indicated ignorance.

"We can only know it will be unbearably tedious,"

replied Charlotte as they walked down the steps together.

❧

Peter strode down the hill away from the oldest part of Alberdene, the Norman tower receding above him. The wind tore leaves from the trees and whirled them about his head, scraps of orange and yellow, a mockery of gaiety. He settled his hat more firmly on his head. In a few days it would be October, and all too soon winter would descend on the Marches, with its short days and damp cold. As chilling as the future he saw before him. He took a flask from his greatcoat pocket and drank one small, frugal swallow of brandy.

He almost never drank. But he also never kissed young ladies in the dim recesses of his home. And was kissed by them. The lovely, exuberant Ada had certainly kissed him as well, dropping into his life like a glorious apparition. The memory sent desire flooding through him again. He wanted her desperately. He wanted to learn all about her and tell her his innermost thoughts and…and rescue her from mortal peril like a knight of old. A bark of laughter at his own folly escaped him. Unfortunately, in this story, *he* was the peril, the path to a life of privation and probably estrangement and acrimony in the end. He was more dragon that knight. A painful paradox. And yet he still yearned for her.

Was this falling in love? He'd read about falling in love, but he'd never experienced this heady sensation. He felt like a goblet filled to the brim with fizzing champagne.

Champagne that was strictly forbidden to him. Peter considered another swig of brandy, and resisted.

The image of Ada continued to taunt him, out of his reach, a treat he could never have. How many of those had there been in his twenty-four years? He'd lost count long ago.

Of course her parents would never allow a marriage. No one would expect them to. He wouldn't. Every time he let himself think of it, he immediately saw a young wife brought into the scraping and scrimping that was his existence. The picture was painful and humiliating. To tell her she couldn't have something she wanted or needed because there simply was no money. To deny the same to any children who might come. Peter cringed as he walked. Unbearable. It was one thing to stint oneself. Another entirely to deprive your family.

He jumped a stream and started up the other side of the valley below the tower, moving faster as if he could leave these thoughts behind. Exertion felt good. He grew warmer as his breath quickened.

He suspected that Miss Ada was falling in love with him, too. With what she'd done and said, he didn't think he was being arrogant to believe so. And the idea filled him with joy. He couldn't help it. His spirit wanted to soar. He leapt from one lump of stone to another and up over a fallen log. Taking hold of a sapling, he swung around an overhanging crag and rushed up the last, steepest part of the incline. He was panting when he reached the ridge across from the tower and gazed up at it. The old Normans had chosen the highest point hereabouts, so that their defenses couldn't be overlooked. Alberdene's oldest bit dominated the landscape.

From this spot, the building's flaws weren't noticeable. But a few steps along—he took them—revealed the cracks and holes. The elation ran out of him. He felt as if he carried every broken stone on his back.

Turning away, Peter walked to the end of this ridge. A great hump of a boulder hid the tower, with a flat grassy spot beside it. In front, the ground fell away to the river valley. This had been a favorite spot of his as a boy. He'd come here to sit, leaning back against the stone and watching the water and the animals that came to drink. He'd found it peaceful.

He'd showed Delia once, he remembered. But his sister hadn't taken to the place. She'd preferred a view of Alberdene and to make up marvelous stories about their ancestors. She'd written little biographies of those she could trace, he recalled. They would be in the library most likely. Should anyone care.

But he did care. That was the thing. Peter put a hand on the stone, cold and solid under his fingers. This land his forebears had held, his crumbling home, the history his family had made—all of them meant something to him. He could not see so many centuries' heritage lost if he could possibly prevent it. He would not give up. It just didn't seem fair that his reward for caring was solitude.

An insinuating inner voice spoke up. What if they could actually find a Rathbone fortune? Piles of treasure hidden away by his misguided ancestor. That would change everything. Peter almost smiled. He would become a dragon with a hoard in that case. He could offer up buckets full of jewels in exchange for his bride. He could take his chance at happiness, along with many other things he'd dreamed of—a renewed birthright rising from the ruins.

It was true that he'd believed in chimeras too often. And always he'd been proved wrong. But such things did happen, once in a great while. Long-lost items were found. The wheel of fortune turned. She'd said that she would be his good luck. An idea as sweet and lovely as she was herself. Peter leaned against the boulder, wondering. Could he change his life with one wild throw?

Like a hardened gamester or a helpless sot, an inner voice jeered. Repeating the actions that had ruined them. It was idiotic to hope. And worse still to shift the responsibility onto the shoulders of the young lady he loved, still little more than a girl. And yet, it was so hard not to want. He did love her. He faced that bittersweet truth. And he rested against the rock and struggled with himself.

In the end, Peter couldn't believe in the fairy tale. He'd never had good fortune. Indeed, his fortunes had been steadily declining all his life. Ada mustn't be pulled into that melancholy slide. She should go. It was wrong of him to try to keep her, to hope to enjoy her company a little longer. He should give up foolish dreams and return to the solitary duties he'd taken up when his father died, fighting the long rearguard action to sustain an ancient dukedom.

But if he made sure he was never alone with Miss Ada again, perhaps he could wait a bit? No, it wasn't right. She had to see that there could be nothing between them.

A pall descended over Peter. Returning to his empty life and long, slow failure seemed too much to bear. Loneliness hit him like a smashing leveler in the boxing ring. The silence would be so much more vacant, the empty rooms more melancholy.

Macklin would stay a bit, he told himself, though the earl had mentioned obligations that would call him home soon. And in any case, his presence, so welcome in the beginning, was no longer enough. Peter craved more, particularly the company of a certain lovely young lady.

❧

Ada sat at a draped table before a pan of soapy water. With a soft cloth, she polished a crystal from one of the chandeliers in Alberdene's drawing room. Her aunt had criticized the fixtures' condition and had them lowered on their ropes, much to the chagrin of the older Alberdene housemaids. Rose had muttered about interfering outsiders. Ada thought her aunt had heard, but she'd ignored the complaint.

This sort of work was usually left to maids, but her aunt had decreed that they should know how it was done, and would in any case benefit from busy hands. Idleness being the devil's playground.

Charlotte, across the table, was positively seething. The heat of rebellion showed in her burning eyes and clenched jaw. Of course she wanted to be in the secret room, poring over the mass of papers. Sarah did, too, though she looked more resigned. Who could blame them? Ada wanted that herself. She wondered where the duke had gone, and why the hidden documents in his house had made him so angry. She needed to talk to him about that. And other things. There seemed to be so many matters she wanted to discuss. She longed to spend whole days in his company exploring them.

Down the table the four maids polished diligently. Tom had not turned up to join them this time. Probably he had gotten some advance warning and taken himself off, Ada thought. He seemed clever that way.

Adding the crystal to the pile of clean ones on her right, Ada wondered whether Compton was thinking of their kisses right now, as she was, continually. They'd been even lovelier than she'd anticipated. How often did longed-for treats turn out to be disappointing? The thought of Compton as a treat made Ada smile. She picked another crystal from the water, which was warm to soften the dripped candle wax, and began to clean it.

"She'd best not be planning to throw away them old candles," muttered Tess. "They're beeswax and cost the earth."

"Indeed I am not," said Ada's aunt. One might have thought that her piercing voice ruled out keen hearing. One would have been wrong. "They are scarcely half burned. We will put them back when we have finished."

Ada liked the use of *we*. Her aunt wasn't polishing. She patrolled the room, critiquing everyone's technique. Ada wouldn't have imagined there was an approved method for cleaning chandelier ornaments. But it seemed that there was.

"I beg your pardon, ma'am," replied the maid.

"Frugality is always welcome. Unlike impertinence."
Tess ducked her head and polished harder.

Movement at the far end of the room caught Ada's
eye. Compton had come in, pausing on the threshold.
"What is this? You're my guests. You don't have to
work." He sounded chagrined.

Charlotte set down her cloth, poised to take this
opportunity to rise and flee. Like a deer coming alert
in the forest, Ada thought, except with a ludicrously
hopeful expression.

"It is not a case of necessity," replied Ada's aunt.
"Your house is providing a benefit. All young ladies
should have a thorough grounding in household management." Charlotte slumped.

The duke made a wry face, as if he'd bitten into
something sour. He looked around the room. Ada
blushed when their glances crossed. His jumped away
immediately. She racked her brain for a way to break
free and join him. There was so much to say now that
everything was changed, with the discovery of the
lost treasure. The problem, as ever, was to get free of
Aunt Julia.

As if in answer to Ada's prayers, Ella stirred at her
feet, stretched, and walked over to the window, resting her paws on the sill.

At the same time, Una exclaimed as a crystal fell
apart in her hands. "I didn't do it," the young maid
exclaimed. "It was already cracked."

Ada's aunt moved down to the far end of the table
to examine the piece.

"Ella needs to go outside," Ada said. There could
be no argument with this necessity. She summoned

the dog and clipped the lead to her collar. Ella, well aware of what this action portended, panted happily.

Ada headed for the doorway, making sure that her route took her close to the duke. "Would you care to come along?" she murmured to him. Softly, facing away from her aunt.

"No thank you," he answered in normal tones. "I've just come in. I don't care to go out again."

Her aunt heard, and turned, giving them a sharp stare. Everyone else looked at them as well. Ada's cheeks flamed. It was practically a cut direct. The sympathy on her friends' faces made the snub worse. Ada tugged on Ella's leash and rushed from the room.

Peter knew he'd offended her. He regretted that. But surely she understood they couldn't be exchanging whispered messages in front of everyone? They couldn't be making opportunities to go off alone. They couldn't have anything he yearned for. She had to go. He nearly groaned aloud.

"I don't suppose you have a supply of these stored away," said Miss Julia Grandison, holding up a broken crystal teardrop.

"I have no idea," replied Peter. At that moment, he could not have cared less.

The older woman pursed her lips. Her blue eyes raked him.

"There might be a few in the hall cupboard," said Tess.

"I never saw any," said Rose.

"At the back," replied the other housemaid. "Up on the top shelf."

"Please go and see," said Miss Grandison.

Miss Deeping jumped up. "I'll go."

"You would have no idea where to look." The older woman seemed amused. "And I have the oddest notion that you would not come back."

"I'll try to reach," said Tess, rising. "I might have to fetch Conway. He's the one noticed them."

"I will come with you." Miss Grandison moved to join the maid. She was nearly a head taller and no doubt well able to peer onto high shelves. The two went out together.

Miss Deeping shoved her polishing cloth away. "I detest household management even more than deportment lessons," she said. "Was there ever anything more irksome? This is like living under the thumb of a tyrant."

Miss Moran sighed sympathetically.

"Miss Grandison seems to me a very proper chaperone," Peter declared. "Alberdene may look ramshackle in some ways, but I assure you it is not. Sneaking about is…not to be tolerated. I hope you will help me make certain it does not occur."

Every occupant of the room stared at him, the maids looking almost as puzzled as the visitors. As well they might, Peter thought. That had sounded stiff and stupid and detestably pompous. Why had he spoken? And where were his wits? But he knew the answer to that. They were outside with Ada, along with his heart.

"What sort of sneaking did you have in mind?" asked Miss Finch.

Her green eyes might be pretty, but they could be dauntingly sharp.

"And whose?" said Miss Deeping. "Not your own, I suppose?"

Peter froze. Did Miss Ada's friends know what she'd been doing in the night? Was this girl taunting him? He scanned their faces and decided they did not. And they must not. He had to protect her. The best way to do that right now was to leave, before he let fall any more ridiculous remarks. Peter turned and strode out.

"Huh," said Sarah.

"Young gentlemen don't usually appreciate chaperones," said Charlotte.

Harriet indicated the listening servants with an inclination of her head. They all returned to their task.

"Do you think he was referring to a particular incident?" murmured Harriet after a bit.

"It certainly sounded that way to me," said Charlotte quietly.

"What has Ada been doing?" asked Sarah.

Harriet shrugged. "She's always up to something, though her schemes don't usually involve unsuitable young men."

"Is he really so—" began Sarah. She bit off the sentence at Harriet's frown. "I promised to help her evade her aunt. I suppose that is sneaking. I didn't think she'd... You know."

"I sincerely hope I do not," said Harriet.

"Are we going to tell Ada what he said?" Sarah replied.

"She's our friend. He isn't," said Charlotte.

"Right," said Harriet.

"I wonder if we should leave," said Sarah. "There's

a great deal to do, after all, to prepare for the season in London. New dresses. Dancing lessons. Have you seen the waltz?" She sighed.

Harriet nodded in shared longing.

"Not yet," replied Charlotte.

"You just want to solve the puzzle," said Harriet.

"What if I do? There's no problem if Ada behaves."

The three young ladies exchanged a doubtful glance. "When has she ever?" murmured Sarah.

"Here we are," said Ada's aunt, striding in with a handful of chandelier crystals held high. "Success! Why are you just sitting there? We aren't even half done. Where is Ada?"

"She took Ella out," said Sarah.

"That spoiled dog! Miss Finch, go and bring her back this instant." The glance that accompanied this command suggested Miss Grandison intended to keep a closer eye on her niece from now on. Or perhaps on all of them.

❧

Peter found his feet carrying him out of the modern wing toward the room his father and sister had filled with their wild hopes. Despite his doubts, a reluctant fascination drew him. They must have been working in there for months, years. When he had thought them shut away in their studies, they had been digging through archives and storerooms, pulling out bits and pieces, pinning their spoils to the walls, excitedly stretching string to mark supposed connections. The knowledge brought pain. Had they never thought to include him?

But they had. Peter stopped moving as the relevant

exchange came back to him more clearly. It had happened at dinner one day near the end of his school holidays. That visit had been full of awkwardness, most particularly his father's confession that he'd lost two thousand pounds—a vast sum in their position—on an unwise investment. Peter had been looking forward to leaving, even though his school wasn't much more comfortable.

His father and his twelve-year-old sister had been practically vibrating with excitement during that meal, exchanging conspiratorial glances and happy smiles. Peter had of course noticed, and resented it. When the servants had gone, Delia pulled a pile of papers from her lap and his father had sat straighter to make a speech. And together they'd presented their new theory—the lost treasure of the Rathbones.

He'd been flooded with a stripling's anger, Peter remembered sadly. The idea had seemed a pathetic grasping after straws to make up for his father's foolish investment, and he'd said so. Only to realize that Delia hadn't known about that loss. Her stricken gaze had somehow prompted more cutting remarks that he couldn't recall in detail now. His father had been humiliated. Delia had been crushed. She'd fled from the table. And they'd never mentioned the idea of a treasure again. He'd forgotten all about it.

He'd cut himself off from them, Peter thought as he started walking again. And they'd retreated into their shared studies. Afterward, no one had made much effort to reach across the gulf that had yawned that night. It had only widened. Now, of course, it was too late. He swallowed that pain.

In the stub of a corridor, he heard male voices
beyond the half-closed door. He hadn't relocked the
room, or the passage between the parts of Alberdene,
as was his custom. Now, he discovered that one could
be glad to have guests and resent their incursions at
the same time.

Peter pushed through the door and stepped in. The
clutter on the walls seemed to loom over him, like
waves of paper about to break about his head. Macklin
and Tom stood by the desk. The earl was holding one
of the notebooks that had been in the drawer. He
greeted Peter with a nod. "Tom told me about your
find, and I indulged my curiosity. I hope you don't
mind."

He could hardly say that he did when most of his
other guests had looked their fill. And Macklin was the
least intrusive of men. "What do you think?" asked
Peter, really wanting to know.

The earl gestured at the walls. "This represents a
great deal of work."

"Probably futile."

"Do you think so?" The older man looked
interested.

"I don't think it could be otherwise. Alberdene has
no lost treasure. The Rathbones have never had that
sort of luck." Yet he somehow hoped that the earl
would argue with him.

"It's not exactly good luck to have it go missing for
so long."

"And then found in the nick—" Peter bit off the
words. Macklin didn't need to know the extent of his
difficulties. Or of his forlorn hopes.

"Such things do happen," replied Macklin. "People come upon long-lost hoards. Roman coins and so on." He tapped the notebook in his hand. "I was looking at this entry." A folded sheet of paper slipped out of the back of the volume. Macklin caught it and looked. "This appears to be private," he said. He handed it to Peter.

Peter recognized his father's handwriting, the shaky version of his last years. The page held a letter, addressed to him. There was no date.

"*I haven't been well*," it began. So it had probably been written three years ago, during his father's last illness. His tremors would account for the slanting lines and scatter of ink blots. Peter's emotions on seeing them were harder to define. He read on.

I don't believe I will live to complete this hunt, which goes on and on until my faith in it wanes. Or my vitality, at least. I won't lose faith! Yet I grow so tired, so easily. Only Delia's conviction sustains me. She is a positive Joan of Arc of treasure hunting.

But I fear she will make this project her life's work. I've pointed out the dangers, suggested that a time will come to declare failure. But as you know she's a stubborn child. Perhaps spoiled as well. No doubt I am to blame for this, as for so much else.

My son. I can see you, standing in the midst of our untidy researches, your lip curling in contempt, your frown impatient.

Peter winced at this picture. He could have disagreed without being so curt, he thought. If only his father hadn't introduced the idea on the heels of his losses. He turned back to the page.

> The truth is, I yearn to present you with a great pile of gold and jewels, the solution to all our problems, and see the astonishment and relief in your eyes. The joy that might follow. And, dare I say it, respect.
>
> I know you have been disappointed by my efforts, particularly that investment with such a large sum lost. Of course so have I. More than you can ever know.
>
> I maintain that I am not unintelligent. Quite the opposite, I trust. But I have no head for money. I never seem to make good judgments in that arena. I'm not sure why that should be. Something about the pounds and pence makes my head swim. Talk of shares and percent returns and loan guarantees slips away as if it were gibberish.
>
> But the reason hardly matters, does it? The result is the problem. A long excruciating slide into disaster. And I leave you with this. Not an iota of improvement since your grandfather died. Matters are worse, in fact. I am overcome with humiliation.

Peter winced again. Looking up, he found he was alone. Out of tact or discomfort, the others had gone, and he was glad of it. He looked down.

> Peter, there truly is a possibility that the Rathbone fortune was hidden away. There are indications, oblique mentions. Delia is like a bloodhound, tracking

them down. I pray she finds the answer, and soon, for both your sakes.

I know your belief in me died long ago. When we argued over that canal scheme, and then the manufactory. Both times you turned out to be right when I was wrong. I take pride in that, actually. I'm certain you will do a better job as duke than I ever have.

Your loving father,

The signature wandered over the bottom of the page. Peter swallowed. His arm fell to his side, the letter dangling from his fingers. Why had his father not talked to him, instead of writing? They might have resolved their differences. Or, if not that, they might have found paths around them and ended on the note of loving father and loving son. Rather than long silences and simmering resentment.

But he knew the answer to that question. He had been as great a barrier as Papa's reticence. Neither of them had made a place for reconciliation.

He swallowed again, his throat thick. Setting the letter on the desk, he walked over to one wall and examined a curling page. It was a list of household items from 1615. Could his ancestor really have possessed twenty-four gold knives and matching spoons? Next to this was a description of the Rathbone tiara, of which he had never heard until this moment. Diamonds and rubies set in a filigree of gold, he read. Peter touched his pocket, where the small box containing the ruby rested. That seemed to him clear evidence that the ornament had been broken down and sold years ago. Along with the golden spoons and all else. He turned away.

The labor in this room represented just another layer of melancholy in the family's waning history. It made him sad to think of his young sister immured in here.

Once again, Peter was glad that he'd sent Delia to school. She'd found friends. Friends who were determined to take up this quixotic quest, he remembered. In his sister's memory. Their determination was heartening, if futile. A small chamber full of chattering young ladies was a different thing altogether.

Peter folded the letter and put it in his pocket, with the ruby. He decided to leave the doors unlocked. Miss Deeping would be vociferously annoyed if she couldn't get through.

He went out and down the short corridor. When he opened the door to the modern wing of the house, Miss Ada Grandison stood there, lying in wait. Her lovely lips were pressed together. Her dark eyes snapped under those lowering brows. At her feet, her tiny dog barked at him.

Ten

"Be quiet, Ella," said Ada. The dog heard that she meant it and subsided. Ada gave Compton the kind of raking glance that her aunt used to chasten the impertinent. It was the first time she'd really achieved that level of militancy. "You were beastly to me," she said.

"No, I wasn't." He edged sideways as if to get around her and escape.

"Bite him if he moves, Ella."

"What?" He looked down at the tiny dog.

Ada wished there was a chance that Ella would do it. "You *are* going to speak to me. And tell me why you humiliated me in front of everyone."

"That's an exaggeration."

"So you admit the intention but not the degree?"

"No, I… This is ridiculous. You must know that I was right."

Ada hadn't realized that one could actually see red. She'd thought it was just an expression. But at that moment, she did. She'd never been so angry in her life. She clenched her fists at her sides and struggled to be maturely furious. "You called me a sneak!" Ada's friends had told her what he said.

"I did not name any particular person."

"Because it was obvious."

"I don't see that."

"Really? Sarah and Charlotte and Harriet all knew that you couldn't mean them. Or my aunt." She hadn't yet confessed to the kisses. With the way he'd behaved, perhaps she never, ever would.

"I may have chosen the wrong word," he answered. "I'm sorry you are offended. I was trying to protect you. In the drawing room just now. We can't be alone." He gestured as if to say, as we are now. "It's not right when nothing can ever come of it."

"Nothing," repeated Ada. "But that's all changed."

"What do you mean? What change?"

"Now that we know about the treasure—"

"There is no treasure." His voice was harsh.

"But your father and Delia—"

"Clearly spent years searching. With their...obsession, they must have looked everywhere. There is nothing to find."

"But Delia had thought of something new!"

His expression grew sad. "I'm sorry my sister was pulled into my father's plots." He looked away. "She might have married, gotten away from Alberdene."

"She didn't want to! She wanted to save it."

"Papa had more schemes to recover our fortunes than a traveling mountebank, and they all failed. Completely."

Ada wondered if it would help to shake him. "This is not a scheme. It's a hunt."

"Are we children? To believe in fairy tales?"

"*I'm* not a child." She was barely able to control her voice, and just managed *not* to say that he was behaving like one.

"No." He turned back to her, his eyes dark with loss. "So you know that we must observe the proprieties. There can be no more wandering about the house in the night. Indeed, I think it's time for you to go."

For a moment she thought he meant go back to the drawing room. Then she saw that this was more. "You are throwing us out of your house?"

"Hardly throwing—"

"Before we have a chance to solve the mystery?"

His sigh was as irritating as anything Ada had heard in her life up to now. Only to be eclipsed by his woeful expression. "This isn't easy for me."

"Really? Not easy to give up without trying? Not easy to reject help when it is offered? To send me away." Her voice trembled, and she bit off the final word.

"I'm trying to protect you."

Did he imagine this air of smug melancholy looked noble? Ada tried to recall some scathing curse, and was frustrated when none came to her.

"I must take care not to rouse expectations."

"Expectations!" As if she was at her last prayers, setting her cap at him. Ada's anger went cold. How dare he?

"It is another of the things I cannot afford," he said, actually putting a hand over his heart.

Did he imagine she was some sort of purchase? Was

he calling her kisses a commodity? Ella barked, perhaps sensing her agitation. Ada bent and picked her up.

"The very many things," he added with what he might have thought was a soulful gaze.

Did he actually expect sympathy? Ada felt as if steam might burst from her nostrils, like the dragon he'd imagined his house to be. She longed to give him the setdown of his life, but properly searing phrases still refused to come. The muddle of her emotions was too distracting.

"So you must understand," he began.

"I'm sick to death of *understanding*!" Clutching Ella, Ada turned away. She was afraid her face would reveal too much as hurt began to overwhelm her anger.

"You must allow me to escort you back—"

"I don't have to allow you to do anything! You said you want me gone. You mustn't be alone with me. Very well then, go away!"

She had to escape for a while, Ada thought. She couldn't go to her room. Sarah would be there. Perhaps the others as well. They would see her agitation and demand the whole story, which she was in no mood to share. Where else? The thought of a refuge came to mind. Ada pushed around the duke and through the open door behind him.

"You shouldn't," he began.

"Let me be!"

Ada hurried off. She heard no footsteps behind her, of which she was glad, of course. Extremely and wholeheartedly glad!

She reached the entry to Delia's tower. Settling Ella more firmly under her arm, she rushed up the winding stair. She'd forgotten a candle, but the slits of windows gave enough light to see the steps. She raced up several turns, trotted up a few more. By the time she reached the top, she was panting.

Ada pushed into Delia's old bedchamber, shut the door, and set Ella down. As her lungs pumped and her heart pounded, her mind filled with crushing retorts she could have made, if only she'd thought of them in time. Why did the right words never come when they could do some good? And how was she going to show the master of Alberdene that he was wrong?

Gradually, her pulse slowed. She looked at Delia's things, still just as they'd been left before her friend's death. She'd come to Alberdene for Delia, first of all. For her connection to Delia. That hadn't changed. In fact, the impulse was stronger than ever, since she'd seen the mass of information Delia and her father had assembled. If Delia's brother chose to be impossible... Well, let him!

Ella sniffed at the hem of one of the curtains, moved on to the next.

Compton had the key to this room, Ada thought. She couldn't lock it. Should she shove a chair against the door? But he wouldn't be looking for her. He'd been clear that he offered...nothing. He refused to even try.

Fatigue washed over her. She'd been too excited to sleep much last night. Her mind had been full of the duke and his kisses. More than that, of the conversations they'd had, the looks they'd exchanged. What had she thought they meant? Not nothing. But what sort of something? Certainly not that she was offering herself as a thing to be *afforded*.

Ella scratched at the corner of a small rug, turning it up to examine the underside, then as quickly abandoning it.

If only Delia was here, Ada thought. She ought to be. This room, the whole house, felt like her. One could so easily imagine her walking into a room—this room—and pouring out stories about her family, her searches. They would have stood together against her brother, put him firmly in his place. But…she didn't want to oppose him.

Ada remembered the way he'd pulled her close, the sudden surge of urgent strength in his arms, the tenderness of his lips. He'd enjoyed the kisses, she thought indignantly, however he might pretend that he hadn't.

He hadn't said that, she admitted silently. Now that her anger had cooled, she realized that he'd been speaking of the same things Charlotte meant when she called him unsuitable. A man of no prospects. So he *had* liked kissing her, liked it enough that it made him think of an unreachable future. The last of her indignation drained away, to be replaced by uneasiness. Surely they would find a way?

Ella examined the hearth as if wondering why there was no cheery flame to curl up before.

There hadn't been a fire here for months. The room was chilly. Ada rubbed her arms to warm them. She ought to go. But she still wasn't quite ready to see the others. She went over and climbed onto the high bed, burrowing under the thick coverlet and pulling it over her. She wanted to think.

But she found herself lying down instead, nestling

into the thick pillows. She was tired. And it was pleasant to be warmer. She would just rest here a bit. There was time.

Gradually, she drifted from waking into sleep. For some time her slumber was peaceful, but then it shifted into the all-too-familiar dream.

She was back home, moving through the grounds of her parents' house. She knew the path, the trees and bushes. The day was cold and gray, with spatters of rain. Not a time for strolling outdoors, but she had to. She had to find something. The need drove her.

Filled with a rising sense of dread she went on, more floating than walking, it seemed. As always, the scene was curiously colorless. And dark around the edges, as if black draperies fluttered there. There was no sound—no wind, no birds, no gurgle from the stream that ran beside her.

The ground on her right rose into a cliff. Though Ada knew what she was searching for, and what she would find, she couldn't stop. The dream drove her on, pushed her forward, and made her look.

There was the cliff path, slanting up the escarpment, and there was Delia, a huddled heap at the bottom. In a final dizzying rush, Ada was kneeling beside her friend. Delia's face was paper white, her dark eyes vacant, her limbs skewed at impossible angles. When Ada reached out to touch her cheek, she found it icy cold. Just as it had been, just as it always was in the dream. Delia was stiff and still as she'd been when Ada found her.

Now Ada would put her hands on the wet ground to keep from collapsing. She would fight nausea and horror. She would scuttle backward and make herself stand. She would run for help even though it was too late.

That was what had happened on that dreadful day. But this time, in this dream, Delia sat up.

Ada's pulse jumped with startled fear. She jerked back, sprang to her feet. Delia's head turned. Flat black eyes fixed on her. Delia's ashen lips moved. She leaned a little forward, as if the message she wished to convey was urgent, but no sound came. Ada stood frozen with dread.

Delia's white hand reached out. She grasped Ada's skirts, her pale fingers curled tight, ready to hold her there forever. Ada backed away, yanking at the cloth, trying to escape. But no matter how hard she tugged, she was caught.

Ada jerked out of sleep with a gasp, her heart pounding as if it would leave her chest. She was smothered in darkness. She couldn't get out. Something damp rasped on her cheek. She gasped again and flinched away. Then a low whine told her it had been Ella, licking her face.

Reality came flooding back. She was in Delia's bedchamber, Ada remembered, high in her tower, in her great four-poster bed. Ada wrapped her arms around her chest. Despite the coverlet, she was cold.

Not as cold as Delia had been, her mind insisted on pointing out, lying dead on the earth. But she was thoroughly chilled, outside and in. Ella cuddled closer, and Ada held onto her little dog, a warm and living presence.

She'd thought that the dreams reliving her discovery

of her friend's body were a wretched burden. Now she knew there was worse.

Ada set Ella aside and slipped off the bed. She felt her way to the post at the foot and then moved out into the darkness of the room. Two steps and she was lost, still disoriented by the world of the dream.

She tripped over a fold of rug and fell to her hands and knees. An intense need to escape fluttered in her chest. She scrambled up and went on, holding her hands out before her. Where had that candlestick been? Was there a tinderbox on the desk? She couldn't remember.

She knocked over the small table by the armchair, scattering books. When she felt about on the floor, she found no light. She made it to the desk and ran her hands over the surface, encountering many small items but no candle. There had been a lamp. She was sure she remembered an oil lamp. Where had it been? Ada kept groping, but she couldn't find it, and she didn't dare try those twisting spiral stairs in the dark. That would be foolish beyond measure. But that sensible conclusion meant she was trapped in the dark. No one would hear her calling from this isolated room.

Several stories below, Miss Julia Grandison distributed frowns around the dinner table. "Where is Ada?" she asked. Her companions responded with shaken heads and shrugs. "I haven't seen her since we finished our cleaning," said Miss Deeping.

"She was going to take Ella for a good walk," said Miss Moran.

"She went outdoors alone?" asked Miss Grandison. "Why didn't one of you accompany her? And why don't you know where she's gotten to?"

The three girls looked away.

They probably knew Miss Ada had gone off to confront him, Peter thought. They seemed to tell each other everything. Ought he to mention the encounter? How could he put it that would not bring Miss Ada a scolding from her chaperone?

Suitable words didn't come. It had been hours ago anyway. But he had seen her rush into the old part of house. He oughtn't have let her do that. But he hadn't imagined that she'd stay. And he'd felt lacerated by her scorn. Hard to call it anything else, Peter thought. She'd been more than angry.

He'd botched the whole matter, from start to finish, Peter thought. Speaking to young ladies seemed the most difficult sort of conversation. He'd tried to make her understand that he was thinking only of her. And either she hadn't, or she didn't care what he was thinking.

Miss Ada didn't realize how painful it was to admit poverty. None of them did. And why should they? They'd never experienced the thousand disappointments and deprivations it brought. And he was glad of that. Happy for them. He shouldn't have allowed humiliation to make him pompous, however. And tactless. That was not acceptable. "I wonder if she might have gone to Delia's room?" As soon as the words popped out, he saw the likelihood. Of course she'd run there. But why hadn't she returned? A horrific vision of Miss Ada crumpled and broken on the tower steps overcame him. He stood.

All eyes turned to him.

"When did she see it?" asked Miss Deeping. "We didn't!"

"Delia's tower?" asked Miss Moran at the same instant.

Peter had to nod, which earned him reproachful looks from the young ladies and a frown from Miss Grandison. The latter clearly had questions that he did not care to answer. "I'll go look," he said. He wanted to run.

Everyone rose, obviously intending to accompany him.

"It's at the top of a steep spiral staircase," Peter added.

Miss Grandison hesitated, then sat down again. "In that case, I shall leave this to you young people. Macklin can bear me company."

The earl, who had been moving toward the doorway, hesitated. Miss Grandison's imperious stare brought him back to his chair. Peter felt a fleeting pity for him as he led the three young ladies away.

"This is not acceptable," said Miss Grandison.

"Perhaps a misunderstanding," replied Arthur.

"I'm not oblivious," she said irritably. "I know something has happened. Charlotte Deeping is sulking like a child deprived of hoarded sweets. And Ada has been increasingly furtive. My dresser says they've found some sort of hidden room, though she knows no more than that. Very exciting for the young people, I've no doubt."

Arthur endured her piercing gaze as he decided what he wished to say.

"I hope you don't think of interfering."

"I?" He was startled by her sharp tone.

"I've heard you've taken to matchmaking. The Phillipsons make quite an amusing tale of your efforts on behalf of your nephew Furness."

Macklin played for time. "I didn't realize you were acquainted with the Phillipsons."

"Isn't everyone?"

It was true. His nephew's former in-laws were a fixture of the *haut ton*. Entertaining was their obsession. One met everyone in their opulent town house, a beehive of hospitality and gossip. Of course they'd talked about him. It was inevitable, much as he wished it otherwise. He should have expected it. Arthur wondered what sort of amused questions he would face next season.

"Rather an odd pursuit for a man of your disposition and stature," she added. "Not to mention an age that ought to know better."

"'Matchmaking' is not the right word."

"What is?"

Arthur searched for a phrase. "'Compassion' perhaps. A desire to use my experience to help others."

Miss Grandison shrugged. "It seems to have come down to matchmaking."

"I never set out—"

"Young Compton may be a fine young man," she interrupted. "Indeed, I like him. But he's clearly on the edge of ruin and not the husband for any girl in my care. I realize I was indiscreet about Miss Finch's prospects. I trust you will not take advantage of that."

Arthur stiffened. Had he been doing that? "You don't suggest—"

"That you would put the interests of your friend over that of a young lady you just met? Of course I do. It's a common enough impulse. I won't have it, however." She shook her head. "This visit was a mistake. Far more complicated than I anticipated. We will bring it to an end."

He couldn't entirely blame her, Arthur thought. In her place, he might have done the same. He didn't think Miss Harriet Finch was in any danger, however. Even worse, from Miss Grandison's perspective, her niece was exhibiting signs of losing her heart. That formidable lady didn't seem to have seen it yet. When she did, there would be scolds of epic proportions. No doubt he would come in for some of them, deserved or not.

Arthur wished there was something he could do to ease the situation, but he didn't see what. Should he mention the possibility of a hidden fortune and the rehabilitation of Compton's prospects? But he knew what Julia Grandison would think of that tale. He didn't require an outpouring of scorn at the moment.

"A mistake," repeated his companion. "I hoped the journey might do Ada good, but she seems unchanged. And now she's wandered off in this wreck of a house." She folded her hands tightly on the tablecloth. "One can't help thinking of Lady Delia's sad end. If an accident has befallen Ada, I shan't forgive myself."

"I'm sure she's all right."

"Are you? Why?"

Of course he had no answer.

❧

Peter led his small party up the twisting stair, candle-sticks held high.

"This is marvelous," said Miss Moran. "So atmospheric."

"Are you mad?" replied Miss Finch. "Who would live at the top of stairs like this? You might break an ankle at any moment. Or your neck."

Silence fell over them as the reality of Delia's death intruded once more. It *was* ironic that she should have fallen when she bounded up and down these steps every day.

The sound of barking drifted down from above. "That's Ella," Miss Deeping said unnecessarily.

"Ada?" called Miss Moran.

Peter reached the upper landing. He pushed the bedchamber door open, and the young ladies crowded in on his heels. Their candles threw jumping shadows over the walls. Miss Ada's dog circled them, barking frantically.

Her mistress stood in the center of the room, her hair coming down around her ears, her eyes wide and dark. She opened her mouth, but no words came out.

The young ladies rushed over and enveloped her.

"Your hands are like ice!" said Miss Moran, chafing them.

"What are you doing up here in the dark?" asked Miss Deeping, holding her candle higher.

Miss Finch put an arm around her friend and held on.

"I fell asleep," said Miss Ada in an unsteady voice. "I dreamed about Delia." She shivered. "And then I couldn't find the lamp."

The oil lamp sat on the back corner of the desk, where it had been the last time Peter saw it. The candlestick was on the mantel.

Miss Moran and Miss Deeping gazed about the room as if eager to take in all the details while they could.

"We need to get Ada downstairs," said Miss Finch. She frowned at Peter as if he'd done something wrong.

"Indeed," he said. "You walk in front of her to light the way, Miss Finch. Miss Deeping and Miss Moran, you go next. I will bring up the rear." Where had he put the key to this room? Somewhere in his bedchamber, Peter thought. He would add it to his father's ring and return to lock this room. And then he would tell them he'd done it.

They moved out to the landing. "Can you walk down, Ada?" asked Miss Finch. "Who would build such a stair with no handrail?" She looked at Peter again.

"Not I," he replied. "And if you will recall, I said at the beginning of your visit that everyone should take care. That would include not wandering about the house alone."

This brought Miss Ada's chin up and a flame into her eyes.

Peter set his jaw. He hadn't meant to refer to her night walks specifically. Or to offend her, again.

"Of course I can walk down a staircase," she said. "I was only asleep."

"You looked *haunted* when we came in," said Miss Moran, with both concern and relish in her tone.

"No, I didn't." But she avoided their eyes. "Give Ella to me."

The little dog stood in the doorway, looking down the spiral stair without enthusiasm.

"You need both hands free," said Miss Finch. "Ella can walk down."

"She can't. She's afraid." The waver in her voice suggested that she might share her pet's apprehension.

"I'll take her," said Peter. He picked up the little dog, settled her against his chest, and buttoned his coat over her. "Shall we go?" He held up his candle.

They started down, each keeping a steadying hand on the outer wall of the stair. Once again, Peter wondered why his sister had chosen to live up here. There was plenty of room to be private in the house without this climb. But none of those spots had such an air of antique romance, he thought. Delia would have sacrificed all manner of comforts for that.

"I suppose my aunt is angry with me," said Miss Ada as they neared the bottom.

No one denied it. "We'll bring dinner to your room on a tray," said Miss Finch.

"As we used to do at school when one of us was ill," said Miss Moran.

"I'm not—" She paused, and then merely kept moving down the steps.

They reached the ground floor. Peter set the dog down. Ella ran to her mistress and pawed at her skirts.

"I'm sorry," added Miss Ada. "I suppose I am... tired."

Her friends bustled her away as if she'd made some damaging admission. The dog trotted after them, leaving Peter on his own. Apparently, he was expected to explain the results of their quest to the formidable Miss

Grandison, which seemed unfair. *He* hadn't climbed into Delia's tower and fallen asleep and woken up haunted.

Miss Moran had chosen the right word, he thought. Miss Ada *had* looked haunted when they found her. And if Delia's spirit lingered anywhere… But he didn't believe in that sort of thing. His sister was gone, and the old parts of the house were simply empty. They might creak and echo, but there was nothing here.

Peter walked toward the door that led to the modern wing. Behind him the ranks of vacant rooms seemed to stretch out into vast distances. He didn't come here in the dark. Of course he didn't. Who would? There were broken tiles to trip one up and sudden, unidentifiable scuffling sounds. Which would be the cats doing their job, he told himself. And good for them.

Eleven

THE YOUNG LADIES GATHERED IN ADA'S BEDCHAMBER before they retired that night. The other three had returned to the dinner table and played their parts in the drawing room. But they'd come back to Ada as soon as they were free. "I'm perfectly well," Ada told them. She'd gotten warm before the fire and eaten. The feeling of the dream had faded, though not the details. "You're making a fuss over nothing."

"The way you looked when we found you in the tower wasn't nothing," said Harriet. She looked at Charlotte, then at Sarah. It seemed to Ada that they all reached some sort of silent agreement. "You haven't been the same since Delia died," added Harriet then.

"You don't take proper care of yourself," said Sarah.

"You brood," said Charlotte.

"And there are the dreams," said Harriet.

"Your mother is very worried about those," said Sarah. "Just before we left to come here, she asked us to help."

"How did she—" But Ada didn't finish the

question. She knew she'd cried out in the night at times. Of course her mother had noticed.

Harriet nodded as if following her thoughts. "And of course we said we would. But this visit doesn't seem to have helped you at all. I'm afraid it's made things worse."

"You looked positively wild when we found you tonight," said Charlotte. "This can't go on, Ada."

"Have you all been conspiring against me?" Ada gazed at her friends. Through their long friendship they'd never taken her to task in this way.

"Just the opposite," cried Sarah. "We're on your side. That's why we worry when you go off to Delia's room and don't even tell us."

"Twice," said Charlotte. "Apparently."

If they found out about the sleepwalking, they'd be even more worried, Ada thought. She couldn't tell them. The days when they knew every detail of each other's lives were indeed coming to an end. But it was all right. She'd stopped walking in the night.

"What did you dream about Delia?" asked Sarah "You said you dreamed about her up there."

"Was it the same one you often have?" wondered Charlotte.

Their worried gazes unsettled Ada. But this she could share. "It started the same," she answered. "I was walking along the path, and I found her lying there." She did not say *dead*. They knew. Ada was so tired of reliving that dreadful discovery.

"And then?" prompted Charlotte.

"I was kneeling beside her on the ground. And Delia sat up and looked at me."

Sarah gasped. Harriet shivered.

"Her eyes were all black," Ada continued. The words came faster. "She tried to speak to me. Her lips moved. But she couldn't seem to make any sounds. Or I couldn't hear any at least. And then she clutched at my skirts. I was frightened. I pulled away. Then I woke up."

"How utterly gruesome," said Harriet.

"Frightful," agreed Charlotte. In an uncharacteristic gesture of sympathy she squeezed Ada's hand.

"Delia wants us to discover her secret," said Sarah.

"She doesn't want anything," replied Harriet. "She's gone."

"Yes, but…" Sarah shifted in her chair. "She *would* want it. Just think how glad she'd be—would have been if we could solve her mystery."

"I know it's not Delia," said Ada quietly. Her friends gazed at her. "Delia is dead. I don't think my dream was a message from the…beyond. It just showed what I believe—that Delia would have liked the truth to come out. As much as I would. As all of us would."

"Well, we're not going to." Charlotte's tone was flat, as it tended to be when she was agitated. "Your aunt says we're going home. She means to arrange for the post chaises tomorrow."

Ada jumped to her feet. "We can't go yet!"

"Then you'll have to talk her out of it," replied Charlotte.

"Has anyone ever changed Miss Grandison's mind about anything?" asked Harriet.

"You don't understand," said Ada.

"Oh really?" Harriet gave her a sardonic look.

"There's something else."

"Delia's brother," her friends supplied in a singsong chorus.

Ada stared at them.

"It's become rather obvious," said Charlotte.

"It has?" Ada wondered if this was her aunt's real reason for going.

"To us," said Sarah.

"And possibly Macklin," Charlotte said. "I've caught the shrewdest look in his eyes now and then."

"Tom too," said Sarah.

"Tom!" repeated Ada. She felt keenly exposed. "So nearly everyone thinks—"

"That your *liking* for the duke has become something more than that," said Harriet. "And, oh, Ada, I fear you will be very sorry for it."

"I kissed him," she said. It was a relief to tell her best friends. "Several times," she added. "I think I love him."

Sarah clasped her hands to her chest, whether in shock or admiration Ada wasn't sure. Charlotte shook her head as if she'd feared as much. Harriet sighed. "Oh, Ada," she repeated.

"I don't see why that is so bad," Ada said.

"Because he has nothing," Harriet answered. "Hardly a sou. And he should not be luring you off alone and kissing you. That was very wrong of—"

"He didn't!" declared Ada. "I told you, *I* kissed *him*." She could see her friends trying to calculate just when this might have occurred. "I don't care about the money," she added as a diversion.

"That is because you have no idea what you're talking about."

Ada had never heard Harriet speak so harshly. The others looked surprised as well.

"I know what it's like to have no money," Harriet continued, her voice gone flat. "Not just a paltry allowance, but none at all. Before my grandfather changed his mind about his will, we were barely scraping by. I had to tutor younger students at school to make up the fees."

"I thought you liked doing that," said Charlotte, looking shocked.

"I did. It was satisfying work. But I didn't like *having* to do it. Or the way the headmistress twitted me about our poverty in private."

"Harriet! You never said." Ada was remorseful.

"We should have noticed," began Sarah.

"No, you shouldn't," snapped Harriet. "I took good care that you didn't. Being poor is bad enough without having to be pitied for it. It brings a kind of shame, even though you know it's not your fault. I was grateful that no one knew."

"Compton said something like that," Ada murmured.

"Did he?" For the first time in this conversation, Harriet looked sympathetic toward their host.

"And I understand that having no money is very hard. But I love him."

Silence fell over the chamber, broken only by the crackling of the fire and Ella's soft snores from the hearthrug. Ada scanned her friends' face. Harriet looked both sad and impatient. Charlotte was frowning.

"He does seem like an admirable young man, apart from the money," said Sarah finally.

There were nods of agreement. Ada's spirits soared. It would have been unbearable if her friends disliked him.

Charlotte huffed out a sigh. "Well, we're just going to have to find this hidden treasure," she said. "And… endow you with it."

Now that someone else was saying it aloud, this seemed rather unlikely to Ada. She wasn't living in a fairy tale, after all.

"Like a wedding present," said Sarah.

Harriet merely looked dubious.

"But you said Aunt is taking us away," Ada pointed out. "We won't have time to search."

"We'll have to stop her," replied Charlotte.

Everyone looked daunted at that idea.

"Compton told her it would take two days to arrange post chaises in Wrexham," said Harriet. "There aren't nearly as many for hire out here."

"Two days isn't long enough," answered Sarah. "We've scarcely begun going through all those papers."

An idea came to Ada. "I could tell Aunt Julia that I'm not well, after being trapped in Delia's room with no fire. That I took a chill perhaps."

Her friends considered this.

"You said my hands were like ice," Ada added.

"And you said you were perfectly well," answered Harriet.

"To *you*."

"Your aunt is difficult to fool," said Charlotte. "More so than anyone I've ever met."

No one could dispute the truth of that.

"But it's better than nothing," she went on. "We'll spend every waking moment going over the things in that room." She scowled. "If we can dispense with the tedious household management. You must see to that, Ada."

"I?" How did they imagine she could do that?

Her friends simply nodded.

It was fair, Ada acknowledged. They were banding together to help her. She should do all she could to smooth the way. But she had no notion how to convince her formidable aunt.

❧

When Peter woke in the night, his thoughts were full of the way Miss Ada had looked when they found her in Delia's old room. Wild, desperate. His heart had gone out to her. She shouldn't be so burdened with grief. If there'd been anything he could do about that… Well, he would have done it by now, of course. A variety of improbable heroic deeds ran though his mind. Unfortunately, there were no evildoers to challenge or mythical beasts to vanquish at Alberdene. And those sorts of tales had no bearing on her plight in any case. The sense of helplessness that descended on him was hatefully familiar. Nothing to be done, no way out, he was sick to death of it.

He lit a candle, put on his father's old robe, and walked through the house. It was dim and empty, as it always used to be. No delectable sleepwalkers to kiss and then escort back to bed. And he was glad of that, he told himself. Miss Ada should be nestled upstairs, serene, safe from nightmares. But he was sorry, too. With her here, the whole character of his home changed. She brought excitement and freshness and the promise of happiness.

And she would take them away with her in two days' time. "Stop being a fool," Peter muttered to his plummeting spirits. "You'll be no worse off than you were before she came." But that was a lie, and he knew it. He went back to bed. After a while, he even slept.

The next morning, when he entered the breakfast room early, as was his habit, Miss Ada was already there waiting for him. She looked weary, with smudges under her eyes, as if the experience of yesterday still weighed on her. He wished with all his heart that he could remove her burdens. Yet he didn't even know what to say.

"Yes, we are alone together," she declared. "But I don't care. I need to speak to you whether you want me to or not."

"I'm sorry that I spoke so abruptly yesterday. I often manage to use… What is the opposite of the mot juste?"

She brushed his apology aside. "Aunt means to take us away as soon as she can arrange for post chaises."

"So she said." Peter saw the pot of coffee the servants left for him at this hour. He moved toward it.

"I'm going to try to stop her. I'll tell her I'm feeling ill after yesterday."

This stopped him in his tracks. "Are you?"

"No. Not particularly. No more than would be expected."

"And how much is that?"

"I'm only tired. It doesn't matter." She sounded impatient. "I only have to convince my aunt."

"Exactly." He started toward the coffee once again.

"You don't think I can?"

"*I* wouldn't want to try."

"No, you would just slink off in defeat."

"Slink?" He turned, wanting to argue about the unfairness of this characterization. Her questioning gaze silenced him. He wanted her so. And at the same time he wanted the very best for her. She wouldn't find that at Alberdene. "It's probably just as well that you go."

"Just as well."

She could mock his phrasing, but he was right. Her aunt knew it. Her friends most likely did. He'd be surprised if they hadn't told her so. The idea was unappealing. Peter moved toward the coffeepot.

"You don't care?" Miss Ada's eyebrows came together, but she looked more forlorn than fierce.

"Care?" He nearly choked on the word. He hadn't really known the meaning of it until he met her. How it could include desperate desire and acute sympathy and a determination to protect someone at all costs. Which was why he couldn't let her know how much he *did* care. "That reminds me. I hope you've told someone about the sleepwalking. You said you would. When I saw you in Delia's room, in the darkness, all I could think of was—what if you'd stumbled down those stairs." He pushed away that lethal picture.

"I didn't stumble anywhere in the house," she replied. "Which is odd, isn't it? It's as if I already knew my way around it. How could that be?"

"I have no notion. And that is not the point. You should inform—"

"And I haven't gone sleepwalking again since I came downstairs on my own. And found you." Her eyes were steady, not pleading or accusing, but demanding nonetheless.

Kisses, thought Peter. How was he to think of anything but kisses when she looked like that? And more than kisses. If he'd had only himself to consider, he would have consigned propriety to the devil and swept her away. But Ada's future was at stake.

"So you will simply let me go," she continued. "Watch me drive off knowing that we will probably never see each other again."

"What would you have me do?" It burst out of him.

"Fight for something different. More hopeful. But you won't fight."

Anger surged through Peter. "Every minute of my life is a fight. A relentless rearguard action to preserve my family heritage. And a perpetually losing battle, I might add. How much fighting can one man do?"

Miss Ada gazed up at him. Emotions seemed to move in her dark eyes. After a bit, she nodded. "Yes, I see. Well then, I will fight for us both."

"You… No. That's not what I meant." Yet her determined tone touched his heart. "You mustn't do that."

"You can't stop me."

"Ada." He savored her name. "Ada. I really should try."

"There's only one way for you to do that."

"What?" With every encounter he was sinking into a deeper fascination with this resolute young lady, Peter realized. Soon he would be lost.

"Tell me that you don't wish to be with me," she said. "That I mean nothing to you." Her voice trembled a little on the last phrase.

Peter nearly tried. It seemed to be his duty to deny his feelings, to send her off to an easier, happier life somewhere far from his deteriorating acres. But he couldn't lie to her. He would never be able to lie to her. "I can't say that."

"I see." The corners of her lips turned up. The glint in her eyes brightened.

"But you know that I have—"

"Nothing to offer me. Piles of debts. Crumbling walls and derelict gardens. Shockingly so, says my aunt."

Ada Grandison was the most entrancing person he'd ever met. "Yes."

"Desperate tenants. Rampant ivy. Mold, probably. Or is it dry rot? What am I saying? Both, of course. Fraying linens and sofa cushions. Draperies in tatters. Huge wild cats who wish to eat my dog."

"Terrorize her at least." He resisted a smile. "You summarize it well."

"And I don't give a…flying fig. Because I love you."

The words, and the look that accompanied them, shook him profoundly. How had he ever thought her eyebrows fearsome? They gave her face gravity beyond her years. They made one believe that she knew what she thought and meant what she said.

"This is the moment when you respond to my declaration," she added.

"I love you as well. But—"

She held up a hand, palm out. "I think that should be said with more…emphasis, Your Grace."

Peter gazed down at her. All he felt and yearned for flooded over him and into the phrase he repeated. "I love you." The admission was a joy and a relief. "But—"

"No," she interrupted again. "We are not venturing into the realm of *but* just now." She smiled up at him.

It was like sunrise and laughter and the first green haze of leaves in springtime. He ached to kiss her, but at the same time, he didn't need to. The feeling that shivered between them was beyond any single embrace.

"So that's all right then," she said, her voice a bit breathless.

For this one moment, it was. Peter allowed himself to revel in the fact that he loved and was loved. It felt like the greatest triumph of his life so far.

Ada let out a long breath. "So, we must get organized. I do think that finding your lost fortune is the easiest way forward."

And Peter came crashing back to earth. The shock was almost as painful as a real plunge. "Easiest?"

"If you have it back, no one could object to our—" She stopped and glanced at him from under her lashes. "You haven't actually offered for me."

"Because I cannot. Because I—"

"Have nothing to offer," she broke in. "Et cetera, et cetera." She gestured as if she could wave this truth into oblivion. "My friends will be spending every minute in the hidden room going through the items there."

She was an unstoppable force, racing down a road that led nowhere. Peter felt a growing fascination with her confidence. He didn't want to puncture it, and yet he had to speak. "You do know that if my father and sister found nothing, your friends are unlikely to succeed. Delia and Papa were…obsessed."

"Yes." She offered him another blithe gesture. "That is why you and I must try much harder to decipher the paper Delia left at my home. I'm convinced it's the key to everything."

"And how do you imagine we're to do that?"

"You promised not to be sarcastic."

"When did I… Never mind. That was not meant to be sarcastic. I merely wonder what we can do?"

"We should talk to your servants," she replied, as if this was obvious.

"I already questioned them."

"Yes, but I would like to try myself."

"I don't see what good it could do."

"I am more experienced at interrogation. My friends and I have solved several mysteries, you know."

In that instant, Peter believed that she actually might succeed.

"Shall we go?" Her look was bright and determined.

"May I have a cup of coffee, and perhaps a slice of toast, first? But definitely the coffee."

Miss Ada laughed. "Of course you can. It doesn't do to hurry *too* much." She pointed at his feet.

Peter looked down, and saw that he'd put on

mismatched boots when he dressed this morning. The two were very like—worn brown leather, indifferently polished—but not exactly the same. One had a strap over the instep with a small unobtrusive buckle. The other did not. "Deuce take it," he said. "Well, my servants are used to my clothes."

"Not all of them. Marged thinks you're a bit soft in the head."

"One of the new housemaids?"

Miss Ada nodded. "But her sister claims that your odd clothes are pranks, meant to catch them out in some mistake. For which they will then be punished."

"Good grief! Why would I do something like that? And punish them how, precisely? That's ridiculous."

She smiled, looking as if she was quite enjoying herself. "I told them Una was partly right. That you do enjoy elaborate jokes. But that there was no threat of punishment involved."

"I've changed my mind," said Peter. "I don't want you anywhere near my staff."

"It's not as if I *suggested* the idea." Ada went over to the sideboard, poured out a cup of coffee, and handed it to him. He drank as if it was a magic elixir and held out his empty cup. She refilled it, elation bubbling through her. He loved her! Nothing mattered more than that. They would find a way to prevail.

When the duke had finished his toast, they went together to the kitchen. All the older servants were there. Ada supposed they left early-morning chores to the younger staff, which seemed only fair. Gathering Conway, Evan, Rose, and Tess, which earned them a sharp look from the cook, Ada and Peter moved to an empty parlor. "Let us all sit down," Ada said, doing so.

The servants exchanged uncomfortable glances, turned to the duke. "Is something wrong, Your Grace?" asked Evan.

"He's going to dismiss us," said Rose. "Now that he has the young ones, he doesn't want us anymore." She wrung her hands.

"No—" began Compton.

"I can carry the firewood," interrupted Evan. "Always have, always will. Don't need some stripling snatching it out of my hands."

"He isn't—" began Ada. But she was also overborne.

"They've no notion how to set a proper table," interrupted Conway. "That William said the forks all looked alike. Nodcock!"

"I'm not—" tried Compton.

"Una has no more spirit than a rabbit," said Tess. "She doesn't know how to use a flatiron properly either. And when you try to tell her, she whinges."

"That sister of hers is nothing but a bundle of cheek," said Conway.

"This is about something else," said Ada. But none of them listened. She wasn't certain they even heard her.

Rose started to cry as the other three threw out more criticisms of the new staff.

"Stop!" cried the duke. He had to shout to break through their anxious babble. "Silence! I am *not* dismissing you."

The four old servants went quiet, gazing at him with lingering reproach.

"Not dismissing you," he repeated. "I never would, unless you should wish to retire." This threatened to start another round of protests, but he held up an admonitory hand. "How could you think I would do that? When have I ever given you reason?"

"Things have been changing round here," mumbled Conway.

"After a long time when they did not," replied Compton. "I know." He glanced at Ada. She was touched by the concern in his expression. For her, but also for them. He had known these people all his life, she realized.

"Now will you sit down," he added. "Please."

Slowly, with some milling about, they did.

"We wanted to talk to you about Lady Delia's foreign governess," said Ada then.

The servants looked at the duke. "We don't know where she's gotten to," said Tess. "We said so already."

Compton nodded. He seemed to be trying to look reassuring and inquisitive at the same time.

"Things can come back to you when you talk about them," said Ada. "Sometimes. That is all we mean to do."

"Yes, miss," said Conway. Possibly he didn't realize how skeptical he appeared.

Best to start at the most obvious level, Ada thought. Simple questions could lead to more subtle ones. "What did this governess look like?" she asked.

There was a short silence.

"She was small," said Rose then. "Shorter than me."

"And skinny," said Tess. "Even though she ate

like a starving navvy. Huh, I forgot about that." She turned to Rose. "Remember when she snaffled up half a seed cake? You were that angry."

"It was meant for his grace's dinner!"

Conway cocked his head, frowning as if he was trying to think of some lost idea.

"She had light hair," said Evan. "I thought it was gray at first. But then maybe that it wasn't. More silvery. 'Cause she wasn't that old."

"How old, do you think?" asked Ada.

"About the same as us," said Rose. "Tess and me, that is."

Ada didn't like to ask for a number. She decided on late forties.

"She had eyes the color of ice," said Conway. When they all turned to stare at him, he looked embarrassed. "Just a thing that occurred to me, back then," he said. "Never seen such a pale blue."

"Did you like her?" asked Ada, taking in all four of them with a glance.

This seemed to be a difficult question.

"She wasn't much for chatting," said Evan.

"And she spent a good deal of her time with Lady Delia," said Rose. "Talking the foreign lingo."

"When she did speak, it was more like a speech," said Conway.

Evan nodded. "That's right. You didn't want to get her started on the war. She'd go on and on like a speechifying politician."

"She didn't care for Swedes," said Tess. "When she first mentioned it, I thought she meant the vegetable. A turnip, you know. Well, they aren't very tasty. But it was a person from Sweden she was talking about." Tess shook her head. "We never had any such around here."

"No indeed," said Rose.

"Did she talk about her life before she came here?" asked Ada. None of this was helpful so far. But she was far from giving up.

"I reckon she'd seen some hardship," said Evan. "Made her bitter."

"About the Swedes and all," agreed Tess.

"And soldiers," added Rose. "She couldn't abide soldiers."

"How would you know that?" asked Conway. "I don't believe a military man has ever crossed our threshold. Not in my time at Alberdene."

Which was a very long time, Ada understood.

"I mentioned my nephew, who'd joined up," Rose replied. "She said he was a fool. We had a bit of a set-to about that, me and the high and mighty Miss Kos—" The maid fell silent, blinking as if surprised.

"Miss what?" asked Ada, leaning forward. This was the sort of thing she'd hoped for, lost memories popping up.

"Kos," repeated Rose. "Her name started with Kos something."

"Yes," agreed Conway. "It was like a singsong when she said it."

"She had that sort of accent," added Evan.

Ada waited through a longish silence. It was sometimes better to let the memories flow without interruption.

"She had a friend in Shrewsbury," said Tess suddenly. "How did I forget about that?"

"That's right," said Rose. "She visited there a few times, didn't she, on her days off. Found a ride with a carter, wasn't it?"

Tess nodded. "Only it was so far, she gave it up finally," she added. "Too much trouble, she said."

"Shrewsbury," said Ada when it seemed they had nothing more to say.

"Yes, miss."

"Do you know who she visited?"

None of them could recall that.

"If we ever knew," said Conway. "Which I don't think we did, myself. She wasn't one for confiding her personal affairs."

"It was a female," said Tess. "I know that. Nothing scandalous about it."

Conway bridled. "I did not mean to imply that there was."

"Maybe it was the vicar's wife," said Rose. She frowned. "I don't know why I think so."

"But you all remember that she went to Shrewsbury," said the duke.

All four servants nodded.

They tried a few more questions, but nothing further emerged. At last Ada let the servants go, with thanks. When she turned back, the duke was staring at her. "That was masterful," he said.

Ada felt herself flush with pride. "My friends and I learned a great deal about how to ask questions when we tracked down a ring stolen by a crow."

"Did you say crow?"

She nodded. "If you begin by asking very simple things, easily answered, without much thought, the memories start to…flow. And others seem to pop up." She was rather proud of their skills.

"Now I am imagining you extracting a confession from a bird."

"The crow did speak." Ada smiled at his bemused expression. "Just a few words. It couldn't carry on conversations."

"And yet you managed to expose its villainy."

There was warm admiration in his gaze, and Ada basked in it a little. "Hardly that. Mere…acquisitiveness. Sooty just liked shiny things." She headed for the door. "Shall we set off for Shrewsbury?"

He looked uncomfortable. "I shall ride there and poke about."

"I'll go with you. Of course. We must make inquiries. There is no time to waste." And she had just demonstrated her ability to ferret out information.

"It's most likely a wild-goose chase," said the duke. "It's been years since the woman visited there."

"Yes, but this is the only link to her we have. She might have gone to this friend when she left."

"Perhaps, but even so, she's probably long gone."

Ada frowned at him. "But she might not be. She might be right there, ready to translate Delia's note for us. On the spot." Her fingers curled, grasping at the idea. "We have to *try*!"

He was almost afraid to do so, Peter realized. If, when, they did, the effort was likely to prove futile, like his father's many schemes. And then he would lose more than a sum of money. The risk seemed greater than any he'd faced before.

She came closer and put a hand on his arm. "You

can't give up hope. A few failures don't mean the next thing won't work."

Her touch warmed him right through. "More than a few," he had to say. The long string of his father's missteps had brought the estate to the brink of dissolution. But he wouldn't tell her that. It wasn't her burden.

She gazed up at him as if trying to divine his thoughts.

If only there was something to say, Peter thought, some magic words that would remove all obstacles. Unfortunately, he lived in stark reality, not a fairy tale.

"When I fell asleep in Delia's bedchamber," Miss Ada said, "I dreamed of her again. Only it was different. She tried to speak to me."

"She?"

"Delia."

"My sister tried to speak to you." Peter tried to keep the skeptical anxiety out of his voice. Unsuccessfully.

Miss Ada made a dismissive gesture. "The dream Delia. Of course I know she isn't real."

The impatience in her tone was a relief. He didn't want to think that her visit to Alberdene had deepened her grief into something more disturbing.

"It just meant that I'm certain the note she left is important," Miss Ada went on. "I believe it's an important communication." She bent close, fixing Peter with her dark gaze. "And I *won't* give up."

The passion in her voice moved him as much as her nearness beguiled him. In that moment he would have done anything she asked. Scaled mountains, wrestled giants. "Of course I'll go to Shrewsbury," he answered.

"*We* will go. Right now. I must be off before my aunt comes looking for me."

"I can't take you."

She made use of her eyebrows to scowl at him. "You wouldn't even know to ask about this woman if not for me. I have a *right* to come."

"Yes, but…" It was humiliating to admit the truth. "I have no horse for you to ride."

"Any sort of mount will do. I'm a good rider. You needn't worry."

The only decent riding horse in Peter's stables was his own. He'd sold off just about everything else. Alberdene now possessed several broken down carriages that wouldn't make it down the drive, a dilapidated gig, and farm carts that couldn't be spared from their tasks, even if their rough teams hadn't been far too slow for the proposed trip. Once again, he was shamed by the state of his holdings. "You misunderstand me. I have no horse for you."

"*No* horse?"

A ducal household ought to have mounts for guests. Anyone would expect that. But this one didn't. He turned away from the astonishment in her face. "I'll report everything I discover naturally."

"You must have something I can ride." She glared. "If you try to go without me, I'll follow you. I promise I'll find a way."

He believed her. He had a sudden image of her perched on the back of a great bewildered plow horse, clinging like a child, kicking it with her heels. She would be hours traversing the road to Shrewsbury, if she made it at all. "I could ask your aunt to keep you here."

She gasped. "You wouldn't!"

Fleetingly, Peter revisited the days of childhood, when to be a talebearer or a sneak was the biggest sin.

"I brought you Delia's note," she said, her voice vibrating with outrage. "I came here to find out what it said! I thought you would help me."

Her dark eyes burned into his. He wanted to help her. He'd never wanted anything so much.

"There must be something," she added.

"There is a decrepit gig." Peter's horse would pull it. He'd been forced to do so before. He did *not* like it, however. There had been incidents. A stable boy had nearly been kicked in the head.

"Splendid," said Miss Ada. "We'll take that."

"It's seven miles to Shrewsbury. You'll be exposed to the elements. You'll be cold."

"Of course I shan't mind that."

She was difficult to resist. No, impossible. "The gig may well break down," Peter warned. "It's older than you."

"You must learn not to be so negative." She put a hand on the doorknob. "Only give me a few minutes to get ready." She turned back. "You won't leave without me?"

It had occurred to him. If he went directly to the stables, he'd be gone by the time she fetched her bonnet.

"I *will* follow you," she repeated.

This wouldn't be as simple as she seemed to think. She would have to find a farm team and convince its driver. No laborer would want to mount her.

"Please."

Peter couldn't resist that quiet plea. He gave in, despite a head full of doubts. They would be cold. They would most likely find nothing helpful in Shrewsbury. They would have to rush to be back in good time. But he would be with her, an inner voice whispered. He would enjoy her company for a little longer.

He nodded. At least the gig was an open carriage, which satisfied the proprieties. And they would be back before the end of the day. "Come to the stables when you're ready."

In her bedchamber, gathering warm garments, Ada had a brief dispute with Sarah, as she'd known she would. And she prevailed, as she'd also been certain she would. Sarah was the most persuadable of her friends, even agreeing to watch over Ella while Ada was gone. She managed to get away without encountering anyone else. She nearly ran into young Tom outside the door, but she saw him first and ducked behind a shrub until he'd passed.

Twenty minutes later, she was riding away beside Compton in the Alberdene gig. It was indeed old and dusty, but it didn't seem likely to fall apart in the next few hours. They would get to Shrewsbury and back. The horse pulling the light vehicle was restive, obviously not happy to be in harness. But again, it would do.

Excitement and hope surged through her. At last they had taken a real step. They would find this woman, discover the meaning of Delia's last words, and uncover the treasure. Meanwhile, she sat beside her love on an adventure that would make all this happen. This was what life would be like in the rosy future she imagined.

"What is your plan?" she asked as they moved away from the ridge where the house sprawled.

"You wait until now to wonder?"

"Of course I trust you to have a plan. This is your country after all. Although how could this woman be so close and you not know?"

He started to say that she could not, and thus that their journey was useless. Ada could almost see the words forming on his lips. She braced for a dispute. But his answer surprised her.

"We weren't really acquainted. In fact, I barely met her. She would have had no reason to contact me."

"You'd think Delia might have kept in touch," said Ada.

Peter shrugged. "I don't know on what terms they parted. Delia never mentioned her."

"You think they might have been at odds?" And if so, would the woman refuse to help them?

"We have no way of knowing." The horse objected to a touch of the reins, and he had to calm it.

"Still, the town is so close," said Ada when this altercation had subsided.

"I rarely go into Shrewsbury. We do our marketing over in Wrexham. It's closer."

"Oh." Ada wondered if they would be reduced to walking about a strange town asking if anyone was aware of a foreign woman who used to visit and might, possibly, be living there.

"I do know some people in Shrewsbury, however," he added. "I will ask them. A foreigner stands out in a small town."

"Yes." She refused to be discouraged. There would

be plenty of time for that if they failed. Ada fingered her reticule, which held the sheet of Delia's cryptic writing, folded in four. She pulled her cloak closer. As he'd warned, it was cold riding in the open carriage on this gray October day. The moving air penetrated despite her gloves and the wool scarf tied around her neck. She hitched up the blanket that Compton had tucked around her when they started out and put her hands under it.

The horse slowed again and kicked at a bit of harness. The duke gentled the animal and got him going again. "Prince doesn't like pulling the gig," he said, as if Ada had criticized his driving.

She'd noticed that young gentlemen could be very sensitive on this topic. Some of them seemed to see their handling of the ribbons as a measure of manhood. Indeed, one of Charlotte's brothers had actually come to blows with a crony over a carriage race, and it had been bloody noses all around. "You're doing very well," she said.

He gave her a sidelong glance. It was warm with amusement, as if he'd followed some of her thoughts. "Better than you know. Prince is a riding horse. Solely and completely, in his mind. He despises the harness."

"Why use him for this journey then?"

"As I told you, Miss Grandison, I had no others available." His tone had gone clipped.

She'd actually thought he was exaggerating to keep her from accompanying him. Surely no duke had just one horse. "There must be farm teams."

"Which need to be about their work. And are even less suitable for a gig. Would you plod along for two hours on this journey?" He glanced at her. "Perhaps you begin to understand what I mean when I say that my resources are limited."

It hadn't really sunk in, Ada acknowledged. Alberdene's furnishings might be worn, but there were servants to call upon and fine dinners on the table. Did he truly have only one horse? Was it a hardship for him to have guests? The idea that her visit might be a financial strain was embarrassing. She didn't know how to ask without offending him further, however. And if he said yes, what was she to reply? Ada limited her comments to observations about the countryside for the remainder of the drive.

They came into Shrewsbury from the north. It was a pretty town of brick and black-timbered white buildings set in a wide loop of the Severn River. Compton drove to the largest inn, where the gig could be stabled until they were ready to return, and then they walked together to the houses of people he knew.

And then began a frustrating process that made Ada more and more impatient as the minutes passed. They couldn't just step in, ask their question, and leave when they received an answer. Whatever his difficulties, Compton was the highest-ranking resident in the area, and a visit from him was an event. People wanted him to sit, accept their hospitality, and provide a story to impress their neighbors. They had to make a bit of polite conversation. The duke did this with a degree of aplomb that surprised and impressed her, exchanging views about the state of the county and agricultural conditions. She had only seen him with her friends before, and he had seemed much less at ease in his own drawing room.

Ada said little, merely enduring sidelong glances as people clearly wondered who she was and what her relation to the duke might be. No one quite dared to ask them. She fell into a daydream of returning here someday with an acknowledged position—as, in fact, his wife. This pleasant vision helped curb her impatience as the minutes dragged on.

Finally, at the fourth house, they came upon a clue. The wife of a prosperous merchant did know of a foreign lady who gave language lessons to aspiring young people in Shrewsbury. After lengthy pondering and word sent to a neighbor, she was able to come up with an address. She even insisted on sending one of her servants to show them the way. Ada followed him eagerly, her hopes rising with each step.

The man led them to a small wooden house in a narrow cobbled street. It had a steep peaked roof and windows picked out in white. The servant marched up and pounded on the door before they realized that he meant to. When it opened, he announced, "The Duke of Compton," with loud, officious relish.

"Thank you. That will do," said Peter. He gave the man a coin and indicated that he could go. Seeming to feel that he had completed his duty, the fellow strode off.

Peter turned back to face the woman in the doorway. As his servants had remembered, she was small and thin. Her pale silvery hair might be gray or a light sort of blond. It was pulled tightly back into a bun at the nape of her neck, which made it hard to tell. She had sharp cheekbones and eyes of a very light blue that slanted slightly in a wrinkled face. Her gown was gray and very plain.

Since the door opened directly into the front room of the house, Peter could see a girl of twelve or so standing beside a sofa. She looked nervous. "I fear we've interrupted," he said. "I beg your pardon. But we wanted to speak to you. Are you the lady taught my sister for a while at Alberdene?"

The woman nodded.

"Ah, good." Peter glanced at Miss Ada and saw triumph in her face.

"I heard that Lady Delia died," said the woman. Her voice had a subtle singsong lilt.

"Yes."

She bowed her head. "I am sorry."

"Thank you." Peter decided just to plunge in. "She left something behind that we hope you might help us with."

"I?"

Peter nodded, not wanting to say more in front of the little girl. He tried to indicate this desire with a shift of his eyes.

This earned him a long glance before the old woman turned and said, "You may go, Fanny. I will see you for your lesson next week. Tell your mama that there is no charge for today as we were cut short."

The girl slowly donned her cloak, clearly curious and hoping for more information. But they waited until she had gone before moving inside the house. When the door had shut behind her, their hostess bent to add a log to the fire. "Please, take off your things and sit down. I'm afraid I have no servants to help you."

They shed their cloaks and settled around the small hearth.

"I am Miss Inari Koskinen," said the old woman then. "Can I offer you a glass of elderberry wine? I make it myself. At home it would be *lakka*, from cloudberries, but this is not so bad, if I do say so."

"Cloudberries? What a lovely name." Ada wondered if she could mention that she was quite hungry, and decided that it wouldn't be polite.

The old lady eyed her, then disappeared into the back of the house. She returned a few minutes later with a tray holding a bottle of homemade wine and glasses. Sitting down across from them, she poured. Ada gave her a smile as she took hers.

Compton leaned forward as if to speak.

"Please," said their hostess again, gesturing at the tray. "Accept my hospitality."

The duke hesitated. Clearly he shared Ada's wish to get down to business. But their hostess looked equally determined to observe the social niceties. He leaned forward and took a glass. "Thank you," he said. He sipped. "Very good."

Miss Koskinen laughed. "I doubt it's exactly to your taste. But it is what I have. In this place."

"You've lived here for a while," he answered, making it half a question.

"Since I left Alberdene," she answered.

Ada tried the wine, sparingly. She understood that although their hostess had been an employee in the past, she was insisting on the rituals of polite calls now, and that the duke had conceded.

"What brought you here?" he asked.

"I took leave of my home in 1809," the old woman said, taking this inquiry in the broadest possible terms. "When the Russians chased off the Swedes and took over in Finland."

She wanted to talk, Ada saw. She wanted to be… acknowledged as an individual. Perhaps she wasn't often, as a language teacher in this English town. Despite Ada's impatience, she could understand.

"I was sick of wars and tyrants," Miss Koskinen went on. "Who wants a tsar? Who needs one? But there was fighting in the south, too. Napoleon. And so after a while, I came to England. I knew the language. I know many languages. My father was a greatly respected scholar, and I was well educated." She nodded as if to emphasize her point. "I began to teach languages to English people. The ones who wished to learn." She looked at Ada as if she knew that Ada was not one of these. "In London, of course, where such things are more common," she continued. "And then I came upon an advertisement for a governess well versed in languages."

"My father?" asked the duke.

"Yes. He was looking for someone to teach Lady Delia, as languages were a great interest of hers. His offer was generous. I enjoy seeing new places. So I applied and was hired. Your sister was a talented pupil. Most intelligent." She shook her head. "A great loss."

"I think we may have met once," said Compton.

"When you were home from school, yes. You weren't there long." Her gaze on him was acute.

He made a face that suggested the visit had not been a success.

"But after a while, I found Alberdene too isolated." Miss Koskinen shrugged. "I like having more people around me. A town, a city. Lady Delia didn't wish me to go, but I had had enough countryside. I came to live here in Shrewsbury where I teach young ladies and some gentlemen who are thinking of diplomatic careers."

Ada wondered how many of these there could be in this market town.

The old lady smiled as if satisfied now that she'd been allowed to tell her story. She fixed her pale gaze on the duke. "What is it I can do for you?" she asked.

"My sister left a note behind," replied Compton. "We think it may be written in your native language. We hope you can help us discover what it says."

Ada opened her reticule and removed the page. Unfolding it, she gave it to Miss Koskinen.

The old woman bent over it with a sad smile. "Yes, that is Lady Delia's hand, full of loops and curlicues. Sloppy, I used to tell her. Better to take more care." She ran her finger down the page. "Very bad grammar. She should have been able to do better than that after our sessions together."

"But can you tell what it says?" asked Ada.

"Oh certainly."

A thrill shot through her. She'd waited so long to learn this. She felt as if she was teetering on the verge of some amazing discovery.

Miss Koskinen held up the page and translated as she read.

> *The hiding place can be nowhere that one would commonly search, because we have. Inch by inch. But then I thought—what has been forgotten? And what always remains? And in that, I knew the answer.*

The old woman raised her head. "I believe she means 'answer.' She has written it a bit wrong. She might have been trying to say 'secret.'"

"Is that all?" asked Compton.

"Yes. The passage is not long."

Ada sat quite still, running over the phrases she'd heard and battling a wave of crushing disappointment. She'd expected a revelation, clear instructions, a path to a treasure. She'd gotten more obscurity. Delia's final communication told them nothing!

Frustration threatened to choke her. Had Delia really needed to be so cryptic, writing in a language that no one could read? That seemed to be taking secrecy too far. It was true that Delia had adored secrets as some other girls loved sweets, but this was ridiculous.

"We need to write it out in English," the duke said. "If you wouldn't mind repeating."

"Of course," replied Miss Koskinen.

Charlotte would leap upon the words and wrest meaning from them, Ada thought. Surely she would. They would remind her of some page on the walls of the hidden room. Or an entry in the notebooks. And that would lead them to the lost treasure. She mustn't give up.

Pen and paper were fetched. Miss Koskinen repeated the contents of the page. Ada wrote them down. "Thank you," she said when they were done.

"You are most welcome." The old woman looked curious. "Do you know what it means? What it is for?"

"Yes," declared Ada, earning a questioning glance from the duke.

Miss Koskinen waited. Ada said no more. Of course, she had no more to say.

"We must be going," Compton said. He glanced out the window as if gauging the afternoon light, then rose and acknowledged Miss Koskinen with a bow. "You have my thanks as well. Please send word if I can do anything for you."

"Very kind, Your Grace," she murmured. She watched them put on their cloaks and only stood when they were ready to depart. The farewells were brief.

"Did you understand something from the message?" Compton asked as they walked away from the small house. "Because it sounded like gibberish to me."

"No," answered Ada. She would not feel forlorn, she told herself. They would analyze Delia's note word by word.

"Ah." He looked thwarted and moved faster.

He walked so rapidly that Ada had to trot to keep up with him. And as soon as they reached the inn, he called for the gig.

"Could we have something to eat?" asked Ada. She

felt positively hollow. It had been a long time since their hurried breakfast.

"No time." Peter was seething with impatience. And discouragement, he admitted. This had been a wasted trip. Delia's note had told them nothing. His sister's affection for conundrums had never been so maddening. She'd been writing in an unintelligible language, for God's sake. She could have simply stated her discovery. The last thing he needed at this moment was a riddle.

Now the day was waning. He had to get Miss Ada home before dark. The proprieties demanded it. Her aunt was no doubt already fuming. Also, he was pretty sure his horse wouldn't pull the gig in the dark. He could only push Prince so far. Thus, when Miss Ada turned to enter the inn, he said, "Where are you going?"

"To ask for some bread and cheese," she replied over her shoulder.

"We must get on the road."

"I'll be back by the time the gig is ready."

She wasn't, of course, even though Prince prolonged the harnessing with a flurry of outraged kicks. Peter nearly went to drag her out, until it occurred to him that she might have had other needs to attend to. They'd been walking about for hours. He visited the privy himself, then stood by the gig tapping his foot.

At last she emerged, carrying a packet wrapped in a napkin. He handed her into the carriage and convinced his horse to pass under the arch and set off through the streets. Prince seemed even more unhappy about his position than earlier. Several times he shied and tried to kick off the reins.

Peter was thankful that his passenger said nothing about this. And very glad when they left the town behind and he could let the horse go faster. Perhaps Prince would tire of fighting him with a clear path ahead.

Miss Ada held out a rough sandwich, a slab of cheese between two slices of bread. Peter took it in one hand, realizing he was close to famished. As he bit in, he saw that she'd nearly finished her own. She'd been quiet because her mouth was full. "Good," he said when he'd swallowed. "Thank you."

She nodded and ate.

A gust of wind caught the napkin that had held the food and swept it from Miss Ada's lap into the air. She grabbed for it and missed. The bit of cloth billowed and flopped, coming to rest on a tree branch well off the road, and well out of reach.

Following its flight, Peter noticed the sky and nearly groaned aloud. Of course luck had turned against him. When did it not? The day had been clear when they left Alberdene, but now a storm was sweeping in from the southwest. A distant rumble suggested thunder. And Prince absolutely detested thunder, almost as much as he loathed lightning. He might just tolerate a storm when he was saddled. In harness, he would put forward the strongest possible objections.

"Shouldn't we try to get it back?" asked his companion.

Get what? His equanimity?

"The napkin," she added, pointing.

"Too high up in the tree. And no time," he replied.

He encouraged Prince to go faster and received an irritated snort in return.

"You needn't be so short with me," she said.

He paused and throttled his temper. "I beg your pardon. I'm rather concerned about getting you back in good time. And now the weather has turned against us."

She brushed crumbs from the front of her cloak. "I saw the clouds. We won't melt away if we get a bit wet."

"No, though I would prefer you didn't." Peter told himself not to resent her shrug. She didn't understand. And they were both irritated by the outcome of their journey, he thought. "The thing is, my horse hates thunderstorms," he added. "On his back I can control him. But here." He waved his sandwich at the harness.

"Should we stop and wait for it to pass?"

"There's no place to shelter along here."

She looked at the empty countryside. "No. Though we could stop, and you could hold his head while I take the reins. I've driven gigs before."

"We can't take the time. It'll be dark in two hours." Peter finished his sandwich. At least he had some sustenance for the coming tussle. "We must get back."

"Yes." Miss Ada watched the passing meadows. "My aunt will be annoyed."

He might have said she should have thought of that before she insisted upon coming. But he didn't. He wasn't entirely oblivious.

"I did know that," she continued, as if she'd read his mind. "But I so wanted to be there to find out what Delia wrote. You'll say you would have told me. But that wouldn't have been the same."

He nodded, understanding.

"I thought, since she'd gone to such lengths to disguise it, that the note would have important information."

"Indeed." A rumble of thunder in the distance made Prince roll his eyes. Peter braced himself for a battle of wills.

"I don't see why she didn't write more clearly," Miss Ada complained.

"Delia loved being mysterious. And she never much cared if her obscurities vexed people. Or me, at any rate." His sister would have smiled at their befuddlement, Peter thought. She would have gloated as she led them to whatever secret she'd deciphered. But she wasn't here to do that.

Rain came sweeping across the fields, cutting off any reply Miss Ada might have made. She pulled the carriage blanket from her knees and draped it over their heads, but it was soon wet through in the downpour. Lightning flashed nearby, and with the boom of thunder that followed, Prince leapt into the air, all four hooves off the ground, and then broke into a frenzied gallop when he came down.

The gig lurched off the ground and slammed down again. It bounced and tilted as Peter struggled to get the horse under control. Prince kicked out with his back feet, tossed his head, and tried to wiggle out of the harness straps. He shied at a windblown shrub, flattening his ears and racing around a curve.

The gig tipped. It was going over. He wasn't going to be able to stop it. Gripping the reins with one hand, Peter twisted to pull Miss Ada into his arms. He curled around her as the vehicle went over, and they were flung out into the long grass at the side of the road. His back hit the ground hard. Miss Ada came down on top of him with a solid thump. Between the two, the breath was knocked right out of him. Prince careened off, pulling the overturned gig behind him.

For a long moment, they lay there, stunned. She was draped over him in a limp heap. If he could have spoken, he would have asked if she was all right.

The answer came when she sat up, tugging at her wet skirts. "Oh. Oh. You saved me."

Peter stayed flat, fighting for air. His chest refused to pump.

"Are you all right? Compton? Peter!" She bent over him, eyes wide with fear.

With a great gasp of relief, his lungs recovered. He could breathe again.

"Oh thank God! Are you hurt?"

"I don't think so." He pushed slowly up to sitting. "Not…not really. Just knocked about a little. What about you?"

"The same. Less so because you shielded me."

They huddled together side by side, recovering, the rain pelting down on their heads.

"I must go to Prince," he said, pushing himself upright.

His horse had dragged the overturned gig only a little way along the road. There he had stopped, trembling and furious, and indulged in a temper tantrum, trying to rid himself of the hated burden. He was still writhing and kicking when Peter arrived. He tried to bite the source of his indignity as soon as Peter was in reach. Miss Ada came up in time to witness it.

He was absolutely going to find a way to afford a carriage horse for the gig, Peter thought as he dodged his mount's teeth. Neither he nor Prince deserved this. Slowly, he calmed him, then ran his hands over the animal's legs and was relieved to find him uninjured. When he went on to straighten the harness Prince glared with livid incredulity, stunned that he wasn't going to remove it. "Can you hold his head while I see if I can right the gig?" Peter asked his companion.

"Of course." Miss Ada moved toward the horse, leaving the soaked blanket she'd been dragging behind her.

"He'll try to bite you," Peter warned.

"He will not succeed." She took charge of Prince with gentle authority. The horse actually settled further under her hand, Peter saw with admiration.

The gig was a lightweight vehicle, and fortunately it had come to rest against a slight rise. By hanging with all his weight on the upper side, Peter was able to rock it back onto its two wheels. Prince objected strongly to the thump as it returned to the earth, but Miss Ada managed him. He appreciated the way she combined a soothing voice and a strong grip. Peter threw the sodden blanket into the gig and climbed up to take the reins. He'd have to hold Prince while Miss Ada got in. There was no other choice. She saw it at once, and climbed nimbly up.

A few minutes later they were traveling along on the road again, soaked through and spattered with mud but otherwise unharmed. Prince, perhaps tired by his trials, kept up a steady pace.

"You saved me," she said again.

Peter was tired and cold. It would have been far better to spare her the ordeal in the first place, he thought. As a man with a proper carriage could have done. Didn't this just show that he was in no position to take a wife? As if he'd needed a lesson. And they'd accomplished next to nothing in return for their mishap.

"Are you sure you're all right?" she asked.

"I'm as wet and battered as you are, Miss Ada. Let us just get back. I'm sure you want that as much as I do."

They drove for a while in silence. The rain slackened and finally ended. But the relief of that was lessened by the rush of chill air across their wet clothes. He saw her shiver. "Put the blanket around you," he said. "It will help even though it's wet."

She pulled at the heavy sodden wool and got it around her shoulders. Peter didn't dare drop the reins to help her. She huddled under the inadequate wrap, and he cursed his luck once again. "Only another half hour or so," Peter said.

Miss Ada nodded. She pulled the fabric closer. "I wonder if Delia felt like that when she fell," she said then.

He glanced over at her. The accident and the fear had reminded her of his sister's death, he supposed.

"Only worse, of course. She had no one to catch her. And the end was—"

"I'm very sorry you were the one to find her,"

Peter said. Had he said this before? He had certainly *thought* it, many times. He groped for some further comfort.

"Yes. I know her accident was not my fault, but—"

"Not in the least!"

She nodded, the brim of her bonnet drooping with wet. "And I don't feel it was. But I can't seem to forget about it. She'd been so…lively. Full of life. And then she was so empty."

The sadness in her voice wrung his heart.

She huddled deeper into the blanket. "I counted on the translation of the note to be the answer."

"Yes." He had allowed himself to do so as well when they were directed to Miss Koskinen's house.

"But it didn't seem to help at all."

"No. Delia didn't like revealing her secrets."

"Except when she could arrange some great dramatic presentation to dazzle everyone."

Peter didn't recall any such occasion. Except perhaps the dinner when his family had told him their theory about the treasure. That hadn't gone well either. He made a noncommittal sound.

"I knew you'd understand."

"I don't think I do, really. I've told you I didn't know her as well as you. Your grief is greater than mine."

"But the same *sort* of thing. We can comfort each other." She put a gloved hand on his arm.

"How can we?" Peter kept his eyes on the road. "We thought Delia's note would make some difference, but it has not. We are just where we were before we went to Shrewsbury. Look at this carriage. Think of everything you've seen at Alberdene. I am not in a position to comfort you." The reality of it tore at him.

"That's not true!"

"It is, as the world sees it. And as I do myself, actually."

"That doesn't—"

"It matters a great deal. To me. You should look to your friends for comfort. I'm sure they're glad to help."

"Who helps you?" she asked.

He was surprised into glancing at her. When their eyes met, they both understood that each of them was thinking of the other. More than of themselves. A strong mutual yearning vibrated between them, a longing to solve every problem, heal every hurt, offer every delight. This was love, Peter thought. And also despair. Because of course all that was impossible.

Then a distant roll of thunder offended Prince, and Peter had to devote himself to managing the horse. By the time Prince had calmed down, they'd entered the valley below Alberdene. And a few minutes after that, they reached the house.

They'd obviously been watched for. The front door opened as they pulled up, and Miss Ada was swept away by a bevy of exclaiming females. Peter drove the gig around to the stables, thinking it would be best if he unharnessed Prince himself. No need to expose the young stable boy to the horse's thirst for revenge. This also put off any confrontation with Miss Ada's aunt, which was a distinct advantage. He would sneak up the back stairs to change out of his wet garments before he faced her.

Twelve

ENGULFED BY THE ATTENTIONS OF HER FRIENDS AND
the Alberdene maids, Ada was hustled up to her bedchamber, divested of wet clothes with many exclamations about the state of them, and chivvied into a hot
bath before the fire. The warmth was welcome, and
the barrage of questions was so thick that she didn't try
to answer them.

She shoved her reticule—carefully kept dry in the
pocket of her gown—at Charlotte, who removed
Delia's note and pored over the translation. Sarah sent
Una for sustenance, and the girl returned bearing a
laden tray. Harriet sent her off again with the sodden
garments to tend. Marged combed out Ada's hair and
spread it over a towel to dry.

All too soon, however, Ada was warmed and fed
and dressed. Her aunt had apparently followed her
progress, because she came in at that moment. "Go,"
she declared with a shooing motion. "Ada and I are
going to have a talk."

Ada's friends filed out with many sympathetic
glances over their shoulders. Aunt Julia settled her

large frame in an armchair and gazed at Ada with sorrowful impatience. "What am I to do with you?" she asked.

Ada wondered what *she* was to do. Her aunt wanted to take her home. She thought it was for the best, and she was a woman of strong opinions. Ada was just as determined not to go. She had to change her aunt's mind. But that was not a thing she had seen happen more than once or twice in her life.

One thing she mustn't do was tell Aunt Julia that she loved the duke. She knew what she'd say about that. Ada had also abandoned the idea of pretending to be too worn down to travel. She didn't think she could be convincing, even if she had been willing to lie to her aunt. She'd realized that she didn't want to do that.

But the rest. If Aunt Julia understood the mystery they'd uncovered, surely she would be intrigued? And so Ada gathered her faculties and told her aunt about the page of Delia's writing, the odd room they'd found full of clues to a treasure hunt, the foreign woman in Shrewsbury who'd translated for them. She considered leaving out her recent dream, but then she included that, too.

That part of the story earned her a piercing look. "Dreams," said her aunt.

If it had been a mistake to mention that, it was too late to take it back.

"I've heard much of this tale before," Aunt Julia continued.

"You have?"

"Miss Tate keeps track of the servants' talk."

"Oh. Yes." Ada felt a bit deflated. Of course her aunt's dresser listened in, and of course the maids chattered about what they overheard. How had she not thought of that? Well, nothing to do but move forward. "Only think how wonderful it would be if we discovered the hiding place," she finished. "And the treasure!"

"Why?" asked her aunt.

"Well, because." Ada was startled by the question. "It would be a splendid thing to do. A triumph."

"For Compton." Aunt Julia watched her as if waiting for a mistake in her answers.

"For Delia as well. To show everyone that she was right."

"Is that so important?"

Ada leaned forward, realizing as she spoke that she felt this deeply. "I think it is, Aunt. It would mean that her life wasn't entirely wasted. Even though she died so young."

Aunt Julia looked uncertain.

"She would have saved her family from beyond the grave," Ada added.

"There is no need to be melodramatic." But Aunt Julia looked moved.

"She was trying to tell me." Her aunt's expression shifted, and Ada realized she'd gone too far. "I mean, she would have been, if such a thing were possible. Which it isn't, of course."

"I don't like all this talk of death," said the older woman. "Or these dreams. They are not healthy."

"I don't mean to have them," Ada murmured.

"They ought to be fading away, not becoming more…fantastical," replied her aunt.

Ada couldn't deny this. Indeed, she wished for it.

Aunt Julia sighed. "I fear I have carried my enjoyment of contradicting your father too far. I shouldn't have agreed to this journey."

"No, it was very good of you. You wanted to help me, and you are."

"How, Ada?"

She struggled to put it into words. And then understanding came to her. "I feel that when I—we finish Delia's task, make use of her discovery, then I won't think of her anymore. Or…I will, but not in a melancholy way. Things will be…complete. And I'll be glad."

Her aunt examined her face as if some crucial message was written there. "If Compton had this treasure you speak of, he would be very grateful."

Ada looked down. She hadn't wanted to bring the duke into this conversation. She wasn't confident she could hide her feelings. Aunt Julia was too acute. And if she found out about everything that had passed between them, all would be lost.

"He might feel he owed some…recompense."

"Of course we don't expect any payment!" Ada exclaimed, deliberately misunderstanding. She rushed on before her aunt could point this out. "Please let us stay until we have seen what we can make of the translation. A few more days."

Her aunt looked at her for so long that Ada grew anxious. Then she spoke slowly. "Compton seems to have no acquaintance, so there is little chance of gossip. No one in town will hear what you get up to out here."

Hope held Ada quite still.

"But my dear Ada, can you imagine what your parents would say to me if they heard about your disastrous expedition to Shrewsbury?"

She could, easily. Or uneasily, Ada thought. She suppressed the impulse to argue over the word *disastrous*.

Her aunt's sardonic expression suggested that she followed this process. "They would be justly angry with me for my failure to supervise you," she went on. "And that takes no account of the carriage accident. You might have been seriously hurt. The hair nearly stood up on my head when I heard about it."

"It came out all right. Compton was splendid."

This earned her another sharp look. "Or lucky. Ada, as I have taken on the role of your chaperone, I am obliged to do it well. I am finding that remarkably difficult. I feel *you* are making it difficult."

"I'm sorry, Aunt."

"An apology is no substitute for gaining permission. Despite the old saying. Which I have always thought specious. You do understand that being labeled fast is fatal to a girl's introduction into society?"

"I am not *fast*!" Unless perhaps she *was*? Wandering dark mansions and kissing penniless dukes. The idea, and the memory, gave Ada an anxious thrill. But she wouldn't trade those stolen moments for anything, and as her aunt had implied, no one would know about them. She could safely hug them to herself.

"That won't matter much if people say you are," said Aunt Julia.

"Why would they?"

"Because you are behaving carelessly?" The older woman reacted to her puzzled frown. "Oh, the gossips revel in missteps. Enough to make them up, or at least magnify the smallest hint. That is their nature."

"How dreadful!" exclaimed Ada. "And grossly unfair!"

"Fairness is not a central concern of fashionable society," replied her aunt dryly.

"Then perhaps I shouldn't care what they think!"

"You shouldn't," said Aunt Julia, surprising her. "Not deep in your heart. Not when you are deciding what is ultimately right and wrong. But you should still *take care*, Ada. Getting along is also important. Gossip can be quite painful. I know this."

"No one here would gossip," Ada replied. She could rely on her friends absolutely.

"As I said," replied Aunt Julia.

Ada clasped her hands together. "So we can stay a little longer, can't we, *dear* Aunt Julia? I promise to behave with *absolute* propriety. I give you my word of honor."

"That is not a phrase to be used lightly."

"I know, Aunt."

Aunt Julia gazed into her eyes. Ada saw concern and sympathy and doubt in her expression. After a worry-provoking silence, the older woman said, "Very well, we will try another few days. And see how matters unfold." She rose. "I am choosing to trust you, Ada." She sighed. "Or giving in to pathetic sentiment," she murmured, almost inaudibly.

Ada stood with her. "Thank you, Aunt."

"You are not going to lie down on your bed?"

"It's time for dinner."

Aunt Julia shook her head as she turned toward the door. "Oh to be young, come home covered with mud after being tossed from a carriage, and still be ready to dine."

They walked together along the hall to the stairs. There, they found the Earl of Macklin stationary on the upper landing. Familiar voices echoed up the stairwell.

"How could you be so irresponsible?" said Harriet.

"She insisted on going," replied the duke.

"You intend to blame *Ada* for this fiasco? What a gentleman!"

"Of course I don't. I merely point out—"

"You took her out in the cold and rain with a poorly trained horse pulling a gig. A gig, for heaven's sake! In this weather."

Ada started forward, but her aunt put a hand on her arm and held her back.

"I tried to convince Miss Ada not to come along," said Compton stiffly. "She would not listen. She swore she would find a way to follow."

This earned Ada a fulminating glance from her aunt.

"And there was nothing you could do about that," said Harriet. "Such as telling *me*. I would have kept her here."

"Do you make decisions for her?"

In the short silence that followed Ada gave a satisfied nod. Harriet was being officious. She did that sometimes. But Compton had stopped her.

"Neither do I," said the duke. "In any case, we got the translation she wanted."

"Which turned out to be gibberish." Harriet sounded vastly irritated. "I liked Delia, but she could be even more annoying than you are."

"I understand that you are concerned about your friend, Miss Finch. But I don't see that gives you license to—"

"Well, you see very little," interrupted Harriet. Her sigh could be heard from the landing. "Really, I think this place must drive people mad."

After a short silence, the duke said, "Do you?" He sounded subdued suddenly.

"I beg your pardon if I offended you," replied Harriet. "But look at your clothes, the state of your stables, your game with the bats."

"My father's muddled mass of *clues*," he responded.

Another silence. Ada imagined that Harriet nodded. "Oh, let us go to dinner," said her friend then. "There's no sense talking about this."

"Indeed," was the cold reply. Footsteps moved away below.

"I don't think you have any reason for concern," said the earl to Ada's aunt.

Ada wondered what he meant. Or rather which thing he meant. There seemed to be quite a few worries floating about Alberdene.

"Disputes can conceal quite a different set of feelings," replied Aunt Julia.

"They can." Macklin started down the stairs. They followed him. "I have certainly seen it. But I don't think they do in this case."

"I believe you may be right."

The two elders exchanged a glance.

"The tone at the end," said the earl. "Miss Finch sounded like a weary headmistress with an uninteresting pupil. One she intended to abandon to his ignominious fate."

Ada didn't understand her aunt's bark of laughter. Indeed, she was bewildered by the entire exchange. "Well put," said Aunt Julia. "I noticed something similar myself."

"That's settled then," Macklin said.

"*That*, yes."

Ada's two older companions exchanged another glance that seemed laden with meaning. She had no idea what it was, however. And they obviously weren't going to tell her. Ada darted down the stairs after her friends.

"I have agreed to extend our visit by a few days," said Miss Grandison as they followed at a more stately pace.

Arthur nodded. He was glad to hear it. Tom had told him about the new developments, and he was interested in what might unfold as the young ladies tried to solve the mystery.

"My niece has promised to behave with rigid propriety."

He knew better than to comment on that.

Miss Grandison sighed. "A resolution that will last until some fascinating development occurs, which she *must* pursue."

That seemed very likely to Arthur.

"I should like your promise to help," Miss Grandison continued.

"I beg your pardon?"

She looked over at him as they left the staircase and turned toward the dining room. "Are we to turn mealymouthed now? We've spoken frankly before."

She had the keenest gaze, Arthur thought. This was not a woman who could be easily deceived. "You want my help in—"

"Keeping things within bounds. Banning any hint of matchmaking. On any front." Her eyes bored into him. "Otherwise I shall have to take my charges away."

"A touch of blackmail, Miss Grandison?"

"An agreement between the two most responsible members of our small society. About the care that is *owed* to my young ladies, in particular." Her tone was steely.

She had a point, Arthur acknowledged. "Of course."

"I have your word?"

"You do." The arch leading to the dining room was just ahead. "If Compton finds a treasure, however, the case would be altered."

"I had no idea you were susceptible to fairy tales," she answered dryly.

"No, it is quite a recent thing with me," he replied. His smile appeared to surprise her.

❧

"We've gone over and over the translation," said Miss Deeping the next morning.

Peter sat with his young lady guests and Tom in the room where his father and sister had covered the walls with their researches. They'd brought in more chairs to accommodate everyone, and the small chamber was crowded. He would have preferred a place with windows. It still sometimes felt as if the mass of information was closing in on him. But obviously all this couldn't be moved. Charts and lists were spread over the desk, with Delia's last missive at the center.

"Ada is certain she copied it down correctly," Miss Deeping continued. "And Compton concurs."

He nodded.

"Read it again," said Miss Finch. She sounded weary.

Miss Deeping picked up the page and read aloud. "'The hiding place can be nowhere that one would commonly search, because we have. Inch by inch. But then I thought—what has been forgotten? And what always remains? And then I knew the answer.'"

They all contemplated this silently for a moment. As they had numerous times before. No fresh ideas came to Peter.

"So in terms of these *wrong places* where they've looked, Sarah and I have read all the notebooks in the desk drawer," Miss Deeping added. "Delia and her father measured every room in the house, including the attics and the cellars. That's what she meant when she said inch by inch. They made certain there were no unknown hidden spaces. We checked some of that."

This sent Peter's thoughts to the attic and his encounter with Miss Ada there. He was wearing one of the shirts he'd found on that occasion, altered by the seamstress. Which was irrelevant. But his mind wandered when it came up against an intractable problem, he'd found.

"They mapped the grounds, too," said Miss Ada. She tapped a detailed drawing on the corner of the desk.

"Though they didn't really think the treasure was buried in the garden," said Miss Deeping.

"Too easy for someone to stumble on it," said Miss Moran.

"No way to lock it up," added Miss Deeping.

"Makes sense," said Tom. "You could sneak in with a shovel and be off before dawn."

"Nonetheless, they did excavate several unusual spots." Miss Deeping touched the pile of notebooks to indicate where she'd learned this.

"Finding nothing?" Peter asked. He was amazed at his family's industry. And that he had missed all this activity.

"The graves of two dogs and a very old refuse heap," answered Miss Ada.

"Full of bones and broken crockery," said Miss Deeping.

"Ah." Peter gazed around the room. The press of words and images was overwhelming. "If all this effort came to nothing, I really don't see how we can expect to do better." He didn't want to be the discouraging voice in the group, but one couldn't ignore the truth. "I still fear there's nothing to find."

"There are records of purchases," replied Miss Moran, tapping a list with one finger. "Bills for plate and jewelry and expensive ornaments."

"And no record of their being got rid of," said Miss Deeping.

"No pawnshop receipts?" asked Peter. "Perhaps they were given as security to moneylenders."

"Which would have been noted. As would bills of sale."

"That sounds more organized than my family ever has been."

"Yet they kept the purchase receipts," Miss Deeping pointed out.

"True. But perhaps they were ashamed of the sales. Or they lost the things at cards."

"Do you *want* them to be gone?" asked Miss Ada. "It's almost as if you don't wish to repair your family fortune."

"Of course I do!" He could see the longing in her eyes and knew his own mirrored it. The gaze was as tender as an embrace and, on her side, utterly determined. If he had the means, he would offer for her in an instant. Of course he would. And she would accept. She'd practically said as much. He could see that she trusted that this would happen. She was resolved upon it.

Her belief was so compelling that Peter let go and allowed himself to believe in a cache of hidden valuables. Enough to repair the decay of his acres and bring home a wife. What would it feel like to stop worrying? A state he'd scarcely experienced since he was six years old.

The rush of hope was intoxicating. He felt himself come alive at idea of taking the risk, making a leap of faith. He hadn't dared in such a long time. But with Ada at his side, perhaps he could?

A familiar tide of doubt threatened. He had more to lose now. His newfound love as well as his tattered heritage. The pain would be redoubled if this all came to nothing. He nearly turned away. But no. He was going to hope. She gave him hope.

Peter became aware of a whole battery of glances. They were all staring at him, even Tom. Feeling like an actor who has forgotten his lines onstage, he bent over the translation. "So perhaps each of us should say what we think this message means. And then offer an idea of what to do next."

"What always remains," said Miss Ada, who also looked self-conscious.

"The house might not," replied Miss Moran. "It could be altered or burn down."

"And we have mentioned the problem with the gardens," said Miss Finch.

"What about that tower up top?" asked Tom. "It's been there for a good long time, eh?"

"A thought," said Miss Deeping. "When did it fall down?"

They all turned to Peter. "I'm not sure precisely, but it was well before the civil war," he said. "The ruin is shown in a portrait of the third duke. So it was already down at the time we're speaking of."

"I suppose they might have grubbed through the stones for a hiding place," said Miss Ada doubtfully.

"The thing is, the builders were all over the ruin when they put up Delia's aerie," answered Peter. "They took out piles of stone to use in the construction, and they didn't come across anything then."

"That you know of," said Miss Finch.

Peter shook his head. "My father told me stories about that project. The fifth duchess hovered over it like a hen with one chick. The workers had no opportunity to haul out a treasure."

"You have an objection to everything," said Miss Deeping.

"They aren't objections," he protested. "I'm simply supplying facts."

"Discouraging facts."

"That will keep us from haring off in the wrong direction."

"Well," said Miss Moran, with the air of one stepping between combatants. "We must keep thinking. What's forgotten?"

They all looked at him again. "If I knew, it wouldn't be forgotten, would it?" responded Peter. He heard the sharpness in his tone. Miss Deeping had a unique ability to annoy him. "I beg your pardon."

"How can we look for forgotten things?" asked Miss Ada. She gazed around the room. "It scarcely looks as if they forgot anything."

"If only Delia had been clearer," said Peter. He flicked the translated page with one finger.

"She didn't know she was going to be…gone. She thought she'd come back and unveil the treasure."

"Just like the old duchess who hid it," said Miss Moran.

"If there is a Rathbone curse, it must be a penchant for keeping secrets when you shouldn't," Peter declared.

"You must watch yourself then," said Miss Ada. "Make certain to be honest and open." She gave him a teasing smile.

Peter's heart turned over. For a moment, her face was all he could see.

"So we're looking for something that Delia

remembered," said Miss Moran. She sighed. "Which doesn't really narrow it down. Her head was positively stuffed full of learning."

"I just don't see how a treasure could be lost all these years," said Tom.

"You have to know something exists in order to look for it," replied Miss Deeping. "I don't think anyone did until Delia and her father assembled all this." She indicated the walls of papers. "We will simply have to go back over everything. The maps and charts and documents. And find the little item we've missed."

Peter nearly said that didn't sound likely to succeed. But he managed to stop himself. And then had to smile at Miss Ada's approving nod.

❧

Arthur sat in the drawing room wishing he was part of the investigation into the mystery. But his presence put a damper on the young people's efforts. That had been made clear. He could rack his brain for ideas and pass them along as they occurred. But he wasn't welcome into their group. The exclusion seemed another sign of endings. His foray into the lives of the young men he'd met in London was nearly over.

"The girls' families have written to inquire when they are coming home," said Miss Julia Grandison, who sat across from him with a pile of correspondence. "October is passing."

She wouldn't be surprised by his situation, Arthur thought. It proved out her view that people of different degree couldn't be friends. He still resisted that opinion.

"Macklin? Are you listening to me?"

"Of course." He had been given, by default, the task of entertaining the older lady. He understood that.

"Next season should be interesting," she said. "With Ada and her friends making their bow to society. You intend to be in London, I suppose?"

Arthur nodded. The London season was part of the round of his life. He'd be returning to that routine when he left Alberdene. The prospect felt a bit stale after so many years.

"I too," she said.

"Really?" He didn't recall seeing her at *ton* parties in the last few years.

"For Ada's debut," she said. "To see that my brother doesn't botch it. And perhaps to pay him back, just a little, for his behavior at mine."

"Indeed?" This sounded chancy.

"Would you care to lend a hand?" Her smile was thin and sharp.

Arthur mustered his considerable ability to be noncommittal. Miss Grandison wasn't fooled, but neither did she extract any sort of promise from him.

Thirteen

ADA CAME DOWN THE STAIRS, TICKING ANOTHER SET OF shelves and chests off her list. She saw Sarah going into the drawing room. Harriet moved through the hallway above. The duke was at the medieval end of the house; he had reserved the ancient part for himself because of the hazards up there. Through a window, Ada noticed Charlotte and Tom in different parts of the grounds. Tom had climbed a tree. People were poking into every nook and cranny of Alberdene. Even her aunt and the earl had joined in now. A searcher was liable to pop up anywhere at this point. Ella trotted over to a shadowed corner and sniffed. "If only you could smell treasure," Ada said. The little dog looked up at the sound of her voice, panting cordially.

Ada was proud of her friends and admired everyone's energy, but she couldn't help feeling that they were not making progress. Delia and her father had looked in all these places already, and they'd known the house far better. The chance of finding something they'd forgotten seemed slim. Why couldn't Delia have been more specific?

Her aunt had told her about the letters from parents wondering when they would be home. Time was running out. What if they failed? What if they couldn't solve Delia's conundrum? The duke could continue the searches when they'd gone. But he might lose heart and give up.

She went on down the steps. She needed to talk to him. The impulse felt nearly as important as breathing. But she'd promised to behave with rigid propriety. Well, she would. She snapped on Ella's lead and slipped through the door into the older part of Alberdene. She wasn't *searching* for the duke. Exactly. She was doing her part in the group endeavor. If she happened to encounter him, she would have to be polite, of course. She couldn't just turn and run. They could exchange a few unexceptional remarks. There would be no kissing. Not even one soft, melting... No. No kissing.

She walked through the empty rooms toward the oldest parts of the building. Ella stuck close to her side. Presumably this area smelled of cats, though not in a way that reached her nose.

At last, after a good deal of wandering, Ada heard a rattle of loose tile and a muffled curse. Following the sound, she discovered the duke in a dilapidated chamber, peering into an ancient cabinet. A fine film of dust covered his clothes and hair.

Ella uttered a sharp bark.

Compton started, bumped his head on a shelf, and practically growled as he turned around. "What are you doing up here?" he asked. "I told you the floors are unsafe." He kicked at a bit of broken tile.

"Just looking into things," said Ada.

"Things." He kicked the side of the old cabinet as well, making no impression on the aged oak. "Alberdene has far too many things, all of them broken down and useless. You know that Delia and my father sifted through them for years and found nothing."

"It we keep looking—"

"*You* have to go. Your aunt sent one of the new footmen into Wrexham to arrange for post chaises."

"She did?" Aunt Julia hadn't shared this detail with her.

Compton nodded.

"When? Not tomorrow?"

"Three days from now," he replied. His shoulders were slumped.

Ada couldn't bear to see him looking so beaten down. "You can keep looking."

"I shall." But his nod was unconvincing.

"And you could come up to London for part of the season." Surely he could manage a short visit? So many people did that. "We could see each other again then."

"To watch you being courted by all the town beaus? I don't think I could stand that."

"I would always pick you."

"Not when you compare me to men with money and sophistication."

"Nonsense. Of course I would. It's just stupid that money should make so much difference."

"Would you like never to have a new gown?" the duke asked. Noticing the dust on his coat, he brushed at it.

"I would make them from the silks and satins in those trunks, as Delia did. A good dressmaker could make *sumptuous* dresses from such cloth."

"And you could wear them as you wonder how to afford good schools for your children," he replied.

His tone was so dolorous that she didn't even blush at the subject matter.

"Then, when you took them to visit your family, and they saw the things other children had, you could explain to them they that there was no money for such fripperies. And they must be satisfied without."

She bit her lip. That wasn't a pretty picture.

"Come, I will escort you back to the safer parts of the house."

"We can't just give up!"

"I am not giving up." He looked fierce suddenly. "But I will not ask you to wager your life on such a slender chance."

He walked out of the room. After a moment, she followed, blinking back tears. They'd had similar exchanges before, but this one felt like an ending. And she didn't know how to make it stop.

They moved in silence through the old parts of the house. Ella growled softly at one point, but Ada didn't pause to see what had set her off. Undoubtedly it was one of the cats.

At the entry to the modern wing, they came across Tom. "I was looking for you, my lord," he said. "I've been climbing all the trees in the garden, and I found out one of the walls is actually two."

"Oh, yes," said Compton. "There's a path between them."

Tom's face fell. "You knew already."

"When the gardens were expanded in the early days of the estate, a duplicate wall was built for some reason. I always suspected it was a mason padding his bill."

"A secret passage?" asked Ada hopefully.

"Not actually secret. Just unused. It goes along to the village. Very overgrown, I think. Did you look?" he asked Tom.

"I went over the wall and along the passage for a good bit."

"I don't believe there's room to hide anything in there."

"There warn't much," Tom acknowledged.

"And those walls are as likely as any others to be torn down," the duke responded.

"Right." Tom was obviously disappointed. "I'll go on looking to the edge of the gardens," he said and slipped away.

"Let's look at Delia's note again," said Miss Ada.

"I've memorized it," Peter replied.

"The translation," she said. "We've just been looking at that. Perhaps there's some sort of secret writing on the original."

He thought she was grasping at straws, but it was an excuse to spend a bit more time with her before she was swept away from Alberdene. He followed her into the treasure room.

On the desk, she set Delia's original note and the translation side by side and pored over the two. "A place that always remains." She scowled at the words. "It's such a useless way of putting it."

He would have used a stronger word. He felt

surrounded by meaningless strings of words, on the page, pinned all over the walls. "Unhelpful," he replied.

"*Remains* just makes me think of death." Miss Ada scowled.

Peter went very still.

"Of course Delia didn't know she was going to——"

He held up a hand to silence her, his brain suddenly teeming. "Remains," he said. The word did point to death, and the rituals that came after.

"Have you thought of something?"

Was it possible? Peter ran over the idea in his mind. If Tom hadn't just reminded him of the old path, he might not have remembered.

She put a hand on his arm. "You have. Tell me at once!"

"I don't want to say until I have——"

Ada leaned forward, took hold of the lapels of his coat, and shook him. "No! You will *not* be mysterious. Like Delia and your wretched ancestor. You will tell me exactly what you're thinking right now." She shook him lightly again.

"This is my only good coat."

"Deuce take your coat! And *good* is not an accurate description."

"Miss Grandison!" He could hardly endure the hope that had begun coursing through him. If he was wrong... Well, they wouldn't be any worse off, would they? "We will go and see," he said.

"See what?"

"Whether I have remembered something important."

"Remembered." She looked down at Delia's note. "What has been forgotten?"

"Certainly that." He turned toward the door.

"I should fetch Charlotte and the others."

Peter wavered. He might be wrong. He probably was. It would be humiliating to have that exposed before everyone. "I'd prefer not."

"They've worked so hard," said Ada.

"I would like to go and see first. If it turns out I'm right, we'll return with everyone." Could he be? Peter didn't dare think further than the next step.

After a moment, she nodded. "If I go for warm clothes, the others will notice."

"I can give you something of mine. I have a few preparations to make as well."

They set out ten minutes later, Ada swathed in an old cloak that dragged on the ground at her heels. She glanced curiously at the lantern Compton carried. It was broad daylight.

They slipped back into the older part of the house and out a door into the gardens. "This way," said the duke. He led her through the overgrown plantings, holding back encroaching bushes to help her through. The October sun flashed through ruddy leaves.

They crossed the grounds, moving toward the rear corner of the gardens, where Ada had never been. It was clear that no one walked here now. The shrubbery had taken over. In several spots they had to beat their way through. "Where are we going?" Ada asked after a while.

"To the remains," he replied.

Here in the overgrown wilderness, the phrase sounded eerie. "What remains?"

He simply beckoned. Ada held up the folds of the cloak and followed.

They came to a row of tall evergreens against a high stone wall. Compton pushed thick branches aside to reveal a small iron door at the base. The panels were rusty but still sturdy. Vines twined over them. The door clearly hadn't been used for years.

"This goes to that old path Tom discovered," said the duke. "Nearly forgotten."

"But not quite," Ada said.

"Not quite," he agreed. They shared a look so laden with hope that she could hardly bear it.

He took an aged key ring from his pocket. It looked far older than the one they'd found in Delia's room and held four keys. He worked one in the lock. It didn't turn. He tried another with the same result. It seemed at first that the third wouldn't work either, but then the mechanism turned with a rasping squeak. Peter pulled at the door. He had to shove quite hard before it opened, dragging a trail of ivy behind it.

They squeezed through. Ada didn't ask again about their destination. He wanted it to be a surprise, and she had no doubt it would be. Also, she wanted to live in hope. She didn't want anything to interfere with that.

Excitement built in her as they pushed their way along a path that centuries of use had sunk below ground level. Wildly overgrown yew hedges pressed on them from either side, the branches scraping their clothes and hair. Weeds poked through the earth under their feet.

Slowed by the vegetation, they walked for nearly half an hour. Movement kept Ada warm enough, but she felt the chill that permeated the path. Under the arching yews, it must see sun for only a few minutes at high noon.

Their trek ended in a short tunnel that dipped under another wall. There was an iron door at the end, the twin of the first they'd come through. Peter opened it on the second try, and they emerged into an open space dotted with low stones. "Is this the village churchyard?" asked Ada.

"The very back part of it, yes. The oldest."

Ada waited. "And?" she said finally.

"The Rathbones have an old mausoleum here," he responded.

"The remains!"

Compton nodded. "That is my thought. The place hasn't been used for burials for many years. I believe I once heard that it had no more room. My grandparents, and my parents, and Delia were buried in a new plot nearer the church. No one comes here anymore."

"And so it was forgotten."

"Yes."

"Until now."

He nodded.

"But your ancestor would have known about it."

"And had a private way to get here," he replied, indicating the path.

"The remains," Ada repeated. She clasped her hands to contain the excitement that raced through her.

"Well, let us go and see."

They waded through long thick grass, past old monuments and weathered gravestones. A row of tall yews bisected the churchyard, screening this part from the newer graves. Another further on hid the church itself. A wall surrounded the whole.

Ada stumbled over a hidden lump. The duke caught her and supported her through the unkempt grass. "Does no one mow here?" she asked. It seemed disrespectful.

"Once a year, I think," he replied. "These graves are very old. People visit the newer ones, mostly."

"Forgotten," she repeated.

He led her to the most overgrown corner. "It's somewhere here, I think."

"You don't know?"

"I haven't actually seen it. We never came back here when I was a child. And my father stopped attending church after my mother died. He and the vicar had a quarrel about the afterlife."

"The—?"

"Indeed. They both had strong opinions. Which differed radically. Ah, this may be it."

They'd come to a mound covered with snaking ivy. Peter led the way around it, raising his feet high and tramping a path through tangled vines and spiky weeds. It looked as if no one had been here in years, he thought. Perhaps they'd given up the annual mowing.

They finished their circuit, finding nothing. This seemed to be a mere lump of earth in a forgotten corner of the graveyard. He walked around again, anxiety rising. Was this to be another disappointment?

"Here," said Miss Ada. He turned to find her dragging a dead branch nearly twice his height. "We can probe it with this," she added.

"Good idea." He set aside the things he'd brought and took hold in the middle. She balanced the far end, and they moved around the mound again pushing the branch into the ivy.

Repeatedly, they hit solid ground. And then, on the far side, the stick lurched into vacancy, overbalancing them. Peter dropped it and caught her before she could fall. She gripped his shoulder, grinning up at him. "Something."

"Yes." He didn't want to let her go. And he wanted to see what was there. Both at once and equally. Which was impossible. Peter stepped away to attack the ivy. The vines resisted, clinging to the earth and each other. He had to brace his legs and yank, scraping skin from his hands.

And then a big swath of ivy came free, revealing an upright slab of stone. Peter redoubled his efforts and uncovered another. He scrabbled and heaved and at last exposed a low stone doorway. Pulling a final strand of ivy from the lintel, he saw the word *Rathbone* carved there in ornate letters. A gate of iron bars filled the opening.

"It seems that your father and Delia would have thought of this place," Ada said. "They examined everything."

"Everything at Alberdene. All their attention was concentrated on the estate, and they rarely left it."

"Well, they clearly never came here," she said.

"No." He pushed at the gate. It rattled but didn't open.

"Is there a key?"

"Lost long ago," Peter replied. He retrieved the

short metal bar he'd brought—a tool he used to pry up splintered floorboards before replacing them—then paused to light the lantern. Setting the light before the gate, he inserted the bar near the lock and pushed. Ancient metal groaned. He leaned all his weight on the bar. There was a deeper groan, and a snap, and the gate sprang open. Beyond was darkness.

Peter picked up the lantern. Holding it up before him, he moved inside. Miss Ada followed.

They crowded into a dim, cramped space with large niches on three sides. Stone coffins filled them all, the last resting places of his ancestors. He turned, lantern in hand, to survey them. There was barely space to move. The ceiling brushed his head.

Shadows danced in the lantern light. The mound muffled sound. There was, thankfully, no particular scent. Air from the churchyard stirred around them.

"Which shall we try?" he asked. The words settled with the opposite of an echo; the earthen walls seemed to absorb them.

Miss Ada huddled deeper into the cloak. She turned as if uncertain. Finally, she pointed at one of the coffins.

Peter handed her the lantern. As she held it high, he set the bar into the crack between the coffin and its lid. It was a tight fit. He wiggled the bar farther in to get more leverage and pressed as hard as he could. Stone grated. The slab was heavy. Instead of trying to lift it up, he pushed sideways.

The lid moved. Peter thrust the bar deeper and levered. A narrow triangular opening showed, grew wider—a hand's-breadth, then a foot of blackness. Miss Ada made a small anxious sound.

He set the bar aside, took the lantern back, and held it up over the coffin, braced for the sight of grisly desiccated death.

The light caught on a gleam of some kind. Peter bent over the opening to let the lantern shine in more directly. There was something there, not a pile of bones. He set the lantern on the lid, reached in, gingerly, and grasped at the gleam. There was a tinkling sound as he pulled out a small golden chalice. Jewels sparkled on its sides, ruby and sapphire. Astonishment flooded through him. "It's actually here," he said.

He turned to Miss Ada, the chalice held up between them. Their eyes met, wide and wondering. Their faces mirrored incredulous smiles. She threw her arms around him.

Catching her, Peter nearly dropped the first bit of his family's lost treasure. She pressed against him, hugging him close. He held her, a warm, heady invitation along the length of his body. The future expanded before him, longed-for possibilities opening out in triumph. Elation flamed down every nerve.

You are assuming there is more than this one random piece in the tomb, a skeptical inner voice remarked. It might be a solitary offering. He wasn't home free yet. "We'll have to look through them all," he said, scanning the rows of stone coffins.

Miss Ada drew back, her eyes gleaming. "We must let the others help. Charlotte will be over the moon. Sarah too. And if we *don't* tell them, they'll murder us."

He nodded. He felt a bit dazed as the discovery sank in.

"Let's fetch them."

"I'm not leaving here." Peter imagined going away and returning to find that he'd imagined the chalice. Or the whole tomb. That the contents of the coffins had been swept away by some arcane thief. The fear was ridiculous, but he couldn't help it. Too much had been lost over the years. He would not leave this place until he'd explored it thoroughly. "You can go. Bring them all back if you like."

She hesitated.

"I am going to guard whatever of my inheritance lies in here. You won't convince me otherwise."

Miss Ada nodded as if she understood. "You won't look at everything while I'm gone?"

"I'll wait. I promise. You can take the lane from the churchyard. It's a little longer but easier walking. And perfectly safe."

She turned to go.

"Ask Tom to bring some bags," he added. The lad would surely want to accompany the young ladies. His strong back would be welcome. If there was enough here to require his help. "And more lanterns."

She nodded again and ran out.

Silence fell inside the mound. The birdsong drifting in from outdoors seemed distant. Solitude settled over Peter and with it a sense of his macabre position. The bodies of his distant ancestors were somewhere here, mute sentinels. They would wish him well, he supposed. But their presence wasn't comfortable. He pushed this idea aside.

Time passed; he grew chilled. He walked out of the mound, stamped his feet and waved his arms to warm them, went back in, counted the coffins. Fifteen, six on each side and nine along the back.

Surely it had been long enough? But he knew Ada hadn't had time to gather the others and return. He walked outside again, circled the mound, went back in.

Finally, he couldn't resist opening another coffin. He strained at the metal bar and shifted the lid, again braced for the sight of a dried-up corpse. But this one contained piles of smaller boxes, the wood cracked and fragile with the weight of years. He had to look inside one. It held an emerald necklace, brilliant even in the dim light.

Peter's breath huffed out in an astonished sigh. He'd seen the receipt for this necklace pinned to the wall in the treasure room, which had at last earned its name. How his father and Delia would have exulted to see it. He could imagine their triumphant expressions. Delia would have shrieked and danced like a dervish around the mound.

He itched to open other boxes. But his houseguests would never forgive him, and the young ladies were Delia's representatives here, in a way. He had to allow them the thrill of discovery. He'd promised. He closed the wooden box and replaced it.

After what seemed like hours, Peter heard a babble of voices. He stepped around the mound and saw all of his guests approaching. The four young ladies rushed toward him, a lantern-carrying mob in bright dresses. Miss Julia Grandison came behind them, her hand on Macklin's arm, holding him to a more stately pace. At the back Tom trundled a wheelbarrow filled with cloth bags over the long grass. Peter moved forward to meet them.

He looked so completely himself, Ada thought. With his slightly odd shirt and worn buckskin breeches, unaware of the streaks of dirt on his coat sleeves. She felt a wave of tender amusement. This discovery would change his life, but she hoped he would never alter. She loved him just as he was.

"You didn't *tell* us there was an ancient family tomb," Charlotte said to him accusingly when they came near.

"I'd forgotten about it," he replied. "Everyone had forgotten about it."

"Just as Delia said," noted Miss Moran.

"Until Miss Ada said *remains* in a way that made me recall."

His gaze warmed Ada to the core. "Delia had only just remembered it, too," she said. "How I wish she was here to see this."

There was a brief silence. Delia's death would always be tragic, Ada thought. That could not be mended. But this discovery vindicated her long researches. She would be overjoyed to see her reasoning proved out. Surely she would rest in peace.

"Can we see?" asked Sarah then.

They had to take turns in the mound, which could only hold a few people at a time. There were gasps and exclamations. The golden chalice was handed around and admired, as was a glorious emerald necklace. "There was a receipt for that on the wall," said Harriet.

"I thought those matched," replied Compton.

"*Now* you are convinced!" said Charlotte.

The duke gave her an ironic bow. And then they settled down to work.

Peter and Tom levered off the coffin lids. Ada and her friends formed a human chain to ferry out the contents to the spot where Macklin was sorting them. The earl had been unanimously judged the one best able to gauge the value of each item, and he was obviously enjoying the process. His smiles were brilliant as new finds were placed before him. Aunt Julia, who had thought to bring paper and pencil, compiled a list at his dictation. She seemed bemused by these developments.

They found silver and gold plate; bags of old coins, mostly gold; various precious objects like the chalice; and a duchess's ransom in jewelry—rings, brooches, more necklaces, earrings, tiaras and a coronet with a missing piece. "That ruby we found came from here," Charlotte said, pointing out an empty spot in the design. The others bent forward to look.

A shout from within the mound brought them upright. Ada ran to the door. "Is something wrong?"

Compton and Tom stood just inside. "Two coffins at the back have all the skeletons crammed inside," said the duke. "When we opened them—"

"There was a heap of skulls grinning up at us," said Tom. "Gave me quite a start."

"As you say," agreed Compton.

Ada peered around them. Did she want to see? She wasn't sure. Perhaps not.

"We've emptied all the others," the duke added. He was dirt-streaked and sheened with sweat despite the crisp autumn air. He also looked wildly elated.

"That's it." He looked over at Macklin and the piles of booty surrounding him.

"You do indeed have a fortune here," said the earl. "I can certainly say that much. You will have to consult experts for exact values, and about converting any objects to cash. Should you decide to."

"I can improve my acres," said Compton, as if he could scarcely believe it. "And the house. Pay off the mortgages. And—" He turned to Ada.

Speculative looks passed around the group. Ada saw them, and she willed her friends not to speak. She wanted, deserved, a private talk with him first.

"We should have brought champagne," said Sarah. "This calls for a toast."

"We can have as many as we please at dinner," replied Harriet.

The group gathered around the glittering array on the grass.

"How did they get it here?" asked Sarah.

"Bit by bit, I expect," Compton replied.

"There's a hidden path from the garden," Ada said. "If they came at night—"

"That would have been eerie," said Sarah, looking around the overgrown churchyard.

Ada thought of this place in darkness, of moving the dead from their resting places. She nodded.

"They used a handcart or a wheelbarrow, I wager," said Tom, indicating the one he'd brought along.

"I think perhaps we should take it back the same way," said Macklin.

Everyone turned to look at him.

"This will cause a sensation when it becomes

known," the earl continued. "And possibly a wave of treasure hunters rushing in to dig up the churchyard."

"But we've found it all," replied Compton.

"*We* know that. But rumors will run wild, believe me. Who knows what stories people may tell? We need to get all this into safekeeping before they begin."

"There's a strong room off Alberdene's records chamber, with a good lock," said the duke. He looked over their haul. "Probably much of this came out of it in the first place."

"I suggest we take all of this there by your hidden path," said Macklin. "And keep the discovery private for a time."

"I can get the wheelbarrow down it if I push hard," said Tom. "I could take a good load. The plate and all."

"We can each carry a bag," said Ada.

Everyone nodded, even Miss Julia Grandison. They all looked pleased for him, Peter realized. He was moved almost to tears. But he smiled first at Ada. He could smile all he wanted now. He could have new tenant cottages and carriage horses and vehicles for them to pull. He could support a family as they deserved. He felt his eyes burn with longing. Ada flushed and looked down. He did the same and turned to organizing the relocation of his astonishing fortune.

Fourteen

PETER HAD EXPECTED THAT HE AND ADA WOULD MEET for a private talk at breakfast the next morning, as they had on other days of her visit. There had certainly been no opportunity to speak to her the previous evening. Moving the items had taken quite a time, and then everyone had wanted to exclaim about the amazing discovery. People couldn't stop talking—reviewing each individual item, comparing them with those noted in his family's researches. The marveling and speculation had raced on through dinner and afterward. Miss Deeping had dropped a number of sniping comments into the conversation. She clearly did not forgive him for solving the mystery himself.

Peter had abandoned hope of talking to Ada then. But he had made careful preparations for a morning encounter. There was no sign of Miss Ada in the breakfast room when he arrived, however. He found Macklin at the table, genial and welcoming but not what he wanted. And when Ada's friends appeared for the meal they professed ignorance of her whereabouts. His inquiries were met with arch smiles but no information.

He left his guests eating and walked through the public rooms of his home. Automatically, his eye noted lacks and needed repairs everywhere. The downward pull at his mood was so familiar that it was a moment before he remembered that he had the power to restore the place now. Those ancient hangings could be replaced. The cracked paneling could be repaired. The fraying cushions could be recovered. His life was undergoing a revolution of *re* words.

But the triumph wasn't complete without Ada. Where had she gone?

Delia's room, he thought suddenly. He should look for her in Delia's room.

He climbed the long stair as quickly as he could and found her in the tower chamber gazing out one of the windows, her little dog sitting at her feet. She turned with an absent smile when he came in. "I dreamed of Delia again last night," she said.

"Oh." Peter gazed at her, concerned.

"It was partly the same," she continued. "She was lying at the bottom of the cliff. I suppose I will always see her there."

"Perhaps in time—"

She held up a hand to stop him. "But in this dream, she wasn't all…tumbled about from the fall. She looked peaceful. As if she was simply asleep." Ada folded her hands at her waist as if demonstrating. "I know dreams are just dreams and nothing mystical, but I choose to believe that she knows we found what she'd been looking for all those years. And that she's happy."

He nodded. And added a hope that this might apply

to his father as well. How Papa would have savored the vindication!

Silence fell. This room was so quiet, Peter thought. No fire crackled. Would it ever again? Would they use this chamber? Not right away, he thought. It would remain Delia's until...something else felt appropriate.

Household noises were inaudible from up here. He could practically hear his heart pounding on the edge of the most important question of his life. "I wanted to speak to you," he said.

Ada smiled at him, and words went flying out of his head.

There were rituals, Peter thought, prescribed courses of action. How did it go? He went down on one knee. Ella came over and put her front paws on his thigh, as if his sole intention had been to pat her head. Peter complied.

Ada laughed. He looked up at her, flushed and beautiful, and nearly lost his voice again. But he had to speak. Nothing happened unless you hoped, and then dared; he'd learned that over these last weeks. "Will you marry me?" he blurted out. He fumbled at his waistcoat pocket. The dog lunged after his hand.

"Ella!" said Ada.

Peter pulled out the ring he'd fetched from the recovered hoard and extended it. "I recognized this from a portrait in the gallery," he said.

The great sapphire winked in the sunlight from the window. The circle of small diamonds around it sparkled.

"The second duchess was wearing it," he added.

"Family stories say she and Tobias Rathbone were very happy together."

"Oh, Peter."

What did that mean? He thrilled to hear her use his name, but *Oh, Peter* was not a yes. Thankfully, it was not a no. Surely she must say one or the other? Not the other, please, he prayed.

"Of course I will marry you," she said. "I have been determined to do so for ages."

Relief crashed through him, followed by wild exultation. Seeming to sense the emotion, Ella began to bark and dance around him.

"Ella," said Ada again. She held out her hand. After an instant, Peter understood and slipped the ring onto her finger. When she held it up to admire it, he thought he would burst with joy and pride.

"You should stand up now," she said with laughter in her voice.

It was strange. He didn't mind the laughter in the least. On the contrary, he hoped no day went by without that warm lilt. He would try to see that they did not. Her laughter would be the music of his existence.

He sprang up, and she moved toward him, and they fell into each other's arms. He held her, conscious that there were many more things he ought to say, if he could just think of them. And knowing that he would find his way there, eventually, as he now had all the time in the world.

She raised her head from his shoulder. He kissed her. She kissed him as well. It was the kind of kiss that absorbed every faculty, fired the body, fed the spirit, sealed the promise of a future that he'd never thought to claim. His luck had turned, after a lifetime, because of Ada.

The kissing went on. And on. Desire surged through Peter. The great four-poster bed was right there, beckoning. Ada pressed eagerly against him. All the longing they'd held back was released.

But this was his sister's bed. Ada's dog danced around them. Her friends might come looking. This was not the time or place.

He drew back on the edge of losing control, and yet without the desperation he'd felt in the past. They were pledged to each other. Every delight would come in time. The path had opened out before them against all the odds.

They stood apart, breathing rapidly. She gave him a little nod, as if she understood his conclusions. "We should begin making our plans," she said.

It turned out that Ada had many plans. He was amazed by the extent and detail of them. She'd been thinking about their future when he hadn't dared. They spent a blissful half hour setting out choices before they went to rejoin the others.

Downstairs, they didn't have to announce the news. The glow on their faces and the ring on Ada's finger told the story. As congratulations filled the air, Ada's Aunt Julia said, "Of course we will have to consult your parents. Nothing can be final until then."

"Of course," said Ada, though her expression said that they had better agree at once.

"As if anyone would refuse a duke who is now rich as Croesus," murmured Charlotte, loud enough to be heard but not so loud as to absolutely require a reprimand.

"Thanks to all of you," said Peter.

Ada smiled. He didn't realize that one was supposed to ignore such muttered asides. He never would. Oddly, it was one of the things she loved most about him.

"I would like to offer each of you a jewel," he added, bowing to the ladies. "For your help and for insisting we must persevere."

"Well, I didn't, really," said Aunt Julia.

"You let us stay on," Ada said. "That turned out well." She smiled at Peter and watched warmth fill his dark eyes. She would never tire of that.

Aunt Julia pursed her lips as if considering, or perhaps suppressing a smile. "I *was* rather taken with those cloisonné earrings."

"You shall have them," said Peter. He turned to Tom and the earl. "If there is any object you would like—"

"Can I have that hat hanging on the wall amongst the papers?" Tom asked.

Peter remembered it—a swashbuckling topper that looked as if it had been worn by a cavalier of Charles the Second. He tried to picture Tom's homely face beneath the broad brim. Incongruous was the word that occurred to him. Yet there could be only one answer. "Of course you can." He turned to the earl. "And you, sir?"

Macklin waved the question aside. "An invitation to the wedding," he said. "I have a surfeit of things."

"Naturally you are invited. But I should like to give you some token of gratitude."

"Your friendship is sufficient." For some reason, the earl gave Miss Julia Grandison a satirical sidelong look.

"You will have that always," Peter replied.

"And mine," said Ada.

"Then I am content," the older man said.

❧

Three days later, Peter said farewell to his love on Alberdene's doorstep. Though it wasn't nearly the rupture he had once feared, the parting was still difficult.

"I will see you in a month," she said as they stood together beside the hired post chaises.

"That seems like forever." It had been agreed that he would visit her home to become better acquainted with her parents and to conclude the marriage arrangements. His joking comments about elopements had been given the consideration Ada thought they deserved. Namely, none.

"We both have much to do," said Ada. And with one last kiss, she stepped into the carriage and was gone.

Peter watched the post chaises move down the drive. The weeds along the verge made him think of gardeners. He needed to hire those as well. The lists of his tasks were lengthening daily.

But Alberdene wouldn't be left empty at the departure of his guests. The newer servants were staying on, and the first workmen had already arrived to begin repairs. He had to ready his home for a bride after all. Ada had promised to send along a first-class housekeeper, with the aid of her mother. He would begin refurbishment of the estate's tumbledown cottages and much else. The knowledge was almost overwhelming after years of scrimping and decay.

Only one fly in the ointment, Peter thought. He had to go to London for the next season. Ada had decreed it. She would not miss her presentation. They would *enjoy* the festivities together and then be married in town. Peter didn't think *enjoy* would exactly describe it from his point of view. But he wanted to do what she wished, even when he didn't want to at all.

Well, he had to go to town to deal with his recovered fortune. Macklin had promised to help him find people to handle sales. He would also gratify his banker with substantial deposits. All very well, but the *ton* parties loomed over him like a huge cresting wave ready to smash him down.

"You will be in London for the season?" he asked Macklin over dinner that evening.

The older man nodded.

"I suppose you find it entertaining."

"In general I do."

"Perhaps I can take advantage of your advice when I make my bow to society. Continue to do so, that is. You've done so much for me already."

"I wouldn't say that," replied the earl. "I did very little."

"You give a fellow confidence," said Peter. It was true. The earl made him feel…capable and…trusted.

"I do?" The older man looked touched.

"It seems like an age since that dinner in London, doesn't it?" Peter added.

"It does. A good deal has happened since then."

"I'd eaten a bad eel pie that afternoon. I worried all through the meal that I might cast up my accounts on the roast beef."

"Really?" The earl's smile was sympathetic. "You did very well under those conditions."

"You think so?"

"Indeed."

Peter let out a sigh. "I suppose I can get through a *ton* party or two on a settled stomach then. Particularly if you'll help me."

"I promise. I'm sure our companions from that dinner will offer their support as well."

"They'll be in town?" Peter asked.

Macklin nodded. "I've had letters about their plans."

"All married now."

"And very happily. As you will be."

"Are you a kind of matrimonial wizard?" Peter smiled to show it was mostly a joke.

The earl smiled back. "Nothing like that. I had no notion what would come of it when I organized that dinner."

But Peter had been diverted. "I nearly forgot. A tailor! I must have a new wardrobe. Ada was extremely clear about that."

"I can recommend my own. He is a master."

"Thank you." Peter felt relief and perhaps a hint of anticipation. With a bit of help, perhaps he'd be all right, even among the town beaus.

❧

"Well, Tom, it seems it's time for us to move on," said Arthur the next afternoon, when his young traveling companion stopped at his chamber before leaving on a ramble about the countryside. "I think you'll like my home," he went on. "It's near Oxford, you know. One day we shall ride in and I'll show you the colleges." He wondered if Tom might be interested in some academic study, eventually. The lad had shown no such bent, but he was still young. And he did enjoy learning. "We'll set off as soon as a post chaise can be arranged. Clayton will be glad to return home, won't you, Clayton?"

"Yes, my lord." The valet folded away an unused neckcloth.

"And in plenty of time for Jocelyn's grouse hunt."

"I'm sure his lordship will be pleased."

Fleetingly, Arthur regretted traveling by post rather than in his own carriage. But as he'd suspected, his equipage and team would have been a burden at Alberdene.

Tom shifted from one foot to the other, looking uncharacteristically uneasy. "Begging your pardon, my lord, but I don't believe I will."

"Will what?"

The lad's face, usually calm and smiling, creased with concern. "Go with you."

"Not?" Arthur was startled.

"I surely appreciate all you've done for me," Tom went on quickly. "You've treated me better than most anybody in my life. I'll never forget it, I swear. Not as long as I live. But—"

"But you are ready to move along now," Arthur finished for him.

"Yes, my lord."

"Of all the ungrateful—" began Clayton.

Arthur held up a hand to silence his valet, just as he struggled to put aside his own disappointment. Tom had always stood on the side of freedom. He'd made no secret of his position. And he wasn't Arthur's ward, or employee or even…friend. As Miss Julia Grandison had pointed out. "Where do you mean to go?" he asked the lad. "I must say I don't like the thought of you wandering the countryside with winter coming on."

"I mean to try my luck in London, my lord."

"London?" This was a surprise.

Some of his customary enthusiasm emerged in Tom's expression. "At the theater."

For once, Arthur was rendered speechless.

"Mrs. Thorpe reckoned as how she could get me a position," Tom continued. "She was most kind about it."

Macklin blinked. His friend Mrs. Thorpe was one of the leading lights of the London stage. Unusually, she was also married to a highly respectable banker. She certainly could help Tom if she wished to. "You want to become an actor?" Of all the predictions he might have made for the boy, this would never have been among them.

"Well, I don't know about that." Tom rubbed his hands together. "There's quite a few other jobs to be done when you're putting on a play. Though I might try acting, sometime, if Mrs. Thorpe thinks I can."

"You've talked with her a good deal about this." And not with him, Arthur noted with a brush of pique.

"Only a bit. Along with some others. I hung about the theater when we were in town."

That, Arthur did remember. Tom had mentioned how much he liked it.

"They've got people building and painting the scenes and running the curtains up and down. I can turn my hand to most anything. I don't mind."

This was certainly true. Tom had demonstrated that willingness over and over.

"And the great thing about it—there's a whole new story coming along every few weeks. Made out of thin air." Tom's eyes glowed with a fervor Arthur had never observed in him before. "You've seen what they do. It's grand!"

Clayton gazed at Tom as if he thought he'd gone mad. "You'd choose to throw in your lot with the theatrical scaff and raff rather than accept his lordship's patronage? Have you any notion how stupid that is?"

"Mrs. Thorpe ain't no *scaff and raff*," replied Tom hotly.

"She is the exception that proves the rule."

"And that's a thing people say that don't—doesn't mean anything."

The valet drew himself up, clearly ready to deliver a blistering scold.

Arthur spoke before he could. "Are you really certain this is what you wish to do, Tom?"

The lad nodded. "The people at the theater… I liked them. I felt…" He paused as if searching for the right word. "At home," he finished finally.

It was true that many actors were as rootless as he, Arthur thought. They formed a class of their own outside the bounds of conventional society. Tom's lack of antecedents wouldn't brand him there as it would almost anywhere else.

"And there'll always be new things to learn," Tom added. "Remember how Mrs. Thorpe put on those scenes up at Lindisfarne?" He shivered pleasurably at the memory. "Warn't...wasn't she amazing? And then it turned out there was a real king who did those things. Ages ago. Some of 'em, at any rate."

Mrs. Thorpe would look out for him, Arthur thought. She'd see that her friends did, too. And the lad could always change his mind later, should he wish to. "Very well," he said. "I'll arrange an allowance for you."

Tom waved this aside. "You've done enough, my lord."

Clayton snorted as if he agreed.

"I don't want charity," Tom added. "I mean to work hard for my keep."

"Until you're settled at the least. It's expensive to live in London." Unless one was in a back slum, Arthur thought. He didn't want to think of Tom in such circumstances. "We'll ask Mrs. Thorpe's advice on a suitable place." He turned to his valet. "I shall make a short detour into London to establish Tom before returning home."

Clayton's sigh was long-suffering.

"You can take the luggage and await me at Macklin Abbey."

"I would prefer to accompany you, my lord!"

Arthur shook his head. It would be easier to settle Tom without Clayton's disapproving comments. "Unnecessary. I shan't be more than a day or so."

Clayton and Tom protested in unison. Arthur ignored them as he faced the fact that he wasn't eager to return to his home, with its all-too-familiar routine. Indeed, he was positively reluctant. The last few months had been full of novel events and deep satisfaction. All the young men he'd singled out were happily settled. He'd achieved the goal he'd set for himself last spring. Now he would do the same for Tom, as a sort of bonus to the rest. And another ending in a series of them. Then it would be all over.

Melancholy threatened to descend. Nothing waited for him at home but empty repetition, a pattern he'd carried out for years through force of habit. Of course he would be glad to see his children and their families for Christmas. His grandchildren were a delight. But the truth was that his wife had been the glue that held them all together. After her death they'd never seemed to achieve the same connection. There was respect, love, of course, but conversations tended to languish and grow forced. They exchanged news like interested acquaintances. No, that was unfair. They all tried very hard. He saw it in his family, and he knew he did all he could. Yet it remained an uphill battle.

Arthur gave himself a mental shake. He would simply have to make more of an effort. Some of his grandchildren were of an age for deeper conversations. He ought to know them better. He would make certain that he did!

Suddenly he found himself wondering about Miss Julia Grandison's plans for the coming season. Just what did she have in store for her brother? He had no doubt the results would be…interesting.

"I hope you're not angry with me, my lord," said Tom. He looked worried.

"Of course not." Tom had not been put on this Earth to amuse him, Arthur thought. He deserved a chance to carve out the life he wanted. Arthur vowed that he would do what he could to let him. And then he would see what came after.

If you enjoyed *A Duke Too Far*, you're sure to love this enchanting Regency romance from Anna Harrington, first in the Lords of the Armory series.

Publishers Weekly says: "Harrington combines suspenseful mystery and charming romance in this compulsively readable treat."

One

May 1816
Charlton Place, London

MARCUS BRADDOCK STEPPED OUT ONTO THE UPPER
terrace of his town house and scanned the party
spreading through the torch-lit gardens below.

He grimaced. His home had been invaded.

All of London seemed to be crowded into Charlton
Place tonight, with the reception rooms filled to
overflowing. The crush of bodies in the ballroom had
forced several couples outside to dance on the lawn,
and the terraces below were filled with well-dressed
dandies flirting with ladies adorned in silks and jewels.
Card games played out in the library, men smoked
in the music room, the ladies retired to the morning room—the entire house had been turned upside
down, the gardens trampled, the horses made uneasy
in the mews...

And it wasn't yet midnight.

His sister Claudia had insisted on throwing this
party for him, apparently whether he wanted one or

not. Not only to mark his birthday tomorrow but also to celebrate his new position as Duke of Hampton, the title given to him for helping Wellington defeat Napoleon. The party would help ease his way back into society, she'd asserted, and give him an opportunity to meet the men he would now be working with in the Lords.

But Marcus hadn't given a damn about society before he'd gone off to war, and he cared even less now.

No. The reason he'd agreed to throw open wide the doors of Charlton Place was a woman.

The Honorable Danielle Williams, daughter of Baron Mondale and his late sister Elise's dearest friend. The woman who had written to inform him that Elise was dead.

The same woman he now knew had lied to him.

His eyes narrowed as they moved deliberately across the crowd. Miss Williams had been avoiding him since his return, refusing to let him call on her and begging off from any social event that might bring them into contact. But she hadn't been able to refuse the invitation for tonight's party, not when he'd also invited her great-aunt, who certainly wouldn't have missed what the society gossips were predicting would be the biggest social event of the season. She couldn't accept and then simply beg off either. To not attend this party would have been a snub to both him and his sister Claudia, as well as to Elise's memory. While Danielle might happily continue to avoid him, she would never intentionally wound Claudia.

She was here somewhere, he knew it. Now he simply had to find her.

He frowned. Easier said than done, because Claudia had apparently invited all of society, most of whom he'd never met and had no idea who they even were. Yet they'd eagerly attended, if only for a glimpse of the newly minted duke's town house. And a glimpse of him. Strangers greeted him as if they were old friends, when his true friends—the men he'd served with in the fight against Napoleon—were nowhere to be seen. Those men he trusted with his life.

These people made him feel surrounded by the enemy.

The party decorations certainly didn't help put him at ease. Claudia had insisted that the theme be ancient Roman and then set about turning the whole house into Pompeii. Wooden torches lit the garden, lighting the way for the army of toga-clad footmen carrying trays of wine from a replica of a Roman temple in the center of the garden. The whole thing gave him the unsettling feeling that he'd been transported to Italy, unsure of his surroundings and his place in them.

Being unsure was never an option for a general in the heat of battle, and Marcus refused to let it control him now that he was on home soil. Yet he couldn't stop it from haunting him, ever since he'd discovered the letter among Elise's belongings that made him doubt everything he knew about his sister and how she'd died.

He planned to put an end to that doubt tonight, just as soon as he talked to Danielle.

"There he is—the birthday boy!"

Marcus bit back a curse as his two best friends, Brandon Pearce and Merritt Rivers, approached him through the shadows. He'd thought the terrace would be the best place to search for Danielle without being seen.

Apparently not.

"You mean the duke of honor," corrected Merritt, a lawyer turned army captain who had served with him in the Guards.

Marcus frowned. While he was always glad to see them, right then he didn't need their distractions. Nor was he in the mood for their joking.

A former brigadier who now held the title of Earl of Sandhurst, Pearce looped his arm over Merritt's shoulder as both men studied him. "I don't think he's happy to see us."

"Impossible." Merritt gave a sweep of his arm to indicate the festivities around them. The glass of cognac in his hand had most likely been liberated from Marcus's private liquor cabinet in his study. "Surely he wants his two brothers-in-arms nearby to witness every single moment of his big night."

Marcus grumbled, "Every single moment of my humiliation, you mean."

"Details, details," Merritt dismissed, deadpan. But he couldn't hide the gleam of amusement in his eyes.

"What we really want to know about your birthday party is this." Pearce touched his glass to Marcus's chest and leaned toward him, his face deadly serious. "When do the pony rides begin?"

Marcus's gaze narrowed as he glanced between the two men. "Remind me again why I saved your miserable arses at Toulouse."

Pearce placed his hand on Marcus's shoulder in a

show of genuine affection. "Because you're a good man and a brilliant general," he said sincerely. "And one of the finest men we could ever call a friend."

Merritt lifted his glass in a heartfelt toast. "Happy birthday, General."

Thirty-five. Bloody hell.

"Hear, hear." Pearce seconded the toast. "To the Coldstream Guards!"

A knot tightened in Marcus's gut at the mention of his former regiment that had been so critical to the victory at Waterloo yet also nearly destroyed in the brutal hand-to-hand combat that day. But he managed to echo, "To the Guards."

Not wanting them to see any stray emotion on his face, he turned away. Leaning across the stone balustrade on his forearms, he muttered, "I wish I could still be with them."

While he would never wish to return to the wars, he missed being with his men, especially their friendship and dependability. He missed the respect given to him and the respect he gave each of them in return, no matter if they were an officer or a private. Most of all, he longed for the sense of purpose that the fight against Napoleon had given him. He'd known every morning when he woke up what he was meant to do that day, what higher ideals he served. He hadn't had that since he returned to London, and its absence ate at him.

It bothered him so badly, in fact, that he'd taken to spending time alone at an abandoned armory just north of the City. He'd purchased the old building with the intention of turning it into a warehouse, only to discover that he needed a place to himself more than he needed the additional income. More and more lately, he'd found himself going there at all hours to escape from society and the ghosts that haunted him. Even in his own home.

That was the punishment for surviving when others he'd loved hadn't. The curse of remembrance.

"No, General." Pearce matched his melancholy tone as his friends stepped up to the balustrade, flanking him on each side. "You've left the wars behind and moved on to better things." He frowned as he stared across the crowded garden. "This party notwithstanding."

Merritt pulled a cigar from his breast pocket and lit it on a nearby lamp. "You're exactly where you belong. With your family." He puffed at the cheroot, then watched the smoke curl from its tip into the darkness overhead. "They need you now more than the Guards do."

In his heart, Marcus knew that, too. Which was why he'd taken it upon himself to go through Elise's belongings when Claudia couldn't bring herself to do it, to pack up what he thought her daughter, Penelope, might want when she was older and to distribute the rest to the poor. That was how he'd discovered a letter among Elise's things from someone named John Porter, arranging a midnight meeting for which she'd left the house and never returned.

He'd not had a moment of peace since.

He rubbed at the knot of tension in his nape. His friends didn't need to know any of that. They were already burdened enough as it was by settling into their own new lives now that they'd left the army.

"Besides, you're a duke now." Merritt flicked the

ash from his cigar. "There must be some good way to put the title to use." He looked down at the party and clarified, "One that doesn't involve society balls."

"Or togas," Pearce muttered.

Marcus blew out a patient breath at their good-natured teasing. "The Roman theme was Claudia's idea."

"Liar," both men said at once. Then they looked at each other and grinned.

Merritt slapped him on the back. "Next thing you know, you'll be trying to convince us that the pink ribbons in you horse's tail were put there by Penelope."

Marcus kept his silence. There was no good reply to that.

He turned his attention back to the party below, his gaze passing over the crowded garden. He spied the delicate turn of a head in the crowd—

Danielle. There she was, standing by the fountain in the glow of one of the torches.

For a moment, he thought he was mistaken, that the woman who'd caught his attention couldn't possibly be her. Not with her auburn hair swept up high on her head in a pile of feathery curls, shimmering with copper highlights in the lamplight and revealing a long and graceful neck. Not in that dress of emerald satin with its capped sleeves of ivory lace over creamy shoulders.

Impossible. This woman, with her full curves and mature grace, simply couldn't be the same excitable girl he remembered, who'd seemed always to move through the world with a bouncing skip. Who had bothered him to distraction with all her questions about the military and soldiers.

She laughed at something her aunt said, and her face brightened into a familiar smile. Only then did he let himself believe that she wasn't merely an apparition.

Sweet Lucifer. Apparently, nothing in England was as he remembered.

He put his hands on both men's shoulders. "If you'll excuse me, there's someone in the garden I need to speak with. Enjoy yourselves tonight." Then, knowing both men nearly as well as he knew himself, he warned, "But not too much."

As he moved away, Merritt called out with a knowing grin. "What's *her* name?"

"Trouble," he muttered and strode down into the garden before she could slip back into the crowd and disappear.

Two

DANIELLE WILLIAMS SMILED DISTRACTEDLY AT THE story her great-aunt Harriett was telling the group of friends gathered around them in the garden. The one about how she'd accidentally pinched the bottom of—

"King George!" The crux of the story elicited a gasp of surprise, followed by laughter. Just as it always did. "I had no idea that the bottom I saw poking out from behind that tree was a royal one. Truly, doesn't one bottom look like all the rest?"

"I've never thought so," Dani mumbled against the rim of her champagne flute as she raised it to her lips.

Harriett slid her a chastising glance, although knowing Auntie, likely more for interrupting her story than for any kind of hint of impropriety.

"But oh, how high His Majesty jumped!" her aunt continued, undaunted. As always. "I was terrified— simply *terrified*, I tell you! I was only fourteen and convinced that I had just committed high treason."

Although Dani had heard this same story dozens of times, the way Harriett told it always amused her. Thank goodness. After all, she needed something to distract her, because this evening was the first time she'd been to Charlton Place since Marcus Braddock had returned from the continent. The irony wasn't lost on her. She was on edge with nervousness tonight when she'd once spent so much time here that she'd considered this place a second home.

"A pinch to a king's bottom!" Harriett exclaimed. "Wars have been declared over less offending actions, I assure you."

Dani had been prepared for the unease that fluttered in her belly tonight, yet the guilt that gnawed at her chest was as strong as ever…for not coming to see Claudia or spending time with Pippa, for not being able to tell Marcus what kindnesses Elise had done for others in the months before her death. But how could she face him without stirring up fresh grief for both of them?

No. Best to simply avoid him.

"Had it been a different kind of royal bottom—say, one of the royal dukes—I might not have panicked so. But it was a *king's* bottom!"

She had a plan. Once Harriett finished her story, Dani would suddenly develop a headache and need to leave. She would give her best wishes to Claudia before slipping discreetly out the door and in the morning pen a note of apology to the duke for not wishing him happy birthday in person. She'd assure him that she'd looked for him at the party but had been unable to find him. A perfectly believable excuse given how many people were crammed into Charlton Place tonight. A complete crush! So many other people wanted their chance to speak to him that she most likely couldn't get close to him even if she tried. Not that she'd *try* exactly, but—

"Good evening, Miss Williams."

The deep voice behind her twined down her spine. Marcus Braddock. *Drat it all.*

So much for hiding. Her trembling fingers tightened around the champagne flute as she inhaled deeply and slowly faced him. She held out her gloved hand and lowered into a curtsy. "Your Grace."

Taking her hand and bowing over it, he gave her a smile, one of those charming grins that she remembered so vividly. Those smiles had always taken her breath away, just as this one did now, even if it stopped short of his eyes.

"It's good to have you and your aunt back at Charlton Place, Miss Williams."

"Thank you." She couldn't help but stare. He'd always been attractive and dashing, especially in his uniform, and like every one of Elise's friends, she'd had a schoolgirl infatuation with him. And also like every one of his little sister's friends, he'd paid her absolutely no mind whatsoever except to tolerate her for Elise's sake.

Although he was just as handsome as she remembered, Marcus had certainly changed in other ways. The passing years had brought him into his prime, and the youthful boldness she remembered had been tempered by all he'd experienced during his time away, giving him a powerful presence that most men would never possess.

When he released her hand to greet the others, Dani continued to stare at him, dumbfounded. She simply couldn't reconcile the brash and impetuous brother of her best friend with the compelling man now standing beside her, who had become one of the most important men in England.

Harriett leaned toward her and whispered, "Lower your hand, my dear."

Heavens, her hand! It still hovered in midair where he'd released it. With embarrassment heating her cheeks, she dropped it to her side.

She turned away and gulped down the rest of her champagne, not daring to look at the general for fear he'd think her the same infatuated goose she'd been as a young girl. Or at Harriett, whose face surely shone with amusement at the prospect of Dani being smitten with England's newest hero.

No. She was simply stunned to see all the changes that time and battle had wrought in him. That was all.

But then, Marcus Braddock had always been the most intense man she'd ever known, with brown eyes so dark as to be almost black, thick hair to match that curled at his collar, and a jaw that could have been sculpted from marble, like those Greek gods in Lord Elgin's notorious statues that Parliament had just purchased. Broad-shouldered, tall and confident, commanding in every way…no wonder she'd not been surprised to learn of all his promotions gained from heroism on the battlefield or to read about his exploits in the papers. Only when she'd learned that the regent had granted him a dukedom alongside Wellington had she been surprised—not that he'd been offered the title but that he'd accepted it.

"You seem well, Duke." Harriett had the audacity

to look him up and down from behind the quizzing glass she wore on a chain around her neck. But her seven decades of age gave her the right to take liberties that few others would deign to claim, including so shamelessly scrutinizing the new duke when she should have done it surreptitiously. The way Dani was doing.

She gave him her own once-over while he was distracted with her aunt, deliberately taking him in from head to toe and finding him more impressive than ever. Despite her nervousness at seeing him again, a smile pulled at her lips. Only Marcus Braddock could appear imperial standing next to a papier-mâché statue of Julius Caesar.

Harriett finished her examination with an approving nod. "Life in London must be agreeing with you."

His mouth twisted with amusement. "I feel as if I've just been put through a military inspection, Viscountess."

Harriett let out a sound halfway between a humph and a chortle. "Better grow used to it, my boy! You were the grandson of a baron before, but now you're a peer. A duke, no less. Privacy has just become a luxury you cannot afford."

Although his expression didn't alter, Dani felt a subtle change in him. A hardening. As if he'd already discovered for himself the truth behind her great-aunt's warning.

"Lovely party." Harriett waved a gloved hand to indicate the festivities, the rings on her fingers shining in the torchlight. "So kind of you to throw it and invite all of London."

Dani blanched. Of all the things to say—

"Couldn't invite the best without inviting the rest," he countered as expertly as if the two were waging a tennis match.

Her eyes gleamed mischievously. "And which are which?"

"If you don't know—"

"You're part of the rest," the viscountess finished, raising her champagne glass in a mock toast.

In reply, he winked at her.

Harriett laughed, tickled by their verbal sparring match. "You happened by at exactly the right moment. I was just telling everyone about the first time I met His Majesty. Have I ever told you—"

"If you'll pardon me, Viscountess," he interrupted politely to avoid being caught up in the story. *Smart man.* "I'd like to ask Miss Williams for the next dance." He turned toward her. "Would you do me the honor?"

Dani's heart slammed against her ribs in dread. Being with him like this, surrounded by a crowd of friends and acquaintances where the conversation had to be polite and impersonal was one thing. But dancing was something completely different and far too close for comfort. There would be too many opportunities to be reminded of Elise's death, for both of them. *This* was exactly what she'd hoped to avoid.

"My apologies, Your Grace." Dani smiled tightly. "But I'm not dancing tonight."

His expression darkened slightly. Clearly, he wasn't used to being refused. "Not even with an old friend returned from the wars?"

Especially not him. "Not at all, I'm afraid."

Something sparked in the dark depths of his eyes. A challenge? Had he realized that she'd been purposefully evading him? The butterflies in her belly molded one by one into a ball of lead as he smiled at her. "Surely you can make an exception."

Dear heavens, why wouldn't he let this go? "I haven't been feeling myself lately, and a dance might tire—"

"Danielle," Harriett chastised with a laughing smile. Beneath the surface, however, she was surely horrified that Dani was refusing not just an old family friend and the man of honor at tonight's party but the most eligible man in the entire British empire. "One dance will not overtax you."

Without giving her the chance to protest, he insisted, "If you grow fatigued, I promise to return you immediately to your aunt." Marcus turned the full charms of his smile on her and held out his hand. "Shall we?"

Now she knew what foxes felt like when they were cornered by hounds. With no more excuses for why she couldn't dance, the only way to avoid him now would be to flat-out cut him in front of his guests. *That* she would never do.

Marcus didn't deserve that. Truly, he'd done nothing wrong, except remind her of Elise.

She grudgingly nodded her consent and allowed him to place her hand on his arm to lead her away.

Once they were out of earshot of the others, she lightly squeezed his arm to capture his attention. "While it's kind of you to request a dance, it's perfectly fine with me if we don't take the floor. You shouldn't feel obligated."

"But I want to." He slid her a sideways glance that

rippled a warning through her as he led her toward the house. "I was very happy to see that you'd attended tonight."

"I wouldn't have missed it." Although she'd dearly tried to do just that. Swiftly changing the topic away from herself, she declared, "This party is a grand way to celebrate your return as a hero. I'm certain that Claudia and Pippa are thrilled to have you home."

Regret surged through her as soon as the words left her lips, because her mention of them would surely only remind him of Elise's absence. She hadn't wanted to cause him more grief. After all, that was why she'd been avoiding him since his return. How could he not look at her without thinking of his sister's death? God knew Dani was reminded of exactly that every time she thought of him.

"And you—" she rushed to add before he could reply, pivoting the conversation in a different direction. "You must have missed England."

"I did." The way he said that sounded faintly aggrieved. "But I'm not certain England missed me."

"It did, a great deal." Part of her had missed him a great deal as well.

He chuckled at that, as if it were a private joke. "Very little, I'm sure."

Yet his amusement did nothing to calm her unease, which wasn't helped at all by the hand he touched briefly to hers as it rested on his sleeve. The small gesture sent her heart somersaulting. But then, hadn't he always made her nervous?

Yet he fascinated her, too. Something about him stirred her curiosity... Of course, she'd found his life as a soldier intriguing and had loved to hear Elise talk of his adventures. His sister had been so proud of him that she couldn't stop bragging, and Dani had soaked up all the stories, especially those few she'd been fortunate enough to hear him tell himself during rare visits home before the fighting grew so fierce on the Peninsula that he'd not been able to leave Spain.

"But you're right. I did miss my family, and I'm very happy to be back with them." Another brief rest of his hand on hers, this time with a reassuring squeeze. "Although I suspect that they're ready to toss *me* back over the Channel."

She shook her head. "Not at all."

He lowered his mouth to her ear so he wouldn't be overheard by the other guests. "Then why else would Claudia torture me with a party like this?"

"She's not torturing you."

"Oh?" As if offering irrefutable proof, he muttered, "A plaster model of Vesuvius is set to erupt at midnight."

She laughed, her gloved hand going to her lips to stifle it. Amusement mixed with surprise. Being with him was quite enjoyable, when he didn't remind her of how much she missed Elise.

"And you, Miss Williams? Are *you* ready to toss me back?"

Her laughter died against her fingertips at the way he asked that. Not an innocent question. Not at all a tease. A hardness lurked behind it that she couldn't fathom.

"Of course not." She smiled uneasily as he led her through the French doors and into the house toward the ballroom that had been created by opening the connecting doors between the salon, dining, and drawing rooms. "Why would I want to do that?"

"Most likely for the same reason you've been avoiding me."

Guilt pierced her so sharply that she winced. This was what she'd feared during the past few months, why she hadn't come to Charlton Place—coming face-to-face with his grief over his sister and her guilt over avoiding him. She wanted no part of this conversation!

She tried to slip away, but his hand closed over hers again, this time pinning her fingers to his sleeve and refusing to let her go. Aware of every pair of eyes in the room watching them and not wanting to create a scene, she walked on beside him until he finally stopped on the far side of the ballroom near the musicians.

She pounced on this chance to flee. It was time for her headache to arrive. "If you please, General—" Remembering herself, she corrected, "That is, Your Grace—"

"Has your absence been because of Elise's death?"

She flinched beneath his bluntness. There would be no avoiding this exchange. This was the reason he'd refused to let her decline the dance.

"No," she whispered, unable to speak any louder past the knot in her throat. "It's been because of you."

About the Author

Jane Ashford discovered Georgette Heyer in junior high school and was captivated by the glittering world and witty language of Regency England. That delight was part of what led her to study English literature and travel widely. Her books have been published all over Europe as well as in the United States. Jane was nominated for a Career Achievement Award by *RT Book Reviews*. Born in Ohio, she is now somewhat nomadic. Find her on the web at janeashford.com and on Facebook at facebook.com/JaneAshfordWriter, where you can sign up for her monthly newsletter.

Also by Jane Ashford

The Duke's Sons

Heir to the Duke
What the Duke Doesn't Know
Lord Sebastian's Secret
Nothing Like a Duke
The Duke Knows Best

The Way to a Lord's Heart

Brave New Earl
A Lord Apart
How to Cross a Marquess

Once Again a Bride
Man of Honour
The Three Graces
The Marriage Wager
The Bride Insists
The Bargain
The Marchington Scandal
The Headstrong Ward
Married to a Perfect Stranger
Charmed and Dangerous
A Radical Arrangement
First Season/ Bride to Be
Rivals of Fortune/ The Impetuous Heiress
Last Gentleman Standing
Earl to the Rescue
The Reluctant Rake